12.01.17

When it showers, it pours.

Donald Trump has had an interesting week.

He ignored an intelligence report claiming Vladimir Putin influenced the election to help him win but found it harder to ignore a report that said he engaged in unseemly behaviour in a Moscow hotel suite with two ladies that were paid for their time.

They were said to have engaged in a "sex act", which sounds like a branch of show-business.

He spent considerably more time rubbishing these claims than attending to the security services who used the $57bn of staff, infrastructure and experience at their disposal to conclude that the Russians had struck at the heart of American democracy and assisted Trump in winning the White House.

Trump claimed that Russian hacking had no effect on the outcome and dismissed the concerns of the security apparatus about ten seconds after he was told about it. He barely waited 'till he left the room before tweeting his disdain.

The official finding of the NSA, FBI and CIA is that Putin 'ordered an influence campaign in 2016 aimed at the U.S. presidential election.'

It said 'Russia's goals were to undermine public faith in the US democratic process, denigrate Secretary Clinton, and harm her electability and potential presidency,'

Armed with no information of any kind whatsoever, apart from the conviction that he is very smart, Donald Trump said: oh no they didn't, and even if they did, what difference does it make, the right man won.

Senior Republicans think differently, the spooks think differently and the public are beginning to re-evaluate their opinion of the man that appears to value Vladimir Putin's word over that of America's own security services.

His reason seems to be that he thinks that Vlad is a really great guy. So that's settled then.

A politician who has yet to take office is usually in their honeymoon period with the electorate. That often lasts for the first hundred days before the press evaluate what he or she has achieved so far.

Donald Trump has skipped the honeymoon. His ratings are down already, and he hasn't even started yet.

A national poll by Quinnipiac University finds that US voters think that Trump will be a worse president than Obama.

Those approving of the job that the outgoing president has done number 55%. Those disapproving of Trump's tenure already amount to 51%, with just 37% approving.

Those are pretty alarming numbers for a man who has not even placed his unusually small hands on the desk in the Oval Office, and quite big numbers for a president that has had eight years to disappoint the American electorate.

Trump's loss is also that of the Republican party. They now have a disapproval rating of 55%.

He might be taking them down with him, which may explain the severe and unbridled criticism that senior GOP panjandrums have been levelling at Trump and his cabinet picks.

A majority of voters surveyed also think that Trump will take the country in the wrong direction, won't help their personal financial situation and do not think he cares about average Americans.

Worse of all, 53% stated that they thought he was dishonest, against 39% who believe what he says.

Celebrities, who are the American royal family, are none too keen on him either.

Obama had a going away party that was attended by rapper Wale, songstress Kelly Rowland, model Chrissy Teigen, John Legend,

Meryl Streep, Al Sharpton, Tyler Perry, Chris Rock, David Letterman, Tom Hanks, Star Wars directors George Lucas and JJ Abrams, Beyonce, Jay Z, Bruce Springsteen, Eddie Vedder, Oprah Winfrey, Usher, Paul McCartney and Stevie Wonder.

Trump, for his inauguration has secured the Mormon Tabernacle Choir, and if the ceremony sags, may give out free hats.

Politics is all about perception these days, and especially so with Trump. He is all Twitter, smoke and mirrors, which is why the revelations about the Moscow hotel room are particularly damaging.

They could be fake news, but it is a bit rich for a man who has embraced that phenomena to complain about it when it does not reflect well on him.

The sex act in question may not have happened, or it may have been a simple misunderstanding.

Just picture an innocent and unsuspecting Donald perusing the hotel's spa menu and being typically drawn to the treatment that had the word "golden" in its name.

13.01.17

Every little injustice matters.

Theresa May has vowed to start tackling 'everyday injustices'. She is going to don her fetish footgear and cow-skin trousers and whip them into submission.

She has plans for housing, education and economic policies. The idea will probably be more housing, better education and a more equitable economic policy, although you never know.

A No. 10 source said that "People feel left behind by economic progress." It only took about 80 million people in America and

Britain screaming that at the top of their voices for the politicians to hear.

In order to tackle everyday injustices, Mrs M promises to deliver a new wave of prefabricated housing, because nothing says "home" like mass produced, factory made, giant slabs of concrete and glass.

There are also proposals to speed up the planning process and force councils to accept thousands more homes in a bid to ease the housing crisis, so expect a chorus of disapproval along the lines of: that's just what we need but not round here of course - too busy, there's no parking, congestion's a nightmare, totally inappropriate, completely out of character.

People are crying out for more housebuilding to be done, just as long as it is not going up anywhere near them.

And the PM has said that new housing won't be restricted to the South East, it will be in other parts of the country too, in order to spread the joy more evenly.

After the everyday injustice of the housing shortage is solved, there's also the Government's forthcoming industrial strategy, designed to boost jobs and economic growth, just as artificial intelligence marches in to take those very same jobs away

Mother Theresa is also keen on dealing with health inequalities. Those born in the poorest areas have an average life expectancy nine years shorter than those born in the wealthiest places.

That is troubling but not entirely unexpected. The causes may be numerous but one might be the average intelligence of the people in those areas.

It is not one of those things that you are supposed to say out loud, let alone put in print, but I would hazard that the average intelligence of people in poor areas is bested by those in rich ones.

How does one get out of a poor area? By being more successful that one's peers.

Success used to be measured by how many woolly mammoths you could slay before dinner. It is now measured, mostly, by the amount of money you can make.

Smart people tend to make more money. There are exceptions of course: top footballers are not famous for their mental agility, bankers tend to earn a fortune whether they know what they are doing or not, and luck is probably the biggest factor in a person's success but on average, people are smarter in Richmond than Tower Hamlets.

Smart people tend to eat better and take care of themselves, because they are smart.

Poor people tend to spend vast amounts on cigarettes and frozen pizza bites.

Add to that the likelihood that if you have some money, the insurance of choice will be health insurance, so they do not have to roll the dice of death with the NHS, and it is not surprising that those in rich postcodes have greater longevity.

So, good luck with solving *that* injustice Prime Minister.

But it is not really an everyday injustice at all. None of them are. Housing, education and health are pretty fundamental issues.

An everyday injustice is when you are waiting at a bar and you have unaccountably become completely invisible to the barman, who only sees the people either side of you, despite you waving a twenty at him over the beer pumps.

An everyday injustice is when you order a frappa crappa mochachino and you are twenty paces down the road before you discover they've given you a peppermint, low fat chai latte.

When you are in, and waiting for the delivery of something you don't need that you bought with money you don't have, and the courier silently posts a "you were not in" note through your door, despite the fact that you were DEFINATELY IN!!!! - that is an everyday injustice.

And so is trying to clear up the mess left by your predecessors, tackle Brexit, placate the press, make your mark, take control and command the country, and all anyone can focus on is your saucy leather trousers and your leopard-print kitten heeled shoes.

18.01.17

If you go down to the woods today, you're in for a big surprise visit to A&E.

At this time of year, it's so cold that squirrels have to rub their nuts just to keep them warm.

Unless, that is, they have discovered that us wobbly, slow moving, ground dwelling meat sacks have all the food they need, and we will not put up a fight when challenged for it.

Some of the fattest squirrels in the country are now so bold that they have started attacking humans for their dinner.

It was predicable that eventually animals were not going to be satisfied with what nature provides and would start to have designs on what us corpulent humans eat, and find that we are not so big and tough after all.

And when the word goes round that we can't defend ourselves against squirrels, what do you think foxes are going to do?

Or cows for that matter? We lead them all passive and pliant to their slaughter; when they get the idea that we won't fight back, we'll get trampled under foot.

In Cornwall, squirrels have had their fill of foraging and have discovered that much tastier fare is carried by people.

When they staged an attack, it left a three-year-old boy needing hospital treatment.

Mother Sophie Renouf, 23, and her little son Finley were spending a pleasant afternoon in the countryside when they were charmed by the appearance of one of the Britain's cutest fauna.

The child proffered it a snack, whereupon the nightmare started. As though in a horror story by Beatrix Potter, while the mother and child were being charmed by the lead squirrel, a gang of half a dozen of them stormed out of the undergrowth and staged an all-out attack.

Ms Renouf, said: 'There was literally one squirrel there and my son, as you would, fed him as usual.

'Next thing, six of them came running out of the hedge and then, all of a sudden, all I remember is him screaming and there was blood pouring out of his hand.'

He was spirited to the hospital and medics spent three hours treating his puncture wounds and bandaging his fingers.

Three hours medical attention after a squirrel attack!

His mother now wants to warn others about the dangers of feeding wild squirrels.

That does not go far enough. There are dangers everywhere. People think that walking through some areas of our big cities are perilous, but they are as nothing compared to the terrors that abound in the thickets and hedgerows of rural Britain.

Rampaging squirrels is about as nightmarish as it gets.

If they ever team up with seagulls, we are sunk.

We must reclaim our advantage. No more Mr and Mrs Nice Guy.

The free ride is over Tufty...this means war.

20.01.17

Making America grate again.

In the National Mall during Obama's inauguration, you couldn't see the grass for supporters.

For the inauguration of Donald Trump, it was occupied by six old white men, who had arrived hoping they might get free T-shirts.

When Obama was sworn in you could barely get into the city. When Trump was sworn in you could have landed a 747 on the Mall and not hit anyone.

Trump spent the morning being introduced to the staff at the Whitehouse - "Jose, you're fired; Manuel, you're fired; Rosita, you're fired; James, you can stay...great guy."

At the Capitol Building, the ex-Presidents gathered, unaware they were about to be insulted by the man of the hour.

The higher-ups of the Republican Party came in, led by House Speaker Paul Ryan who had the smile of a man who thinks it's really going to be HIM in charge and not the giant Tangerine Scream that lumbered in behind him.

Trump came in like Al Capone, swaying from side to side like he was entering a deserted factory to torture a business associate.

His tie was knotted so that it ended around his knees, a giant red arrow which pointed to where he would want us to believe his Donaldhood ends. He has "no problem" in that department, he guarantees it.

His wife was wearing a reinforced powder-blue suit of armour, in case Trump got any ideas and decided to give her a grab when he got bored.

Meanwhile, a short distance away, protesters were hurling stones at McDonald's which is the international sign that they have run out of McFlurries.

The 45th President of the United States was sworn in with the look of someone who would rather be cheating at golf, or picking a Twitter fight with Meryl Streep.

Taking the microphone, he name checked the previous presidents who were lined up behind him: President Bush, President Carter, President Clinton, President Obama.

He did this to get their attention so that they would not miss the part of his speech about them all being terrible and unable to do their job, not like he can, because he is very smart and successful.

Worst presidents ever…SAD!

He spoke like he was still campaigning. He said that under his leadership "we will rebuild America and restore its promise", as though he was taking over a broken down car and not a successful country that had been run by the people behind him.

They had to stay there and take it, while staring at the cloud of gold coloured nylon that almost covers the back of his head.

He said this moment belongs to all the people gathered here, which by that time amounted to three people on the Mall who thought it was a line for soup.

He said January 20, 2017 will be remembered as the day the people became the rulers of the country again. Again? Since when have the people been the rulers of the country? Any country?

And how likely is it that a cabinet of billionaires will make that happen. The super-rich don't seem to be the kind of people that like to give up power.

On guns and gangs, he said this American carnage ends now…and in Chicago they stopped shooting each other for five minutes and fired into the sky in celebration.

He said, "we will put America first, we need protection from other countries stealing our jobs, America will start winning again, like never before.

We will bring back our wealth, our borders and our dreams

We will eradicate Muslim terrorism from the face of the earth, we will be protected by the military and the police and most importantly we will be protected by God.

He knows God. God asked him for a loan just last week. Great guy.

He said the time for empty talk is over, the time for empty tweeting is here.

He said we stand at the start of a new millennium - just 17 years out there Donald but let's not get bogged down in facts.

And to all Americans, he said, "you will not be ignored again…now get out of the way, my gold carriage awaits to take me to my gold lift that opens directly into my gold apartment.

26.01.17

Size matters

It was a week when the word "tumultuous" was wheeled out by anyone that spoke about the new American regime. If that word had not already existed, we would have had to invent it just to encompass what has happened so far.

First and foremost, the new leader seems obsessed with refuting the notion that he is in any way not the most popular person on earth, ever.

Every day, he has returned to the story about the numbers that came out to see his inauguration, or the numbers of votes cast in his favour at the election.

He seems incapable of letting anything go, no matter how trivial. He takes any slight, imagined or otherwise, and feels compelled to smash it into the ground, like a toddler who breaks his toys when he is told it is time for bed.

The press would have moved on from how few people showed up on the National Mall, but Trump won't let them.

He just keeps on lying about it and sending his harassed team out to lie about it, when anyone with functioning eyes can see the huge discrepancy in the crowds that greeted Obama and the new incumbent of the Oval Office.

First, he sent out a man with a shaven head who looked like he had been bricked up in his own suit. Whitehouse Press Secretary Sean Spicer screamed nonsense at the the assembled news corps, as though they could be cowed into agreeing with an obvious untruth by pummelling them with volume.

He shouted that no-one knew the numbers that were present in The Mall to see Trump sworn in and therefore you could not make a comparison with Obama's crowd for his first big day.

Having stated that no accurate crowd numbers could be gauged, he then claimed that Trump's numbers were "the largest audience ever to witness an inauguration, period ".

They don't do irony in the new administration. Irony is for losers with small crowds.

He looked like the world's angriest man, but then he had probably spent the previous day being yelled at by the Tangerine Scream.

Another unhappy traveller was Trump's consigliere Kellyanne Conway, a woman that looks like she was refused a job as an extra in a vampire film because she looked too tired.

She wears the tiredness of a 150 year-old, but she probably doesn't get much sleep these days what with having to tend to a yelling orange baby.

She was sent out to brow-beat the press into believing the lies that Sean Spicer was selling.

In a perfect moment that encapsulated the new era, she said on American national television that Spicer and Trump were not lying about the obvious shortfall in the new President's turnout, they were simply expressing "alternative facts".

If that is not the phrase of the year come December, I will be astonished.

Actually, I will be astonished if the world makes it to December.

28.01.17

Propping up the Special Relationship

Mrs M went to see the Screaming MeMe to tell him how big she thinks his hands are. This was another in her increasingly desperate attempts to get the best out of the bad deal that she was bequeathed by her predecessor .

So much ink was used writing about the "special relationship" that you could have coated a church with it.

It was a toe-curling meeting that the right-wing media covered as though the ghosts of Ronald Reagan and Margaret Thatcher had risen to do the tango.

Trump spoke the words, that someone else had written for him, like an automaton running low on batteries. He talked of deep bonds and ad libbed how great the bond is...it is a really great bond, a tremendous bond...yooge.

When reading a script, he talks like brain surgeon Ben Carson has been operating on him with an ice-cream scoop.

Mother Theresa could not fail to sound perky by comparison.

She described Trump's apparent neat pirouette on NATO, which she insisted he now supports 100%. This is a complete turnaround from his previous ramblings on the subject when he described it as obsolete.

He had also refused to say whether he would come to the aid of another NATO country under attack, which is the principle of collective defence, the heart of NATO's founding treaty.

He implied that in the hour of a friend's desperate need, he would go through their pockets to see if they had any money on them before deciding whether to step in.

Trump talked of his approval of torture and continued to paint the world in apocalyptic tones that do not reflect any kind of reality.

For no understandable reason, standing next to our Prime Minister, he reignited his beef with Mexico (where he got much of his Trump branded goods made) and repeated how bad all the other Presidents had been before him to allow America to be "beaten to a pulp".

Vladimir Putin must be ecstatic. Everything is working out perfectly.

As the new administration has OK'd the use of alternative facts, allow me some of my own.

In the Oval Office, there were photo opportunities in front of the bust of Winston Churchill, a dark brass effigy that Trump refers to as "that black guy".

Behind the scenes he guided Mrs M towards the photographic evidence his staff had cobbled together of the tremendous crowds that greeted his inauguration - they were the biggest crowds...ever.

The dishonest media tried to say they weren't. So dishonest. Sad. They will pay.

Back to reality: on exiting the White House, the shot of the day was Trump and May holding hands. Proof that the relationship is as strong as ever.

If you look closely, however, you will see that Trump grabs on to May's hand as they negotiate a ramp and lets go at the bottom.

He used her as a walking aid.

He's still grabbing crutches.

03.02.17

Flailing and drowning.

Here is the tally so far. This is a list of the people and places that Donald Trump has picked a fight with just two weeks elapsed in his presidency: Iran, Iraq, Libya, Somalia, Syria, Sudan, Yemen, Canada, Europe in general (except Russia), North Korea, China, Australia, and Germany.

And he threatened to invade Mexico - he actually said to the democratically elected leader of the neighbouring country that he had some "bad hombres" down there and he might just send the US army into Mexico to deal with them

Then there was the continuing beefs with all of the past presidents of the US (except Abraham Lincoln), Republican senators Lindsey Graham and John McCain, the New York Times, the Washington Post, Vanity Fair, the media in general (except Fox News), the University of California at Berkeley, women who don't dress like women, whatever that means, and Arnold Schwarzenegger,.

He abused Arny from behind a lectern that had the Seal of the President of the United States on the front, at an event called the National Prayer Breakfast, which is a religious based event organised by Congress and is something that is supposed to be for political and social leaders to gather to exchange views, in a pious and reflective environment.

Trump used it to say how great his audience was when he hosted the Apprentice reality TV show, compared to current host Arnold Schwarzenegger's.

Arnold sent a message in response saying they should swap jobs - Trump could go back on TV, seeing as he's such an expert, and Arny could take over as President and then we will all be finally able to sleep comfortably again

The other speaker at the event was the Chaplain of the US Senate. He did not use his time by saying how much better he was than the person who did that job before him, because, you know, he's a grown up

Trump seems obsessed with making people believe that everything about him is the biggest ever.

He is totally preoccupied by size. It is why he can't get past losing the popular vote by 3m people to Hillary.

He has to invent some reason why he had a bigger vote - it was a lot of dead people voting, or he could have had the biggest vote if he wanted to but he didn't bother, which makes it odd that he's so bothered now..

And its why he sees millions of people that weren't there at his inauguration.

Why would a man with small hands be so obsessed by size?

Well, you don't need Dr Freud to rise from the dead to help us figure that out - the way he has his tie so that it hangs down round his knees is indication enough.

He's Donald T Trumpet...the T stands for Tiny.

There is one thing that he is the best at though. There is one area that he is the most successful of all previous presidents - reaching a majority disapproval rating.

Bill Clinton was the previous record holder to get more than 50% of the American public to register their disapproval. He managed it after 573 days in office.

It took Obama 936 days and George W Bush 1205 days to get the majority of Americans to disapprove of their presidency.

Donald Trump has achieved the same feat in 8 days.

No-one's better at being disliked than the Donald. He's number one.

Now, who's going to be the one to tell him the good news?

04.02.17

The menace of the aerial chip snatchers.

An Honourable Member of Parliament has called for a government crackdown on a terror of the skies.

Oliver Colvile, the Conservative MP for Plymouth Sutton and Devonport, has been granted a debate in Parliament next week on the subject of seagulls.

He said it was a 'big issue' in seaside towns as seagulls 'can be quite invasive'.

This is true. They can also be loud, which is great for a townie on a break, as their song speaks of the sea-side holiday. Their emotive call brings to mind childhood adventures and underlines the fact that you are not in the city any more.

This noise becomes somewhat less delightful when you actually live on the coast and have to put up with their incessant, piercing squawk every day.

Mr Colvile said: 'I was out campaigning with a mate of mine when suddenly this seagull decided it was going to take his fish and chips from him.'

He said, 'I am aware that they are a protected species, but we need to do more.'

Why are they protected? We need protecting from THEM, not the other way round.

It is not the first time this has happened. Tourists have reported seeing their ice-creams disappearing in a co-ordinated attack of fast moving clouds of feathers, claws and beaks.

Some birds have become so bold as to march into shops and take packets of crisps directly from the shelves.

Mr Colvile said many of his constituents have written to him asking for a solution to the problem.

I've got a solution. It is long, comes with two barrels and is deadly even in the hands of amateurs. You just point and shoot.

More considered responses have included replacing eggs in their nests with fakes. This does not appear to have had the result of lessening their numbers, but it has made them angry.

It is not the only wild-life related issue that Mr Colvile is concerned about. He is also planning to present a petition about hedgehogs to Parliament next week.

More than 50,000 people have signed the petition calling on the Government to 'give the hedgehog better legal protection in order to reverse its decline'.

No less a body than the Department for Environment, Food and

Rural Affairs said last year: 'We support measures to help hedgehogs.

However, they added that, 'We do not believe it is appropriate to list hedgehogs as a protected species, which is best reserved for species deliberately killed or injured by humans.'

Do they mean cows for instance, because we kill millions of them?

It's their own fault for being so delicious. If God did not want us to massacre cows, he wouldn't have made them out of meat.

We don't need to put seagulls on the endangered list, we need to put them on the menu.

I bet they taste a bit like chicken.

11.02.17

The elephant in the room.

Would you care to hazard a guess as to who was present when Donald Trump gave his first post-election foreign newspaper interview in the UK to the Times and former government minister Michael Gove?

I know what you are thinking. You are thinking: was it Vladimir Putin?

No, go to the back of the class. You are so wrong that you qualify to be the next US Secretary of Education.

The person in the room with Donald Trump when he gave an interview to the Times and Michael Gove was...Rupert Murdoch.

That is, Rupert Murdoch, the very left-wing owner of giant chunks of the famously liberal mainstream media that you will have heard so much about.

The Financial Times said Murdoch sat through the whole interview. Presumably, the billionaire media titan did that in order to press upon his friend the billionaire property mogul the importance of thinking about the little people.

If there is one thing the financial elite think a lot about, it is the poor. They are very concerned about people less well off than them.

And if you believe that I have a very valuable degree from the Trump University I would like to sell you.

Donald loves to tweet, but after Twitter, the Murdoch empire is Trump's favourite media outlet; he has had Sean Hannity, of Murdoch's Fox News, over more often than he's seen Melania these past few weeks.

A video clip of the interview shows Gove asking the president if the UK is now "at the front of the queue" for a US trade deal.

Not that we are desperate or anything but we're begging you Donald...we'll crawl across the carpet and bark like a dog if you like.

We'll go out and buy all that unsold stock of the clothes your daughter is selling, just don't hang up on us like you did Australia.

There is a consumer boycott against Trump - it is the sort of thing that will drive him crazy because his brand is based on the spurious notion that everything he touches turns to gold

Declining sales of anything that has the word "Trump" on it underlines the (not alternative) fact that his popularity has taken a nosedive since Russia helped him win the presidency.

Ivanka Trump's fashion brand has taken another kicking after the bosses of stores TJ Maxx and Marshall's demanded staff throw out her advertisements and take down her special displays.

Her clothes have already been dropped entirely by a string of retailers, including luxury chains Nordstrom and Neiman Marcus, because of a major anti-Trump boycott called GrabYourWallet.

This is troubling for Trump because you can't send the national guard out to force people to buy Trump clothes, so he tweeted about it instead.

He wrote 'My daughter Ivanka has been treated so unfairly by Nordstrom.' 'She is a great person - always pushing me to do the right thing! Terrible!'

Well, push harder Ivanka!

Nordstrom shares rose by two points in the hours after Donald Trump's furious tweet, which will also drive him crazy.

By the way, Ivanka Trump's clothing is made in America as you would expect, because Trump is all about buying American and hiring American.

Just kidding, it is of course made in Indonesia, Vietnam and China.

12.02.17

Making Ivanka's profits great again.

Donald Trump's daughter has a fashion and jewellery range. These days, who doesn't?

You probably do too. You may not have realised because you haven't received your year-end accounts yet. Check the spam box on your emails.

Ivanka has been caught up in the wave of popularity that has greeted her father since he took over as The Big White Chief.

People are so thrilled with the job he is doing that they have organised a boycott of anything Trump, so as to demonstrate their support.

It is called the GrabYourWallet campaign and it is coming to a Trump product retailer near you soon.

To mitigate the losses from having been dropped by a slew of stores, Trump got right-hand woman Kellyanne Conway to try to persuade the country to buy Ivanka's clothes and accessories from the home turf of the Fox News channel..

He did this to underline the fact that Trump has really distanced himself from all his family businesses.

It's not like he's doing this to get richer or anything.

Conway told Fox News viewers to "go buy Ivanka's stuff,"

She said, "This is just a wonderful line." "I'm going to give a free commercial here. Go buy it today, everybody. You can find it online."

That leaves little room for doubt as to her loyalty to the brand, or that it was an advert delivered to the nation from the Whitehouse to buy products that would directly benefit the family of the President.

While Trump has repeatedly stated that he is above the law on conflict of interest, the same can not be said of employees of the state.

Specifically, Conway violated a key ethics rule barring federal employees from using their public office to endorse products.

You are not supposed to use the presidency to enrich your family but it has been happening ever since he took office.

If you look on the Whitehouse website, you see Trump boasting about his success and advertising his own book The Art of the Deal.

When Ivanka was interviewed by the press after Trump's victory, she alerted journalists to the fact that she was wearing Ivanka brand jewellery, which is also not doing too well these days because of that consumer boycott.

Ironically, that boycott seems like the sort of thing that right wingers would do - to go after any target they can to progress their agenda.

Perhaps the left have finally learned their lesson from the right, which is, in a nutshell: stop being so nice.

The right have never been hampered by being nice. They get what they want by stirring fear, refusing to talk, shouting down the opposition, and basically doing anything necessary to get their way.

Just look at the Tea Party, the gun lobby and the Christian

fundamentalists who boycott, protest and flood their government representatives with phone calls and letters to get them to bow to their collective will.

Now those in the centre and on the left are starting to fight back using the same tactics.

It's about time.

It has only been a couple of weeks but so far the Trump administration and the newly emboldened Republican Party is getting rid of the rules about the coal industry polluting the environment - specifically to allow coal mines to dump toxic heavy metal waste into rivers, the ban on which the coal companies say is restricting their ability to make money.

They have cancelled the rules on capturing methane leaks from oil and gas drilling. Unfortunately for those of us who do not think that climate change is a Chinese conspiracy, methane produces 21 times as much warming in the atmosphere as carbon dioxide.

The administration has also dropped the rule about disclosing bribes that oil and gas companies give to foreign governments. This was intended to cut down on corruption.

Rex Tillerson, the new Secretary of State lobbied against that rule in 2010 when he was running the oil giant Exxon Mobil, arguing that preventing corruption would put his company at a disadvantage.

He lost then under Obama. He has won now under Trump.

They are looking to change the rule about banks and financial companies having to work in the interests of their clients, which was put there to stop people from being ripped off.

Banks and financial advisors could go back to selling you something they know is rotten and then making a side bet that it will fail.

And they've made it legal to sell guns to the mentally unstable without any background checks.

All of that was done while our attention was taken by the constant inane twitterings from the Whitehouse and the fight about the immigration ban.

You really do have to have eyes in the back of your head with this lot.

19.02.17

Lax Tax Fax

In the past ten years, Her Majesty's tax inspectors overpaid themselves £22million.

I know what you are thinking - they deserve it! They work hard, they should share the spoils.

Oh, you weren't thinking that?

In the 2015/16 financial year alone, the overpayments averaged about £5,600 extra for each staff member.

They did not all get that amount but if the £1.4m overpayment was shared out equally, that is what it would come to.

If you have recently been fined by HMRC for late filing of your tax return, or some other simple mistake, you will be surprised to learn that they are not so strict with themselves when it comes to their own tax affairs.

Oh, you aren't surprised?

The overpayments were revealed by a Freedom of Information request.

It is the sort of thing that you would think they would do everything in their power to keep from us.

They could have used any number of available excuses not to release that news. They could have said that it would cost too much to find out that information. They could have said that they did the research but the dog ate it, or they left it on a bus, but the truth came out anyway.

Perhaps they were too busy celebrating their windfalls to notice the press looming on the horizon, sharpening their pens.

Of course, this does not look good for a revenue service that has been treating ordinary, non HMRC staff quite harshly for minor infractions of the rules.

The tax man doled out a new record of 143,000 penalties last year to people who had not taken what they call 'reasonable care' to fill in their tax returns correctly.

This includes a large number of people that have made innocent mistakes, which are understandable, as a tax return is about as complicated as the operating manual for the International Space Station.

While they have been handing out punishments, 245 HMRC employees were overpaid more than £1,000 last year.

Many of them do not even work for the Revenue any more, having left, presumably to enjoy a prosperous retirement on all the cash that still pours in to their bank accounts from an organisation that is supposed to be good with money.

It is not like they have been distracted by concentrating on the big fish tax avoiders.

Just last month, the Public Accounts Committee said HMRC collected £1 billion less from multi-millionaires, six years after setting up a task force to collect more money from multi-millionaires.

Aren't you shocked? The poor get clobbered for sending in their tax returns a few days late and the super rich get a pass on £1bn worth of taxes that they actually owe.

Oh, you're not shocked?

25.02.17

An inconvenient fruit picking truth.

This week, an expert said it will take "years and years" before British workers are ready to fill the low-skilled jobs left by EU migrants.

He said the UK was not about to "suddenly shut the door" on low-skilled EU migrants.

That is because UK nationals were not likely to take up the low-paid jobs in care, farming or hotels and restaurants for some time.

And which loony left winger said that? It was chief of the hard-line anti-EU Ultras, the Brexit Secretary David Davis.

He even went further than that. He said, "We're a successful economy, largely or partly at least because we have clever people, talented people come to Britain."

And we are a successful economy because we have non clever, untalented people coming as well - the ones that are serving us food and washing our plates afterwards, bending over in a field all day to pick fruit and vegetables and wiping up after us in care homes.

They are the ones cleaning our offices and our streets, helping us to make the right decision on where not to park and making us pizza.

Migrants make up a third of the people engaged in cleaning, food preparation and hospitality.

If they downed tools for just one day, it would cost the country £328m, according to the New Economics Foundation.

'Cos they come over 'ere...and help make our economy successful.

The Prime Minister has consistently said the UK wants to continue to attract talent, but she always goes on about the highly skilled workers in industries such as finance and technology, not the industries that employ the most migrants - the NHS, care-work, agriculture, retail, hotels and restaurants, bars and coffee shops.

Brexiteers will be concerned about that because they think that leaving the EU will mean fewer foreigners but it won't because we fat lazy Brits won't do all those jobs that are currently being done by immigrants.

We won't even, as David Davis said, do them in "some time". We won't do those jobs at all, ever.

The only way we Brits would deign to get our hands dirty like that is if the pay for those jobs was greatly improved.

Unfortunately, that would cause much of those industries to shut down. Companies would go out of business, prices would shoot skywards, unemployment would soar and the government tax take would plummet causing more cuts.

So, we will either see the collapse of the restaurant trade and the health service and the farming sector or we will continue to have migrants coming in at the same rate to do our dirty work for us, whether we are in or out of the EU.

However, the Tories gave campaign pledges to bring down the numbers of low-skilled migrant workers. The Government has put a number on it. They claim to want to bring net migration below 100,000.

It is about 300,000 now, from inside and outside the EU and yet unemployment is at a long-time low of 4.8%.

That is the best figure for 10 years and before that, you'd have to go back to the early 1970s to get anywhere near it.

The total on unemployment benefits is about 745,000, the lowest since 1975.

People not in work or seeking work is about the same now as it was in 1971, so the inescapable conclusion is that all the migration into this country has not caused mass unemployment - those that have come in are working and helping the country to function and without them we'd be in big trouble.

Brexiteers should not take it from me, they should take it from their headbanger-in-chief, the man so great they named him twice.

25.02.17

<u>A cunning feat of prestidigitation?</u>

I think I have figured out what is going on here.

The six-foot, bright orange, whiny carnival barker lumbering around the Whitehouse is a giant distraction machine.

He is the only fine-tuned machine in the whole place.

On Wednesday, Donald Trump's administration revoked a key piece of guidance to public schools, which allowed transgender students to use the bathroom of their choice.

You would hardly think that was top of the list of priorities in a country that is beset with gun violence and poverty and health problems.

Republicans and the religious right-wingers are thrilled because they would like to ban everything that happens between a person's knees and waist, but Trump is not really a Republican or religious, so why spend time on this, knowing the public storm that will accompany it?

In May 2016, President Obama instructed schools to allow transgender students to use the bathrooms they feel most comfortable with.

The decision had been hailed as a victory for human rights in general.

The new administration bizarrely placed rescinding those rights at the top of their to-do list and it was championed by the new Attorney General Jeff Sessions.

Education Secretary Betsy DeVos was initially against the revocation, and it was only after the President compelled her to sign the directive that she did so, according to the non-fake, highly reliable New York Times.

Why would he be insistent on this, especially as he previously stated that if the newly transitioned Caitlyn Jenner wanted to visit Trump Tower, she could use "any bathroom she chooses".

This all came after the furore about the Muslim ban and the "big beautiful wall" and the Mexican stand-off and the Australian telephone incident and the constant trolling on Twitter.

Commentators were predictably furious and fascinated about all of those things.

But what if that was the plan?

What if all those demented missives and Tweets pouring from the freakishly small hand of the Screaming MeMe from Mar-a-Lago were designed to distract the public from what was really going on right under their noses?

What if Trump was acting like one of those magicians that wave one hand in front of your face while picking your pocket with the other?

Because, while all that was happening, the Trump administration and the Republicans controlling government have:

- voted to abolish the rule brought in by Barack Obama to subject those with mental illnesses to a background check before they could buy guns.

- overturned an Obama administration rule that sought to reduce climate change by decreasing the emissions by the oil industry of the harmful gas methane into the environment.

- quashed an Obama era regulation that prevented coal mining companies from dumping toxic waste directly into rivers and streams

- moved to eliminate Obama's fiduciary rule on financial advisors that required them to act in the interests of their clients and not just sell whatever products that would generate the highest returns for the advisors.

All that has been done pretty much under cover and was barely discussed because of the attention generating tool that is the unhinged 70 year-old toddler in the Whitehouse.

Now it all makes sense. The blatant lies, the fights with the press and celebrities, the unhinged outpourings of Captain Chaos - they were all classic diversion tactics.

The Trump administration will be great for Americans, as long as they don't like air, water or money and don't mind being shot.

04.03.17

Lib Dems Li lo.

The Liberal Democrats are camping.

To be clear, they are camping indoors, not camping it up, although the two are not mutually exclusive.

Lib Dems have ordered 90 blow-up beds so that their peers can stay overnight in Parliament to tweak Theresa May on the nose.

They plan a pyjama party stand-off with MPs on the Brexit Bill, with which Mrs M wants to fire the starting gun on leaving the EU in the next few weeks.

On Wednesday night, peers voted to amend the Bill, to force the government to guarantee the post-Brexit rights of 3.3million EU citizens living in the UK, which seems like the right thing to do.

The problem is that the PM wants to use those people as bargaining chips to discuss the rights of 1.2million Britons living in other member states.

That is the position we find ourselves in: four and a half million people don't know whether they will be allowed to stay in the country they now call home. For a bright new dawn, that seems pretty dark.

Government ministers are itching to overturn the Lords' vote when the legislation goes back to the Commons this month.

It will then "ping pong" between houses as the Lords will want to insert another amendment which the government will also fight.

It could ping back to the Lords at any moment, hence the ruddy faces on the Lib Dem benches as they strain to put enough puff in a Li-lo to catch a few winks before they are needed to stymie The Will Of The People.

That second opposition amendment would require Parliament to be given a 'meaningful' vote on Britain's final withdrawal.

Who could argue against that? That's what the leavers wanted wasn't it - a return of complete power to our elected representatives?

Was not the whole referendum on asserting the primacy of the British parliament? Or did the leavers only want our parliament to have its say when they agree with it?

How weird a place we are in right now. Our MPs are fighting for the right to have no say on the future direction of the country.

This is because the government seems to believe that last summer the people weighed up the issues, considered the implications, understood the byzantine complications of the economic and social consequences and have wisely spoken.

What is alarming is that millions of pounds of advertising was used to directly target voters on social media, paid for by a few of the super-rich who, for whatever reason, wanted us to leave the EU, and it worked very well

What we have now is a country run by not the political elite but a much wealthier, shadowy business elite, as in America.

They have very cleverly packaged both Trump and Brexit as a return of power to the little people, where quite clearly the opposite is true.

And "truth" has been the casualty on both sides of the pond - the most obvious example here was the "£350m extra to the NHS per week" bus advert.

Buses have not lied quite so much since they advertised how comfortable and convenient they are compared to cars.

Then there were the lies about all of Eastern Europe flooding into the country and the EU being a completely unelected dictatorship, which was so successful a lie that people still think that today.

What's most worrying is not that the people heard the arguments from both sides, thought about the issues and voted accordingly, it's that the people only heard carefully directed messages that showed up in their Facebook feeds and on Twitter and on phoney news sites.

The personalised messages were designed around their interests and internet histories by clever algorithms and direct marketing techniques, placed there by billionaires, using the latest technologies and propaganda tools.

Meanwhile, the Remainers were still trying to reach people the old fashioned way, by reasoned argument and pushing leaflets through people's doors like they were fighting a campaign in 1975.

Coincidentally, that was the last year that anyone slept on a Li-lo.

05.03.17

Bananas, boobs and Brussels.

The Liberal Democrats are hoping to elicit the help of pro-Remain peers to help them 'ping-pong' amendments to the Brexit Bill between the houses.

The party has 102 peers in the Lords. This number infuriates some people because it is much larger than the number of Lib Dem MPs in the Commons but 102 is about 16% of the number of Lords in the upper house, which is about where they were nationally just a few years ago. They polled as much as 23% in the 2010 general election.

Ninety folding beds have been ordered by the party in preparation for all-night sessions so they can be ready to vote at any point during the night. This means that 12 may have to bunk up.

A party strategist said: 'We are planning for every eventuality and preparing for all-night sessions. If that means pizza delivery at 3am then so be it."

The intention is to defend the rights of 3.3million EU nationals who have made their home in Britain and to be allowed a final say on the terms negotiated for our exit from the EU.

This is also known as Undermining The Will Of The People.

What the people think is very important all of a sudden.

I do not recall MPs being so exercised about it before. In fact, they have a history of blithely dismissing what The People think, and with good reason.

The people think that Brussels insists we eat straight bananas, that EU laws are made in secret and imposed on us without debate, that the EU wants all flags but its own banned at sporting events, that good old British Bombay Mix be renamed Mumbai Mix, that the EU has designs on banning prawn cocktail crisps, that barmaids showing cleavage is against EU rules and that the evil EU bureaucracy want to ban custard creams.

The People particularly believe that the EU is so chock full of frauds, crooks and ne'er-do-wells that auditors have always refused to sign off on the EU's accounts.

None of that is true, but The People think that it is.

Let's not get bogged down in forbidden biscuits and boobs because that is so silly it is hard to believe that anyone thinks it to be true.

On the subject of fraud, The Court of Auditors has signed the EU accounts every year since 2007.

The problem arises in the individual countries once they receive the EU funds. The rate of misuse of these funds is about 4.4% of the total budget.

Misuse can take many forms and mostly it is counted as such if the country in question spends the money without regard to the applicable rules and regulations.

You've got to have some rules regarding how the money is spent or it would all go on sweets and comics.

The EU's accounts are scrutinised by the Court of Auditors, which checks what goes where.

As for actual fraud, the Court says it makes up about 0.2% of the EU budget. That is still a hefty chunk of change but it is better than the 0.7% of Britain's own benefit payments that were lost to fraud in 2013.

The Court of Auditors did point out that some of the funds - 4.4% of the total in 2014 - were not used in accordance with the EU rules. But they said typical cases involved roads or airports that were not used enough to justify the expense.

These funds are not even mostly administered by the EU. They dole the cash out and 80% of it is put to use by the individual countries themselves.

We do so poorly on this score that on 28 April 2016, our own, very British House of Commons Public Accounts Committee called on the UK government to improve how it spends EU funds.

The committee found that UK departments contribute "additional complexity" to the implementation of EU programmes, especially agricultural and rural development ones, which drives up errors.

If we meddled less we would waste less.

And as for being an out of control bureaucracy, the entire EU staff is about the same number as that employed by one-and-a-half typical British councils.

There are 46,000 people employed by the EU, that includes the Commission, the Parliament, the Council and the Court of Justice.

By contrast, 33,000 are employed by Birmingham City Council alone.

They also have no one regulating the straightness of their bananas.

11.03.17

You ruined it, you clear it up

The Chief Executive of the oil company Shell, Ben van Beurden, said there will be falling oil use as soon as the 2020s.

He's talking about a peak in our oil consumption, and it can't come soon enough.

He went further - the boss of Shell said those who trivialise the threat of climate change will exhaust public tolerance for fossil fuel companies if they are not careful.

Is he talking about the Screaming MeMe in the Whitehouse?

He said "Social acceptance is just disappearing. I do think trust has been eroded to the point that it is becoming a serious issue for our long term future,"

That is because in the long term, the best customers don't tend to be dead, and you can't fill your car up with petrol if it is covered in water.

He said, "It is not a rational discussion any more, it's emotional", which is exactly what the world thinks every time Trump opens his mouth or goes into a tantrum on the internet - it's not a rational discussion any more, it's emotional.

Trump is emotionally wedded to the idea that fossil fuel companies should be able to do whatever they want to the environment to maximise their short-term profitability, as long as it allows him to Tweet something self-aggrandising about "jaaabs".

Almost all of the world's climate scientists think the fossil fuel industries are contributing to catastrophic climate change, but 100% of the owners of oil and coal companies think those industries are causing them to earn a ton of money, so no wonder they don't want to stop, or go to the expense of cleaning up their act.

I know we are no longer interested in science, or facts, but allow me this one: the 12 hottest years in history have all been in the last 20 years.

In the parts of the world that Donald Trump is not currently running, individuals and regulators are starting to demand that fossil fuel companies account for the financial risks from climate change.

This is huge. There was a law suit in Germany featuring German coal company RWE which was being sued by a farmer in Peru for the potential disaster that could be wrought by a flood caused by climate change melting glaciers.

He claimed that the company would be at least partly responsible because pollution and harmful emissions know no boundaries. What is emitted in Germany does not stay in Germany.

The case was dismissed, but then so were many cases against the evil tobacco companies before they were defeated for the first time.

The Peruvian farmer only wanted €17,000 from RWE towards a dam to protect up to 50,000 people at risk, due in part because of the utility's historic contribution to greenhouse gas emissions.

But the judge ruled that while there was "scientific causality", the farmer's lawyer had not demonstrated "legal causality".

In other words, the court was not convinced RWE was legally responsible for protecting this farmer, despite evidence that its activities had contributed to the town's predicament.

The ruling was important to RWE, not because they saved €17,000, they could afford that in the spare change they've got in their car ashtrays, but because it would set a precedent by which the polluters would be deemed responsible for their mess, just as you would be sued by the council if you just threw your rubbish into the road.

It seems fair that the polluter *should* pay. Air pollution in this country costs the UK economy £54bn a year, according the World Health Organisation - that's almost 4% of GDP, which is a measure of all the money we make.

They got to that number by allocating a value to each death and disease caused by pollution.

If we forget about the disease and the lower life expectancy and the lower IQ scores and the lower job prospects, and just concentrate on the deaths, pollution kills 40,000 people in this country every year.

If you ran a business that was in some way responsible for killing 40,000 people in Britain every year, you would expect the government to do something about it.

At the very least you would have to pay a fine and clean up your act and you should prepare to go to jail.

But like the cigarette companies before them, the fossil fuel giants get a pass because they have a wall of money to throw at any impediment that gets in the way of doing whatever they want, and successive governments have just gone along with it.

Just remember that when the authorities slap another tax on alcohol or maintain the ban on marijuana and they say they are doing it for the good of your health.

12.03.17

No designs on the future

Design and technology GCSE has disappeared from nearly half of schools because teenagers no longer like making things.

They are too busy updating their Snapchat feeds with news of their latest haircut or practising their selfie pout.

Hundreds of schools across the country have axed the subjects from the curriculum in the past year alone, according to a poll of teachers conducted by the Association of School and College Leaders.

The Chief Executive of the Design and Technology Association said the survey results were "worrying". She said, "We know that the subject itself suffers from a bit of an image problem, people see it as a craft based subject, where you just make a bird box or something like that."

This would be a health and safety improvement on my school

metalwork class in which, at the age of ten, we were instructed on how to make an ashtray.

They were different times, when a packet of twenty did not cost £9 and children could afford them.

The news that there is a ten per cent decrease in the number students taking design and technology as a GSCE is worrying because designing things is one thing that can't be done by a robot.

Robots can make products but they can't design them.

Like many things, it is all Tony Blair's fault.

In 2004, the Labour government removed the requirement for pupils to study design and technology at GCSE.

The problem has been exacerbated recently by the introduction of the English Baccalaureate, which focuses on a core of subjects made up of English, mathematics, history, geography, the sciences and a language.

These are important subjects. It is important to know a foreign language so you can tell visitors to "go back to your own country" in their own tongue and it is important to know geography so you know where they are going to be sent back to.

It is important to know history, so you can see it being repeated and it's important to know that 9 times 8 is 63 and that 6+3 is ten, and it's important to know English, cos it's, like, our language, innit?

But design is one of the things we are historically really good at, like music.

Unfortunately, the last big British design launch was a £300 hair dryer and our biggest musical export now is Ed Sheeran.

If we carry on ceding the lead in art and design, we will have to fall back on our traditional skills of invading countries, stealing all their stuff and introducing them to cricket.

At this rate, China will replace us at the forefront of the design world and we will be working in factories for twelve hours a day making cheap plastic crap for THEM.

18.03.17

They bought the land out from under us

Now that Article 50 is about to be triggered and those that wish to thwart Brexit have been vanquished, can we go back to a time when no-one ever used the word "thwart"?

Seriously, where did that come from? It's as anachronistic as a train announcer saying that passengers may "alight" at the next station.

I realise some people would like to go back to when Britain was great (1953) but do we have to use the language of the time as well?

The good old days are gone and were not that good anyway. Mostly they are fondly remembered because that is when we were young and better looking and had more hair coming out of our scalps than our ears.

As an indication that times have moved on, a question: who owns the largest chunk of London, our fair capital city?

An educated guess might be the Queen but that would not be correct. Not by a long chalk, and good thing too.

The repair bill for Buckingham Palace alone is costing about as much as buying the world's most expensive, misfiring Manchester United football player and one of Philip Green's bigger boats. If she owned any more, we couldn't afford it.

So, if it is not the Queen, who owns the most in London?

Perhaps you are thinking it must be the Duke of Westminster, by which I mean Major General Gerald Cavendish Grosvenor, 6th Duke of Westminster, KG CB CVO OBE TD CD DL.

If he had any more letters after his name we would have to get a bigger alphabet.

He owns loads of London because he worked his way up from the bottom and fashioned a property empire from nothing. Or his dad gave it to him, one or the other, but it isn't him either.

Maybe it's the Earl of Cadogan. He's super rich. He owns Chelsea, by which I mean the actual place and not just the football team.

He did it the aristocratic way as well, by having a distant relative who bought the land for peanuts when you could still find room to park your horse.

But it isn't him either. No, the owner of the biggest parcel of property in London is the royal family of Qatar, the quite un-British place which sounds like something smokers cough up in the morning but is actually a spit of land about half the size of Wales, off the coast of God-knows-where in a place that's too hot to live in.

Even camels say, "to hell with this, I'm going to Africa".

Every summer the Qataris come to London to visit the places they already own and to size up what little is left that they don't.

If it is big and shiny and they can see it through the shaded windows of their luminous green Lamborghinis, they'll buy it.

They already own Canary Wharf, not the wharf itself but all of it - everything that you see when you get out of the Tube.

They own the skyscrapers, the bars, the shops, the lot.

Then there's the British Olympic village, which was the site of our glorious games, during which supreme British athletes suffering from debilitating asthma managed to find enough totally legal medicine to pull in a record medals haul for Her Majesty's Team GB.

I don't recall the Qataris winning any medals in that "village", but now they own that too.

They also own the Shard, the tallest building in the country. In fact, they have a great love for tall, thrusting, phallic buildings that only Donald Trump can match.

The massive plot that was the Chelsea Barracks is theirs too. It will soon be a much needed complex of tiny executive flatlets for millionaires to park the money that they haven't invested in highly complex off-shore tax havens.

In total, according to a commercial property data company called Datscha, the Qataris own 21.5m sq ft of London's most prime space, which is a lot. You wouldn't want to have to paint it.

The Queen, meanwhile, has to squeeze herself into just a third of that - 7.3m sq feet.

It is still enough run-around room for the corgis but is a bit embarrassing for us proud Brits who used to run Qatar until the 1970s.

It was a place that used to make most of its money fishing and diving for pearls before they discovered that millions of years ago a mighty forest once stood there and under their feet was so much oil and gas that they leapt out of the third world and put a firm down-payment on the first.

Now that Brexit is happening, thank goodness that we have got our country back.

19.03.17

Please speak directly into the toaster Mr Trump.

I was beginning to miss him. It had been almost a week since Donald Trump had said something un-presidential on the internet

Twitter seemed such a sane place without him, and then he broke cover by spewing up the allegation that he just found out he was being secretly wiretapped in his gold tower by the non-American Muslim terrorist from Kenya, his presidential predecessor, Obak Arama

The internet said, "thank you Donald for bringing back the crazy"

He heard about it on some right-wing shock jocks' radio show, which was totally NOT fake news because Donald Trump believed it.

That is the difference between fake news and real news: whether the

Screaming MeMe in the Whitehouse thinks it is true.

After his Tweet landed, Obama's people said he didn't do it, the FBI said he didn't do it, the CIA said he didn't do it and Homeland Security said he didn't do it.

For all I know, Kermit the Frog and Miss Piggy said he didn't do it, but Donald Trump is not swayed by experts and their so-called facts.

He is a man who has never heard the word "no" and never said the word "sorry", so he sent out his messengers to explain that when he said that Obama had "wiretapped" him, he didn't mean wiretapped, what on earth gave anyone that idea?

He actually meant that Obama had been listening in on him through his household appliances, including but not limited to, his television, through which he hears voices, and his light switches and his microwave oven.

He actually had his top spokesperson, the wicked witch of the West Wing, Kellyanne Conway, appear on TV news and say that the government spies on people by putting cameras in their microwaves.

If they did, what they would mostly get is film of people shouting at them to hurry up.

I would like to see the footage of the camera that is installed in his hair-dryer. Then we might see where the hair comes from and where it goes to.

My bet is that it's one twenty foot long strand that's been woven into that candy-floss cloud that hovers above his head like a hair drone.

When people thought that accusation was silly and that the American government would find much better hiding places for secret Donald Trump camera recorders than a microwave, he did not back down and say that he had miss-spoken because he had been inhaling wig glue fumes.

In fact, he doubled down, dug his tiny heels in and said that Britain had helped spy on him.

He knows that to be true because he heard about it from some conspiracy theorist on Fox News who said that we British had sicked our security services on him and have been bugging his trousers or his chicken wings or his swan shaped solid gold bath taps, which he said was illegal and a disgrace.

It would be disgraceful and illegal if it was true but it isn't. Britain's diplomats went very quietly berserk.

There then followed a collector's item: for possibly the first and last time, Donald Trump sent someone to apologise for his outburst.

He got that angry yappy-dog of a press secretary Sean Spicer to say sorry for him, while Trump himself said he had done nothing wrong and he was merely repeating what he had heard on television.

He will reciting the weather forecast in Tucson next.

Britain's spy chiefs at GCHQ, said that the allegations were utterly ridiculous and should be ignored.

You could say that about the President himself - he's utterly ridiculous and we should ignore him, but unfortunately for at least the next four years, we can't.

25.03.17

"You're going home in a ****ing Krankenwagon"

England football supporters chanted offensive songs and made offensive gestures at the inoffensive German fans and footballers before a "friendly" match this week.

They did that as the German national anthem was being played, which in England is also known as: an incitement to violence.

Football supporters are rude. This is news, just as it gets light when the sun comes up is news.

Football fans make troglodytes look sophisticated. As individuals they may be an unalloyed delight, but as a group they revert to the mouth-breathing knuckle-draggers that we were when we emerged from the swamp.

And now the Football Association is going to do something about it. They have decided to leap into action after only 200 years of this sort of thing since the invention of the beautiful game.

The FA has moved to ban those who bring shame on our nation, and the best of luck with that.

There was a campaign to get racism out of football and there is now another to rid the game of homophobia. How are they going by the way? You might as well try to ban stupidity from the terraces.

If everyone who is rude or loudly threatening and insensitive is going to get banned from the stands at football matches then games will be pretty quiet affairs.

If your team is doing badly, you won't have to leave early to get a head start on the crowds because there won't be any.

You will be able to stroll out unimpeded, at your leisure. You will also be able to sit where you want. You'll be able to lie down and take a nap if you like. It will so quiet you'll hear the grass grow.

The FA must be the most patient organisation in sport. Either that, or they are chronically inept and ineffective in the face of fans' manufactured, effortful boiling rage at anyone and anything that is not wearing the colours of their own team.

This included referees who are subject to so much spittle-flecked abuse at top flight games that they must have to hose themselves down afterwards.

If players are that aggressive and intemperate when millions of people are watching in high definition and close up on television, just imagine what refs have to put up with in the lower divisions.

Their work car should be a tank.

The top players' constant barracking of officials and persistent cheating communicates to the fans that this is how football is done.

I can't recall cricket umpires getting screamed at by some hulking fielders after giving a decision they didn't like. Rugby players do not regularly get so close they are touching noses to yell at an official when a call goes the other way.

This only seems to happen in football, and the players, the coaches and the FA are all responsible.

Nine months after England were almost thrown out of the European Championship for rioting in Marseilles, supporters ignored repeated warnings not to perform the song '10 German bombers' in front of what was a television audience of millions.

It is a song that children used to sing in the Second World War about the RAF shooting down enemy planes in the manner of '10 green bottles sitting on the wall'.

It is still being sung by the childish, seventy years later.

FA chairman Greg Clarke said: "The behaviour of a section of the England support in Dortmund was inappropriate, disrespectful and disappointing.

What he did not say was that it was also entirely predictable and is the sort of thing you are likely to hear at every football match in the land.

You don't even have to go to the match. They bring their stupidity to you.

For instance - try travelling on the District Line when Chelsea have just finished playing, as I frequently used to do and you will hear moronic, drunks trying to outdo their mates in offensiveness, at the tops of their voices, regardless of whether the train is full of families, old ladies or children.

The train winds peacefully from Putney until the mood turns ugly the moment the doors open at Fulham Broadway and the Chelsea contingent lurch on yelling every kind of obscenity that you can think of, and some they have invented especially for the occasion.

What the hell is the matter with these people?

The Football Association said "The FA has consistently urged supporters to show respect and not to chant songs that could be regarded as insulting to others.

They will probably go so far as to ask managers to wear a special respect badge when being interviewed on the telly.

That's bound to work.

25.03.17

<u>Your in-flight entertainment is cancelled for your convenience.</u>

The British government has followed the Americans by banning laptops and Kindles and all that shiny electronica that people use to make time on a flight go faster.

From now on, you are no longer allowed your favourite screen-based waste of time in the passenger compartments of planes coming from some carefully selected Muslim countries.

People on carriers like BA, Egyptair and EasyJet are going to have to put their amusements and work tools in the hold.

This makes perfect sense because if some swivel-eyed terrorist nutcase wanted to plant a bomb in a laptop and it exploded in the hold, the hole that it would blow in the plane would only affect the luggage section which would disengage from the passenger compartment and all the people upstairs would continue on to their intended destination unscathed.

Of course, that's a fantasy - it doesn't matter where the bomb goes off in a plane, the whole thing is going to split into a million bits and rain fire and sachets of complimentary peanuts all over whatever is underneath.

What's the point of telling terrorists that bombs are no longer acceptable as carry-on luggage, they're going to have to put them in their suitcase with their pants and socks?

The government has decreed that no-one flying in from Turkey,

Jordan, Egypt, Tunisia, Lebannon and Saudi Arabia can watch La La Land on their lap top, they're going to have to put up with whatever Adam Sandler film the airline dishes up.

Unfortunately, terrorists are crazy, they're not stupid.

If you were in Turkey and you wanted to blow up a plane going to New York and you weren't allowed to take your bomb in your carry-on bag, and you absolutely totally and definitely wanted to press the switch to blow it up, you'd just cross the border and fly from Georgia instead.

Apparently flights from there are fine. You can take what you like on board a plane from Georgia. There's chickens and goats running up and down the aisle on flights from Georgia.

The authorities say it is all about security. The British government takes security very seriously.

They always say that when they need an excuse for doing something daft or intrusive, but you can be pretty sure that if the security services have found out about some threat from an exploding iPad, the crazies that want to blow stuff up will have moved onto something else.

A while ago it was exploding underpants. You might remember that bloke was able to sail through security with TNT in his pantaloonies, and he got through probably because even if there had been a credible threat, no one wanted to look there.

Security experts who examined them after he tried but failed to light the fuse in his Y fronts said that he'd been wearing them for two weeks straight and the explosive had become what they called "degraded".

I'm feeling degraded just thinking about it.

Then you will recall that fellow with the exploding sandals who just waltzed trough security despite the fact that he was about 8 feet tall, had a giant bushel of pubes on his head and looked so mad that you could have seen his crazy from space.

Richard Reid the shoe bomber actually tried to light the fuse in his boots with a match and the stewardess told him he couldn't smoke on the plane.

He couldn't light it because his feet had been sweating so much he wet the fuse. Everyone else wet themselves laughing.

So now we have to take our shoes off and go through a scanner that takes a picture of our genitals and shares them on Facebook for all we know, and we can't take over 100ml of liquid on a plane, not because you can't blow up a plane with such a small amount but just because the authorities want to be seen to be doing something, and now this.

It is almost as though the romance has gone from flying!

Of course, our British government was just following on from what the Screaming MeMe in the Whitehouse had done and banned electronic devices bigger than a phone from the passenger pod.

Theresa May presumably did this to further ingratiate herself with that orange golfing galumph in Washington in the hope that he will forget we are spying on him through a camera in his microwave and to avoid him slamming the phone down on us like he did Australia.

01.04.17

Back to the past in the future.

A YouGov poll last month asked over 2,000 British adults what they want to see return in the wake of Brexit.

Top of the list for those that voted to leave the EU was a time machine to take the country back to how it was in the good old days before the bloomin' internet and bloomin' teenagers and bloomin' newfangled litres and grams.

Of the available options posed, what the leavers most want is a return of the death penalty.

The pollsters did not ask what they want the death penalty for, so let's assume it is for everyone they don't like the look of.

That would be a long list. We are going to have to get bigger graveyards. Perhaps we could stack the dead on top of one another, or bury them standing up.

The number two most important thing Brexiteers would like to see the return of is - and I swear I am not making this up - their old dark blue passports.

Not that they are going to use them to actually go anywhere, 'cos its all foreign over there and they don't make tea like you get at home.

They'll keep them in a drawer and look at them every now and then and have a British patriot-gasm right there in their front room, all over the antimacassar.

Third on the to-do list for Mrs M, now we have got our country back, is a return of good old fashioned pounds and ounces.

They want to go back to the sensible way of measuring things that were not divided up into multiples of ten.

Leavers want to return to when there were 20 shillings to the pound and 12 pence to the shilling and two ha'pennies and four farthings to the penny.

That way was much better than this decimal rubbish we have got today - all you had to do was be able to multiply by 2 and 4 and 12 and 20 to figure out how much stuff was.

Back then there was 16 ounces to the pound and 14 pounds to the stone and 2240 pounds to the ton.

That made sense. Instead of multiplying by ten - you got to multiply by 16 and 14, so you knew instantly that when you had 17 pounds of something, that was 272 ounces.

Much more preferable than bloomin' round numbers and the ten times table.

God didn't give us 14 fingers for nothing you know.

Those that voted leave also want the return of corporal punishment in school. This is allied with a desire to bring back hanging. If you can't execute unruly teenagers, then old folk should be able to thrash them, as a compromise.

They want to cane the modern world right out of them.

Leavers want to say, "take THAT you young people with your hair styles and your Beatles music and your sexual shenanigans".

And they want them to say "thank you sir may I have another"...and they'd bloomin' well get another too, and no mistake.

They also want the old incandescent light bulbs back 'n' all - 'cos they want to see the suffering in the miscreants' eyes when they are getting their punishment.

Never mind that those bulbs are detrimental to the environment. To Hell with the environment.

They won't be around long enough to see the climate change, and the sea rise, and they're dying of smokers cough anyway, so what's a little extra pollution?

Speaking of which, leavers say: why can't they smoke in pubs like they used to?

Bloomin' moaners put a stop to that - what's a bit of cancer going to do to you? Never harmed no one.

Leavers want to go back to some imagined idyll, when everyone knew their place, when men wore hats, dinner was turnips and corned beef and the loudest thing in the house was the ticking of the clock on the mantelpiece.

Well, that time's up granddad - try stepping into the 1960's before your time on this earth is over. You never know, you might like it.

On the plus side - if you don't like it, it'll give you something else to grumble about.

02.04.17

Incoming!

An enormous asteroid flew closer to Earth than the moon this week.

The object, given the clunky, unlovely, slightly threatening name of 2017 FJ101, zipped past within 202,000 miles of planet Earth.

The moon orbits around 238,855 miles away, so a piece of space rock the size of a bus came around 36,000 miles closer to the Earth than the moon.

Alarming! Not even Ken Livingstone's bendy London buses were that dangerous.

The White House released an official document describing the plan if a meteor or asteroid was to head our way, it said "We're going to build a wall, a beautiful wall and we're going to get E.T. to pay for it."

The document is called the 'National Near-Earth Object Preparedness Strategy'.

It says the US government seeks to improve the nation's preparedness to address the hazard of near-Earth object (NEO) impacts by claiming that they are not real, that scientists do not agree that they are a "thing" and that if the President did not see it on Fox News then we can't be hurt by it.

Actually, that's not true, I made that up.

Dealing with a threatening asteroid would involve sending up a rocket to attack it, and as rockets are giant phallic thrusting objects, Donald Trump is VERY keen on having his name on one.

At the end of last year, Nasa warned we are not prepared for an asteroid strike.

Nasa's Dr Joseph said: 'The biggest problem is there's not a hell of a lot we can do about it at the moment.'

This is the sort of thing you do not want to hear from a scientist that is responsible for saving mankind.

He said: 'They are the extinction-level events, things like dinosaur killers; they're 50 to 60 million years apart, essentially.

This was more comforting, but then he added:

'You could say, of course, we're due.'

So, there's nothing we can do about it and it is just pure luck whether we all survive or we all die, which sounds like our prospects under a Trump presidency.

We might all die if he starts World War Three because Kim Jong-un starts a Twitter fight about who has crazier hair.

Of course, we might all survive if the dipstick in the Whitehouse can be distracted by something shiny for the next 4 years, while the grown-ups take charge.

Maybe a small asteroid will hit Mar-a-lago and do us all a favour, except that would put Mike pray-the-gay-away Pence in charge of the free world.

All things considered, I think at this point, maybe an extinction level event would be better.

Wipe the slate clean and start again.

Who's with me?

08.04.17

<u>Whoopie we're all gonna die</u>

President Donald Trump suddenly got a conscience about the poor people suffering in Syria.

That is the same Donald Trump that banned the poor suffering Syrian refugees from salvation in America.

It seems that he doesn't want to actually help any of them - but he is all for firing off some big weapons to make it appear that he does.

This also has the added benefit of making him feel like a man.

Melania is safely in New York, so she hasn't been making him feel manly, so he has got to get his ego polished somewhere else.

For his inauguration, Trump actually asked whether he could have a military parade of rocket launchers and tanks, like a third world dictator, or a Russian president.

A confidential email released under transparency laws showed that The Presidential inauguration committee requested the Pentagon to - and this is a direct quote - "send us some pictures of military vehicles we could add to the parade".

Trump wanted to vet the vehicles for masculinity. He was looking for something that's longer than it is wide.

Big, thrusting, phallic rockets and guns to project a strong image.

It sounds like an advert for erectile dysfunction pills.

This strike against Syria wouldn't have anything to do with Trump's historically low approval ratings would it?

Even Richard Nixon had better ratings than the Tangerine Scream in his first year in office. In fact, at this point in the presidency, Trump trumps every one of his predecessors for unpopularity.

It's unprecedented!

That must drive him nuts. His orange face must go red watching the TV news reporting that fact. His complexion is clashing with itself.

It is taught in Dictator School Class 101 that when you want a bump in the ratings, which is all he seems to be interested in, then you start a war or you overreact to a terrorist attack.

I think the terrorist attack scenario will play itself out pretty soon.

There will be some outrage and the president will announce that in order to make everyone safe he'll cut the regulations on privacy, crack down on the media, distort the truth and demonise a small minority of the population for people to direct their anger at.

Oh wait, that's right - he's done that already.

In what many assume is an attempt to shore up his ratings, he sent 59 Tomahawk missiles to save the Syrian people, while at the same time refusing to give shelter to the Syrian people.

And, fact fans, he did it on the 100th anniversary of America entering the 1st World War.

Donald's close friends in the Kremlin said they were outraged and very upset and winked so hard they almost swallowed their eyebrows.

The UK government just trailed along behind him like a lap dog.

We had government officials coming out saying that they were fully briefed before hand and they fully support him.

That may be, but knowing about Trump's unpredictability, would you be at all surprised if our government knew about it the moment they saw it on CNN?

What precipitated all this was a gas attack in Syria, in which 70 people died a horrible death.

However, this was after close to half a million people had died by other means in the Syrian war, but we didn't do anything about that.

We didn't send in the rockets and we didn't call for military action and our government spokespeople did not go on TV to rail about it because those half a million people all died a happy, peaceful and legal way, by being shot or blown up, their body parts scattered all over the place, dying slowly in filthy hospitals screaming in agony.

It seems there are only a few horrible ways to kill that we get all superior about and start citing international law and harrumphing that they've gone too far this time.

I don't know if you've ever had your home blown up and everyone you know die all in the same place but I bet that's not too nice either.

But that doesn't get straight to the heart, like pictures of people dying of a gas attack.

In the end the result is the same - a lot of dead people, but we're only interested in lots of dead people if they died nearby, or they died in a place we might go on holiday, or they were British, or if they died in such a way that it momentarily stops us eating our dinner while watching the news.

09.04.17

I'm not angry, I'm disappointed...and I'm angry.

A note to The Guardian newspaper - I am very disappointed with you.

Newspapers are hurting. Sales are falling off a cliff and have been for quite some time.

The official ABC circulation figures say that The Sun is down 3.5% year on year, The Mail down 4.8%, The Mirror down about 10%, and The Guardian flat-lining , despite the gifts to the news industry of Brexit and Trump.

On-line figures give more hope and the Mail Online is doing very well but what is disappointing is that there seems to be a rush to Daily Mail website-ise everything that papers do in this country, and it is getting wearying.

Mail Online increased the reach for their website by 10% last year but does that mean that everyone else has to follow them with tales of gormless 'slebs and endless headlines that are questions:

Is this the worst atrocity ever?

Has this TV chef revolutionised chips?

Have you been cleaning wrong all this time?

I don't know - you are the newspaper - you tell me. It's why I came to you in the first place, not for a game of 20 questions.

Just tell me the bloomin' news and if I want to be bombarded with questions I don't know the answer to, I'll watch University Challenge

And I know that many of these headlines are deliberately designed to annoy, just to make you click on the link so you will see the advert that sits alongside, but really, The Guardian has gone too far this time.

Right there on the front page of their website this week was this headline:

"Harry Styles debuts Sign of the Times."

For those of you who have no idea who, or what, a Harry Styles is, he is one of those tattooed haircuts that is, or was, in the television game show band One Dimension.

I suppose it would have been alright if the headline ended there. I am sure that some of the less mature readers of The Guardian, who do not care much for music, are actually interested in what some boy-band member is doing now, but they did not end the headline there.

It got a lot worse than that, because after saying that Harry Styles has a new song out, The Guardian then asked, in big bold letters:

"Is he really the new Bowie?"

Well, let's think about that for a moment shall we?...NO!

Yes, it's a "no" from me, and for the benefit of foreign readers who may be unsure of my position, that's "nee" in Africaans, "non" in French, "nein" in German, "tidak" in Malaysian, "net" in Russian and "ghobe" in Klingon.

Harry Styles is really NOT the new David Bowie.

Any more stupid questions?

16.04.17

There's a route to happiness, but you won't like it.

According to a new report from the giant brains at Oxford Economics, British households are richer than ever.

However, before you start putting out the bunting and the Union Flags and having a special Brexit I-told-you-so-gasm, there's a "but".

British households are richer than ever, BUT that won't translate to a much-needed boost to the economy in the form of increased consumer spending.

That is because those riches are not shared out evenly among all of us. It is an average trend which hides the fact that this wealth is tied up in house prices and pension funds and mostly because it is tied up in the hands of a tiny number of people who got lucky and sit atop the greasy pole.

At the end of 2016, British households' total holdings of properties and assets amounted to £9.2 trillion — up almost 8% on a year earlier.

Consumer spending did not grow at anything like that rate though, because the 8% increase was not spread out over all consumers.

In fact, Oxford Economics' model suggests that a 10% rise in wealth boosts consumer spending by only 0.2%.

If the money is in private pension funds, it isn't being spent - and pension funds represent about half of the wealth in the country, which won't come as any comfort to half of those in the country who have no pension at all.

If the money is in housing, that is not being spent either. In both cases, those with money are the ones that are benefiting the most.

It is the old that are the biggest winners. They bought houses when they were giving them away free with ten gallons of petrol and now they are worth a fortune. The young aren't benefiting from the house price increase, because they don't have the money to buy them in the first place.

They will also miss out on the pension schemes that previous generations are enjoying.

On top of that, the increase in young renters is raising the income of the property owning class, while depressing the prospects and the spending power of those same young people.

According to Oxford Economics the average household wealth for those in the top 20% of income distribution was £853,000, and just £23,600 for households in the bottom 20%

Despite the obvious disparity of wealth distribution, we are witnessing a further move of wealth from the poor and the young, to the rich and the old.

That could be partly remedied by taxing the rich more and maybe taxing property.

But if you even suggest that, the newspapers will scream about socialism and the Conservatives will bang on about rewarding the job creators, despite the fact that if the money is tied up with the wealthy, who are not spending as much as their wealth is increasing by, there aren't any jobs being created.

What is odd is that people in the lower income brackets go along with all that because they are either easily swayed, or they don't know enough to make a reasoned judgement, or they have never heard of Denmark.

In Denmark, the top line tax rate is about 56% of income. In the UK it is 45% - and guess which of those two countries has happier citizens?

There's a thing called the World Happiness Report, which asks people in 53 countries how happy they are and measures levels of GDP, life expectancy, generosity, social support, freedom, and corruption.

For 2017 it lists the top ten as:

Denmark, Switzerland, Iceland, Norway, Finland, Canada, the Netherlands, New Zealand, Australia and Sweden.

Of those countries, only Switzerland, and Canada pay less tax than we do.

We are 23rd on the list, behind Israel and Mexico, the places with the bombs coming in and the headless corpses by the side of the road.

The countries at the bottom end of the happiness index are, coincidentally, the ones with the lowest tax rates on earth - Saudi Arabia, Qatar, Kuwait, and Bahrain, have a 0% personal income tax rate.

You would think that would make them happy but they are not.

If politicians point out that countries that have a fairer distribution of wealth are full of happier people, they will be shot down in flames, asked to resign, refused a vote and ridiculed by the very same people that would benefit from it.

It is almost as though the poor have been trained to act against their own best interests.

17.04.17

Hair-raising times.

North Korea threatened to 'ruthlessly ravage' US troops and to 'pulverize' US bases and the South Korean capital Seoul if it was threatened by the US military, which is unfortunate because a threatening US aircraft carrier group is steaming right towards them.

Still, I am sure that the leaders of North Korea and the US are sensible, grounded men, so what could possibly go wrong?

China warned the region could go to war 'at any moment', particularly if Donald Trump keeps pronouncing it as "Jyna".

North Korea warned that President Donald Trump's 'troublemaking' and 'aggressive' tweets have pushed the world to the brink of thermo-nuclear war, which is my least favourite type of war.

Pyongyang's Vice Minister said: 'We will go to war if they choose', and that the country would continue developing its nuclear program and conduct its next nuclear test whenever its leaders see fit.

He said: we'll do it if we want and you can't stop us.

We need that nice nanny off the telly to sit these toddlers on the naughty step.

During the election campaign, Trump said he would not be getting involved in any foreign wars.

His presidency is not even 100 days in, and so far he has dropped bombs on both sides of the conflict in Syria, dropped the biggest bomb since Nagasaki on Afghanistan, is sailing an armada to threaten North Korea, has re-started the Cold War with Russia, has threatened Iraq with taking its oil, slammed the phone down on Australia and accused the British of spying on him through his toaster.

On American media, those strikes in Syria and Afghanistan were greeted with the usual whooping and cheering that you get when the military goes into action.

As Trump seems especially interested in people whooping and cheering for him, it is quite likely that he will continue in this vein.

Meanwhile, Kim Jong-un's regime is thought to be considering another nuclear bomb test.

The last one went 'bang', and they want to know if they can make one that goes 'BANG!!'

This week, North Korea marked the Day of the Sun national holiday, commemorating the birth of the country's founding father Kim Il Sung, who was followed by Kim Jong-il who was followed by Menta Lee-il, who is running the country today.

At the celebrations, the North Korean military spokesmodel said: 'Our toughest counteraction against the US and its vassal forces will be taken in such a merciless manner as not to allow the aggressors to survive.'

I think it is probably just the translation into English that makes them sound like puppets from Thunderbirds.

It looks like it is shaping up to be the war of the two Big Chief Crazy Hairs.

It will be a battle to see who is the least suitable person to run a country and the least appropriate to be on a picture in a barbershop window.

22.04.17

UN-nerving.

The United Nations is worried. Having read their latest report, now I am worried too. Let me tell you all about it, so that you don't miss out on the rising tide of panic.

The UN has warned that the risk of a nuclear war breaking out is at its highest ever point.

They say it is because the likelihood of a catastrophic error has never been greater.

It is a good job our world leaders are people stable temperaments, and are not prone to rash judgement.

According to a report by the UN's Institute for Disarmament Research, complex automated systems could malfunction and start a chain of events which could kill millions of people.

I have seen that film and it doesn't end well unless you are Arnold Schwarzenegger, when you get to return for MUCH more money in the sequels.

The whole point of a nuclear deterrent is just that - it is a deterrent. We are not supposed to use it.

Countries spend many billions of pounds to arm themselves to the teeth with weapons that can wipe out everything, except cockroaches and Keith Richards, so that they never have to use them.

This makes sense on paper. What also makes sense is that everything tends to go wrong eventually. Sometimes things go wrong all the time. Just ask passengers on Southern Rail.

The UN document says: 'Nuclear deterrence works—up until the time it will prove not to work. The risk is inherent and, when luck runs out, the results will be catastrophic.'

I have just looked up the word "catastrophic" in a dictionary and it has nothing to do with kittens.

The problem is that the systems connecting all those nuclear bombs has been made by humans. As you will know if you ever met a human being, they should not be allowed to walk a dog without supervision, let alone construct something on which the survival of Planet Earth depends.

The UN report says that the interconnectedness of the systems mean that one error could very quickly be magnified, and warns of the risk of 'accident, misunderstanding or inadvertent escalation'.

This scenario includes the President of the United States of America mistaking the nuke button for the television remote.

Its report states: 'The complex interactions and tightly coupled systems linked to nuclear arsenals (like those for early warning, and launch command and control) have made "accidental war" more likely.'

And so has having a giant, orange, thin-skinned baby in the White House.

Speaking of which, now that Captain Chaos has a taste for warfare, the likelihood of the USA arming itself with nuclear-enabled drones is a further reason to be fearful.

Drones are going to deliver pizza and could also deliver the end of Mankind as we know it.

Total global annihilation in less than 30 minutes, or your money back.

23.14.17

Mop-top flip-flops.

Donald Trump has changed his mind. This is now so common that it should be printed on his baseball hats.

Inside sources in the US and Britain say that Trump will strike a free trade deal with the European Union before it agrees one with Britain.

If true, it would signal a dramatic U-turn on the part of the U.S President. Dramatic but not unexpected.

Trump has changed his mind on everything he has ever said depending on who he spoke to last.

China was a currency manipulator, now it is not a currency manipulator.

He wanted to appoint a special prosecutor to lock Hillary up, but after he had won, he said to one of his hollering fan rallies: "That plays great *before* the election, now we don't care" .

There was going to be a big beautiful wall all the way across the southern border. Now it won't go all the way, it won't all be a wall and Mexico is not going to pay for it, after all.

He was not going to get into any foreign wars, now he's starting them in every country he can name off the top off his head.

He was going to drain the swamp and attack special interests. After the election, he picked his cabinet from the swamp and special interests.

NATO was obsolete, now it isn't. It is almost as though he has no idea what he's doing and is making it all up as he goes along.

According to the Times, Trump has 'softened' his opposition to a US-EU deal after Angela Merkel, the German chancellor, convinced him that reaching agreement would be simpler than he thought.

He likes simple thoughts - they're his favourite type.

Apparently, his administration thought they would be able to open talks with individual EU members. He had to have the concept of the European Union explained to him.

Sources say there has been a 'realisation' in the White House that a trade deal with the EU, would bring greater rewards than a deal with little Britain.

Someone whispered in his ear that the EU has 690m people and the

UK has just 65m...that the EU has a GDP of about $16.5trn and the UK has only about $2.5trn

Mrs Merkel is said to have told senior colleagues that Trump asked her 10 times if he could work out a trade deal with Germany before finally getting the message he had to negotiate with the EU as a whole.

That's probably why he wouldn't shake her hand in the Whitehouse. She had to sit him in the corner with a dunce hat on and he was still grumpy about it.

The US exports five times the value of goods to the EU than it does to Britain, so The Donny has re-thought the queue for a trade deal.

The President has changed his mind.

He is also OUT of his mind.

Twenty-five leading psychiatrists have broken convention to alert the world that the President of the USA is unstable and should not be left in charge of running a bath, let alone a whole country.

They said that he has clear hallmarks of mental illness and it was their 'ethical responsibility' to warn the American public about the 'dangers' Trump poses to the country....and, I would add, to women in particular.

They said the president displays anti-social, narcissistic and chauvinistic tendencies that, they believe, are grounds for impeachment.

One leading psychiatrist objected to that diagnosis, however, saying that, 'He may be a world-class narcissist, but this doesn't make him mentally ill.'

He leapt to Trump's defence by saying that he feels it is an 'insult to the mentally ill, who are mostly well behaved and well meaning, to be lumped with Mr Trump, who is neither'.

That has to be one of the best slights ever – don't call him mad, it's unfair to the mad!

29.04.17

Mugworts, mugwumps and the "C" word.

If I see one more pink faced old duffer spout the phrase "coalition of chaos" on the news, I will heave my TV set out of the window.

The Tories are beside themselves with glee that one of their number, some dull spark, came up with that phrase to describe a band of unity between the other parties that could, in theory, lead the country after the next election.

The phrase is alliterative, it is almost a joke and they are so pleased with it that any Conservative spokes-model that goes on television winds their whole argument up to its deployment.

A memo must have gone round to include it in any appearance before the cameras.

They use it as though it is the wittiest, most devastating political put-down that they have ever heard.

You can see in their eyes as they near it, that they are tickled pink to be using it. They relate to the phrase like it is a safety blanket and cruise missile all rolled into one.

Boris Johnson only used half of it when he branded Jeremy Corbyn a "mutton-headed old mugwump" who would cause "security chaos".

Close, but not on message enough to add to the phrase's cumulative effect.

In fact, the insult tripped over its own shoelaces and fell flat on its face as everyone rushed to a dictionary to find the definition of a mugwump.

It auto-corrects to "mugwort" when tapping it into a search engine. A mugwort is a shaggy unkempt mess of a hedgerow topped with a blond crown.

Remind you of anyone?

The full obligatory Tory phrase is: "we need a strong and stable Conservative government rather than a coalition of chaos under Jeremy Corbyn".

The idea is to repeat that ad nauseum until even the dimmest bulb in the box can remember it and act accordingly, come election day.

The Americanisation of British politics is complete.

Any day now, someone angling for our vote will promise that once in power they will make everything "tremendous and great".

As for the notion that a coalition means chaos, here is a list of some of the countries in the world that are run in just such a way:

Australia, Austria, Belgium, Bulgaria, Croatia, Cyprus, Czech Republic, Denmark, Estonia, Finland, France, Germany, Iceland, India, Indonesia, Israel, Italy, Japan, Luxembourg, Monaco, Netherlands, New Zealand , Northern Ireland, Norway, Pakistan, Poland, Sweden, and Switzerland.

All of those countries are run by coalitions of two or more parties.

None of them appear to be in chaos, apart from Switzerland, of course, but they keep it very hush-hush.

By the way, guess how many of those countries run by coalitions are among the top 10 happiest places on earth?

All of them, except Canada. Nine out of the top ten happiest places on earth are run by coalitions.

And do you know how many of the top ten national economies on earth are run by coalitions?

Most of them. In the world's ten biggest economies, just us, the US, China and Brazil are not governed by coalitions.

Of course, what happens in other countries does not necessarily apply here. A coalition running Great Britain might be a disaster, but that would be on us. It would not be because coalitions equal chaos.

Even a mugwort ought to be able to understand that.

30.04.17

<u>Nukes or knees - select.</u>

Boris "Bozo of the FO" Johnson, was discussing Jeremy "Jezza" Corbyn and warned voters against being lulled into thinking the Labour leader is a 'benign Islingtonian herbivore' because of his 'meandering and nonsensical' public performances.

That was Boris Johnson accusing someone of being meandering and nonsensical.

I shall send Boris a compilation video of his public appearances. "Meandering and nonsensical" pretty much defines them.

Labour accused him of 'demeaning' his role as Foreign Secretary.

I think Mrs M demeaned the role of Foreign Secretary when she selected Boris for the job.

He is our top diplomat. Is there anything in his past that would give you pause to award him such a position? Apart from everything you have ever heard him say or do?

Bozo called Jezza a "mugwump", which, for an insult, is as daft as Johnson's effortfully dishevelled appearance.

A mugwump is someone who remains aloof or independent from party politics

Say what you like about Jeremy Corbyn, he's not exactly that.

Boris criticised Corbyn's record on security issues, his lukewarm support for Nato, his opposition to Trident, and his refusal to countenance ever using Britain's nuclear deterrent.

Unfortunately, it is only a deterrent if you are dealing with sane opposition. No sane person would launch a nuclear attack, so it is as good as useless.

The person who will start a nuclear war will be clearly insane, so it is not much of a deterrent.

This is a country that is cancelling people's knee, hip and eye operations, closing schools early, not bothering to investigate crimes and has a backlog in the courts that stretches to the moon and back, all for lack of money.

For us simultaneously to be spending £205bn (according to the CND), or £167bn (according to Reuters) on the best methods of mass killing is, at the very least, morally questionable.

The people who have led us in recent years have all banged on about their faith and how they are guided by the Lord.

Well, I wonder what Jesus would do...help the sick or invest in ways of killing them?

Bozo suggested Jezza was more interested in 'virtue-signalling' than standing up for Britain's interests.

Apparently, Britain's interests are selling weapons of mass destruction to foreign dictators, shaking the hand of confessed serial killer Rodrigo Duterte of the Philippines in the hope of extracting some money, looking the other way when the Saudis bomb hospitals and schools with the weapons we sell them, and, according to Transparency International, providing the world's number one haven for the stolen money of the international criminal super rich.

Those are supposedly in Britain's interests.

Or rather, the interests of the vanishingly small number of people who profit the most from such enterprises.

Theresa May appeared uncomfortable when questioned about the appropriateness of Mr Johnson's creative use of language when referring to the leader of the Labour Party. She later said he was 'doing a great job as Foreign Secretary'.

He's making the job of Foreign Secretary great again.

He should get a hat made.

06.05.17

Bowing out gracefully

The Duke of Edinburgh stepped down this week from whatever it is he does for a living. He did so in a blaze of flattery by the press that would embarrass even Donald Trump.

They could have drowned a hippo in the ink they used to kow-tow to his royal highness.

The Queen's second son Prince Andrew is known as Air Miles Andy because of his love of travel at other's expense. Mostly ours.

He is now about to emerge from the shadows to take a more prominent role in the family firm.

Insiders at the palace say they are going to rehabilitate him in the public's eyes.

I hate to sound ungrateful for his loyal service but I think that his rehabilitation depends on us, rather than on them. He will be rehabilitated in the public's eye when the public decides, not when we are told that he is now rehabilitated.

If I were him, I wouldn't hold my breath. He is not well liked.

What if your school or club were told that it will be receiving a royal guest?

Everyone goes round painting the whole place from top to bottom and re-lays the grass and breaks the budget on flowers and spends 3 months preparing the most fabulous feast that you have ever seen and when the helicopter lands in the playing field to disgorge the mystery royal guest, out gets Prince Andrew.

Can you imagine the disappointment?

You were all geared up for Wills and Wotsit and you get him. It could only be worse if he couldn't attend and sent his daughters instead, who show up with satellite dishes strapped to their heads.

We are witnessing the beginning of the end for the royal family. The slow fade out has begun.

Once the Queen goes, that's it, game's over.

The coverage of the Duke's "retirement" read like an obituary for the House of Windsor.

The usual royal hem-sniffers piled it on about his lifetime of selfless service, but his job, if you can call it that, was to get driven to some place that had been cleaned and polished to within an inch of its life, to glad-hand some carefully selected genuflecting cap-doffer and say something insensitive that everyone felt required to laugh at and then shoot off in a blizzard of sirens and flashing lights.

And for that onerous task, which he did not have to interview for, he could not be fired from, nor ever had justify his performance, he got more money in one year than the rest of us will earn in our lifetimes.

He got waited on, hand and foot, by literally hundreds of servants and had anything he wanted brought to him where ever he was, on a sold silver platter at the time of his choosing.

For all that selfless service, he and his business partner was given £45m a year and the run of two palaces, three castles, a house and two lodges. All fully staffed with hot and cold running minions.

The patriotic wing of the press came out, all guns blazing, for the retiring Duke, going on about his legendary witticisms, which would be called being rude and insensitive if we had said them.

They chirruped about his hard work ethic of official engagements, each of which we would call the best day of our lives if we were lucky enough to do it.

They talked in breathless tones of the 785 charities that enjoy his patronage

Forgive me, but what exactly did he do for 785 charities?

If the Duke of Edinburgh actually did anything for those bodies, other than lend them his name, he would be visiting them briefly once in a blue moon, an event that would probably cost the charity a good amount of the money they would have raised that year, what with all the sprucing up and the vittles they would feel obliged to lay on.

Assuming that he took 4 weeks holiday a year, and worked 5 days a week, it would take him about 3 and a half years to visit them all once.

Lending your name to a thing doesn't mean you are involved in any way, just as if something has got the name Trump on it, it doesn't mean that the orange nightmare has had anything to do with it.

His business is a branding exercise, just like the royal family is a branding exercise.

The Firm show their face and get their picture taken before vanishing off in a cacophony of sirens, past halted traffic.

They do just enough to titillate the masses and keep the old dears on the pavement with the plastic flags and Thermos flasks happy.

It is work, but not as we know it.

07.05.17

It could be worse – it could be King Andy.

As the Queen nears the end of her reign, the royals are keenly aware that the public's affection for her has failed to find a new home with any of the other members of the House of Windsor.

The queen has longevity and a sense of permanence in her favour.

We have all grown up with her as a fixture on the coins and in the papers but the younger royals just don't have "it" - that indefinable something that I would call the X-factor if that phrase hadn't been hijacked by the toothsome Simon Cowell and his parade of deluded cannon fodder.

We are persuaded to be bowled over when the royal family do just what we would do given half a chance - show up for a free lunch, meet interesting people that are dazzled by us and leave when we want. When someone that enjoys the public's genuine affection does it, it works.

When we are not so keen on them, it does not work at all.

When the Queen gives up the reigns, or passes on to ride the golden carriage in the sky, the fairy-dust will fall flat on the ground like a discarded pizza box.

Wills and Wotsit just aren't that interesting, Harry is too normal to be exciting, and as for Airmiles Andy, well, he's just flat out unlikeable.

That leaves Charles, the only one of the lot of them who has anything of importance to say on any subject, and for doing so has been regularly vilified for meddling and interfering and nannying.

Honestly, can you recall anything that William or Harry or even the Queen has ever said?

Charles talks about important things like climate change and caring for animals.

We like to think of ourselves as an animal loving country, but we actually don't care about them at all, unless we find them cute and can imbue them with human personality traits.

Charles talks about organic food, not just for the protection of the land from pesticides but for the relative kindness that is shown the animals that are farmed that way.

The amount of food that we buy that was created organically is tiny for a country that has convinced itself of its love of animals.

Charles talks about housing and how people are squeezed into charmless little homes for the profit of the construction firms, and about pollution.

All these things that are actually important to people's lives and the press and the public dislike him for it so much that they want to skip him when the Queen dies and make William the king.

But that's not how it works - if we skip Charles, that would make the Queen's second son the king.

All hail King Airmiles Andy.

When The Queen passes on the crown, it will be time to slim down the royal family. We have got plenty enough history to amuse the tourists.

You would have to be seriously deluded to imagine that you are going to get to meet the Queen or some passing prince if you come to London on your holidays, so the institution is an historical attraction.

We don't need them and they don't need our money.

We could take back the palaces, cancel the payouts, have them pay for their own security and spend what we save on the health service.

It would be an extra £350m a year for the NHS.

Someone should write that on a bus.

13.05.17

Don't Spice up your life.

Arfon Jones, a police and crime commissioner in North Wales, this week called for the drug Spice to be legalised and allowed back into shops.

This is the stuff that has people staggering around like zombies, which the papers have recently taken to printing pictures of, having temporarily run out of snaps of Kim Kardashian's bottom.

Arfon Jones knows his patch. He was a policeman of 30 years' experience and is so Welsh that his name is Arfon and he lives in a place called Gersyllt, a name that only a black belt in the Welsh language should attempt to pronounce.

Drawing on his vast experience, he said criminalising the drug, which used to be legal and sold in what hippies used to call 'head' shops, had driven its production underground and made it more deadly.

It is pretty much the same story with marijuana, apart from the selling it in head shops part.

The illegal nature of marijuana has directly led to its increasing potency. It is more profitable to sell the stronger stuff, so why would a dealer sell something weaker for less money?

The penalty is the same regardless of its strength, so the law, and basic economics, have conspired to produce grass that is so strong that Willie Nelson would write a song about it, if only he could remember where he put his pen.

Spice is another thing entirely. It makes skunk seem as powerful as a lime cordial.

It is apparently as addictive as heroin and crack, and costs just £5 per bag.

It has left addicts suffering severe psychotic episodes, hallucinations, vomiting and seizures.

That doesn't sound like a good night out, but the people who are taking it are not doing so for a light relief from their stressful day at work, they are taking it because they want to blot out the life they are leading with the cheapest thing at their disposal.

And like super-strong grass being a result of the underground marketplace, so high potency Spice has been created because there is no regulation on its ingredients and its affects.

Ministers outlawed possession of the drug last year,

That policy is going so well that they have even got a Spice drug problem in prisons.

If you can't keep it out of a secure facility, how are you going to keep it out of Rhyl and Prestatyn, Glasgow and Galashiels?

In Manchester, Spice users are collapsing so frequently that the emergency services are finding it hard to cope.

They say that almost all of the city's young homeless are hooked on the drug.

I would guess that is because, if you have no home, you have no job, no future and are living outside of our comfortable cappuccino society, you want the least expensive way to pass the day you can get, and a fiver for a joint of Spice that is equal to 100 ordinary marijuana joints would seem to be just the thing.

Towns and cities all over the country have also reported problems with this stuff, and if it isn't round your way yet, just wait, it will be.

Arfon Jones, the police and crime commissioner for North Wales said 'I believe that the war on drugs was lost many years ago and that we need a new approach to dealing with problematic drug use,'

He said, 'I have felt for some time that the current prohibitive stance is extremely damaging to individuals and their communities.'

We can add his voice to the myriad experts who have come to the same conclusion and have spoken on this issue frequently, to whom the government never listens.

There's a war on learning the lessons of the war on drugs.

1 4.05.17

Donald Trump has a big one, just not THAT big.

Donald trump has been embellishing the truth.

I know that is about as newsworthy as the sun rising in the east.

The best spin on his behaviour might be that he has lied so often and for so long that he does not realise he is doing it any more.

Rich from an early age from the money his daddy gave him, he has never had to endure hearing the word "No", and no-one around him has ever questioned his version of events, so he has just become used to believing whatever words spill over his luminous white teeth and past his orange, puckered lips.

Mostly he lies about the size of things. He lies about the number of people at his inauguration, the enormity of his achievements, the popularity of his presidency and the length of his ties suggest the reason why.

He also lies about how many floors his buildings have.

Donald Trump boasted that he lives in splendid gold entombment in a penthouse on the 66th to 68th floors of Trump Tower.

The one small problem with that claim is that people with time on their hands have counted the floors of said tower and come up ten floors short.

There are only 58 floors in Trump Tower. Apparently, he does this a lot. Trump exaggerates the number of floors in his buildings because it makes him feel important and also, he can get more rent for units on higher numbered floors.

That is just the sort of huckster we want in charge of the free world. What could possibly go wrong?

The lies don't stop with the numbers in the lifts.

During the Obama Presidency, Trump gave Forbes a tour of his Manhattan penthouse.

Forbes described this as another episode in "a decade-long crusade for a higher spot on our billionaire rankings".

During the tour, Trump said that his flat was 33,000 square feet, which is about 33 times the size of a new-build 3 bedroom house in Britain.

Unfortunately for Donald Trump, journalists are in the habit of checking facts and the scribes at Forbes discovered that Trump's apartment is less than half the size he said it was.

They discovered that Trump first acquired a triplex apartment in the newly opened tower with his name on the front in 1983. It covered 6,096-square-feet.

You would think that would be big enough, but not for Donny's ego it wasn't, so he bought two neighbouring units and merged them into one giant apartment measuring about 14,000 square feet.

Journalists could look this up because of pesky plans that are kept on file in the city of New York.

A flat of 14,000 sq ft is pretty big, but it is not 33,000 sq ft.

Trump probably saw on the news that someone famous had the grandest penthouse in New York, so he just added a bit to their figure and settled on 33,000 sq ft, to make his the biggest.

While taking Forbes round his tower, Trump pointed to a door they passed that he claimed was the entrance to a flat he had leased to Michael Jackson, who he said he knew "better than anybody".

He called it a "little section" that he rented to Jackson, presumably to underline how huge his apartment was in comparison with the one occupied by the planet's biggest star.

The same plans on file in the city showed that the door Trump had motioned to had never been a residence at all, and appeared to be a space occupied by machinery.

But as the current President of the United States would say, it's the best mechanical space in the world...it's a tremendous mechanical space...yuuuge.

20.05.17

There's nothing social about it.

You may have seen gaggles of youths hanging around with each other, all with their necks craned, staring into their phones.

They appear to want to converse with anyone except the people they are with. You may have thought that kind of behaviour is a bit odd and that it might not be very good for them.

The Royal Society for Public Health and the charity Young Health Movement recently conducted a survey of about 1,500 people aged between 14 and 24 in Britain to gain some insight into their use of social media, which is what they are all staring at most of the time, and how it is affecting them.

It turns out your concerns are justified. It isn't doing them any good at all.

They were asked to score how each social media site made then feel. They gave scores on emotions like anxiety and depression, on whether the sites made them feel lonely, or made them lose sleep and about the problems of bullying and how they experienced a fear of missing out.

The latter is pertinent because, like the manufacturers of junk food, social media companies calibrate their offerings to twang the pleasure senses enough to create an addiction, with all the problems that come with that.

Instagram was listed as having the most negative effect overall. In case you have not had the opportunity to waste your life looking at it, Instagram is chock full of hot celebrities and beautiful people uploading pictures of themselves having a fabulous time surrounded by friends who are so tanned and taught they look like they just stepped out of an ad for sunscreen.

Not unsurprisingly, Instagram was said to harm perceptions of body image, increase the fear of missing out and have a detrimental effect on sleep.

The kids are up all night wondering why Kim Kardashian hasn't invited them to a naked jacuzzi party on her yacht. She seems so nice and they are sure they would get along, so WHY HASN'T SHE CALLED?!

Social media is a carefully curated stream of other people's lives that look better than your own. No wonder the kids are depressed, if that is their diet every day.

Snapchat was the second least positive platform, and as far as I can tell, it is the same thing as Instagram – pictures of celebs in Ferraris by a lake in front of a £100m mansion and you're penniless and stuck in your parents house on an estate in Huddersfield and it is raining outside.

Other sites scored badly for on-line bullying. Children are not very nice - they are like adults in that respect, except that they have much greater opportunities to bully each other and a lot more time on their hands to do it. Social media is the ideal weapon.

Oddly, and quite sadly, some of the sites gave the youngsters a sense of community. That used to be held by people that were geographically near to each other.

A sense of community used to be neighbours chatting over the garden fence, now it is solitary individuals thousands of miles apart swapping tales of loneliness and pictures of their personal parts.

One of the few positives that was reported from using social media by the young people surveyed was being able to express themselves.

Looking in from the outside though, it seems that means posting a comment on someone else's selfie, which doesn't really count as self-expression.

YouTube was the only social media platform to have a largely positive effect on mental health, which might be because its where the kids steal their music from.

It is also the young person's television. YouTube is sit-back viewing rather than the tense, shoulders hunched, sit-forward stuff that is the experience of using the so-called social media sites.

The researchers called for a warning to users that would pop up and tell them they had been using the site too much, but that would probably seem like nannying.

They also called for sites to alert users to any pictures that had been manipulated to enhance the appearance of the people in them.

But every photograph of every celebrity and model on earth has been manipulated in some way: lighting, make up, carefully chosen angles and smoothing out the lines, but even knowing that they are doing that does not change the effect the pictures have on us - that depressing feeling that everyone is better looking and more successful than we are.

The answer is not to regulate or change the on-line experience, the answer is for young and old alike to look up from their phones once in a while and change their relationship with these sites, to realise that they are built to create addictive behaviour and a constant nagging fear that if you don't check-in every five minutes you will miss something important.

If people would raise their eyes from their screens, they will find that there is a whole wide-screen, high definition world in surround sound that is going an all around them.

They should try it, they might like it.

21.05.17

Donny does diplomacy.

Donald Trump is taking a break from his very important golfing duties, and the vital business of leaking secrets to the Russians, to head off on his first, and perhaps last foreign trip as President.

For this outing, he is travelling to a select few of the countries that he has insulted on Twitter.

He's going to Saudi Arabia, Israel and the Vatican. What could possibly go wrong?

If you had to put together a list of the places that it is possible to screw up in, those three would be right at the top.

He insulted Saudi Arabia by saying during the election campaign that Hillary Clinton wanted to open the borders and "let the Muslims flood in". He demanded that the Saudis give America free oil or he wouldn't protect their aeroplanes and said they were "nothing but mouth pieces, bullies, cowards. They have the money but no guts".

He should hope that Twitter is as popular in Riyadh as women's rights.

After Saudi Arabia, he is getting a direct flight to Israel. This is not normally possible. They do not like each other much and planes do not fly between the two states for fear of the transmission of toxic or harmful cargoes.

Donald Trump might be harmful but the only toxic thing on board Air Force One will be whatever it is he uses to keep his hair in place.

In Israel, the Trump circus will swerve the Masada mountain fortress, a Unesco World Heritage site that is of profound importance to the Israelis. It was the place where Jewish rebels killed themselves rather than be captured by the Romans in 73AD.

Trump was due to make a speech there but cancelled because they wouldn't let him land his helicopter on it.

From there, it is straight to the Vatican. When on the campaign trail, Trump talked of building his wall, the Pope suggested that people should be building bridges, not walls, which made Trump angry.

He shot back: "If and when the Vatican is attacked by Isis...I can promise you that the Pope would have only wished and prayed that Donald Trump would have been President because this would not have happened."

Speaking of himself in the third person and warning the Pope what to pray for. Classy.

Trump is also visiting Belgium for a NATO summit. He described that country as a "hell hole" and a "mess".

Finally, he will roll through Italy, a country he told all Americans to boycott in 2011, unless they released Amanda Knox because he said she was innocent. This conclusion presumably based on how hot he thought she looked.

It is a big trip for Donny and will be the first time since becoming President that he has slept in a building outside the Whitehouse that doesn't have his name on it.

He is going to places that are among the most treacherous spots for a diplomatic catastrophe on earth.

Can you imagine what the Whitehouse staff who are having to trail after him are doing at the very thought of it all, apart from pulling what's left of their hair out?

Diplomacy is not his strong point. He tends to say whatever he thinks will make him look good at any given moment, which is the exact opposite of what diplomacy is.

Diplomacy is making the other side feel good about themselves, not boasting about the crown size at his inauguration and how his restaurants have the best chocolate cake you have ever seen and whining about how unfair everyone is being to him and how he can't just do what he wants.

He's like a big orange baby - his staff are going to have to schedule regular feeding and nap times or Donny will get grumpy and have a tantrum.

State visits are usually prepared down to their last detail. Everyone knows who they are going to be talking with and what they are going to be saying but Donald Trump doesn't do scripts, he's just a random, bleating, boast generator.

Stephen J. Hadley, was former President George W. Bush's National Security Adviser.

He said "You really hope that he sticks to the script, executes the trip as planned and avoids distractions, because the whole world is watching,"

It's exciting isn't it? It is like a soap opera...tune in next time for more jaw dropping cliff hangers.

If only the future of the world wasn't at stake.

27.05.17

Somehow Getting Away With It

It was a big week for Donny. He was off, away from his troubles at home, but they followed him there like the smell of the bucket of

Kentucky Fried Chicken he left on Air Force One.

He was filmed having his unusually tiny hand slapped away by Melania not once but twice, and barging to the front of a NATO meeting, actually knocking world leaders out of the way, so that he could take centre stage to preen in front of the cameras.

Donny doesn't like shade.

At the G7 summit, he was reported to be Making America First by refusing to agree to the climate change plan that might go some way to saving the planet.

Think about that - it's like he doesn't believe that America is part of planet Earth, or that what happens to our fragile little sphere has any bearing on America or the people that live in it.

What are the American ding-a-lings from the yeehaw states going to do when the rising tide floods their homes...shoot it?

His problem with taking action on climate change seems to be connected to the fact that the energy giants in large part paid his way into the Whitehouse.

He has signed executive orders that removed much of the regulation that requires them to curb pollution and their effect on the world.

They can pollute the streams and rivers and the air, and car companies no longer have to make efficient engines and all that good 'ole American screw-you stuff that his fans love so much.

Maybe they will have second thoughts when they get sick from the water and get lung disease from the air and won't be able to get any treatment because he's taken them all off health care to fund a tax cut for the super-rich.

Even then, I wouldn't be surprised if they all blamed Hillary

What would you think if the prime minister of this country accepted over $2.5 million dollars from the energy industry and then dropped the pollution regulations on coal and allowed coal mining in national parks?

Or if the prime minister of this country said they were going to drain the swamp of special interests and lobbyists and then gave all the plum roles in the cabinet to billionaires that worked in or owned businesses in the same sectors that they would now be regulating?

I would have to assume you would cry foul. His supporters do not. Not only did he not drain the swamp of special interests and lobbyists on behalf of the rich and powerful, he employed those people straight away and immediately gave them what they wanted.

He even said it on the campaign trail - he said "I could stand in the middle of Fifth Avenue and shoot somebody and I wouldn't lose any voters."

That's the amazing thing about this man - he keeps telling people he's a con man and a fraud and they're either not hearing him because of all the whooping and yelling, or they just don't care that he's manipulating them. They seem to actually like it.

He fired the head of the FBI and his staff ran around putting out fires, saying that it was someone else's decision.

They insisted that it certainly wasn't Trump trying to subvert justice, trying to stop the investigation into his ties with the Russians.

Then Trump goes on national television and says...no it was me...it was my decision...I did it.

He ruined his own alibi because he couldn't stand to have it look like someone told him what to do.

He invited the Russians, one of whom was the actual head spy of the country which all 17 of America's security agencies said colluded in rigging the American election.

Then he threw the American media out of the room, kept a Russian press photographer in, and told them state secrets in a boast about military might...and then admitted it to the press, with an excuse which went something like: it's my right, I can do what I want!

It is as though he's daring his fans to think badly of him. It's like a game: how far can I push them?

Well, how about telling them on the campaign trail that he wouldn't throw anyone off health care or reduce their benefits, and his first budget and heath care bill calls for 23m people to lose their health insurance and benefits like food stamps and in-work credits are going to be cut by half.

That is going to affect the exact same poor white people that voted for him. Will that push them to the edge?

What's he going to do next, tell them Elvis was gay and set fire to Dolly Parton?

Everything he's doing in office is the exact opposite of what he promised in the campaign - sticking up for the little guy, protecting the workers, locking her up.

Even all that America first stuff was rubbish.

Do you know where he gets The Donald J. Trump Collection of ties, suits, dress shirts

and eyeglasses made?

Go on have a guess. If you guessed China, you get bright red trucker hat.

28.05.17

An Incident of Upset in the Night Time.

If you are considering contracting an MRSA bug for kicks, don't.

For all I know, licking hospital bedlinen is what the kids are doing today to get high.

They may have exhausted the possibilities of smoking baked banana skins and snorting grated nutmeg, and are bored with the delights of ingesting bath salts and garden fertiliser and are after the sort of buzz that can only come with a good dose of a highly aggressive communicable disease.

If you are thinking: that sounds like a fun weekend, please allow me to share my personal experience of contracting an industrial strength bout of an antibiotic-resistant infectious agent.

I have a tale to tell of the havoc it can wreak to, not just your insides, but everything around you, especially if you do not quite reach the toilet in time.

I was visiting my father, who is in hospital, where you would think he would be safe.

My dad is on a ward that a nurse said has had "some tummy bug problems". This understates the case by some considerable degree.

It is like saying that wearing a centre parting, a cardigan, sandals and socks would somewhat work against you becoming a sex object.

The phrase "tummy bug" implies some benign infection that can be treated with a nice cup of tea and a good night's rest.

What I contracted was the Mount Etna of stomach infections. A great gushing flow of hot lava that exploded out of every orifice I knew of, and some I was not even aware that I had.

It started, as these things often do, in a mild room spin, but not in a good way. This proceeded to a distant rumble of the crisis to come.

Sleep came fitfully, until in the dead of night I was seized by the urge to get up. Two feet from the bed, this urging became the warning bell of imminent catastrophe and exactly one foot from the toilet, all Hell broke loose.

Unfortunately, the toilet seat was down, in the polite manner, and so what ensued covered every surface of the bathroom. In fact it may have covered every surface that Man has ever created.

The volume that a single stomach can hold is really quite remarkable. Mine seems to have held on to every meal I have ever eaten. I am sure I spotted some Farley's Rusks.

But a cursory glance through a fog of dizzy horror revealed that, contrary to popular belief, there were no diced carrots present at all.

I hate diced carrots, an intense dislike that has stayed with me since school dinners. I don't mind carrots; it is the dicing I can't stand. And how much otherwise perfectly usable carrot is discarded simply because it can not be reduced to a perfect three dimensional solid object of six square sides?

There were no cubes of any kind but the roiling intensity of the blasts breaking out from me continued into the night. I tried to quell the grief with a Rennie. This was like placing a damp towel over a meltdown in a nuclear plant.

Time was the healer, and lots of water, which I would always recommend, even when you are well, assuming there is no alcohol at hand.

I am fairly fit and suffered a 7 out of 10 on my personal pain-ometer.

If someone who is already in hospital were to get it, where would the ambulance take them?

03.06.17

Au revoir Paris

Donald Trump has pulled out of the Paris Accord because he does not believe there is any such thing as "Paris".

He said that "Paris" is an invention of the Chinese to make Donald Trump use less make-up.

He did not say that, I made that up. What he did say was just as surreal.

His Orange Magnificence said he made the decision to pull the U.S. out of deal, as it was bad for the environment.

In his brave new world of made up facts, caring for the environment is bad for the environment.

That makes as much sense as anything else that's happening right now.

Trump said, 'We don't want other leaders and other countries laughing at us any more. And they won't be.'

I'm not sure that's true - I get the feeling that since the Screaming MeMe entered the Whitehouse, laughing at America has become the most popular world sport after football and fighting.

He said 'I was elected to represent the citizens of Pittsburgh, not Paris.'

Those words had only just fallen from his puckered lips when the mayor of Pittsburgh shot back that 80% of that city's voters went for Hilary and that he would issue an order ensuring that carbon emissions guidelines would still be followed there despite anything the President said.

They hate him in Pittsburgh, and pretty much everywhere else on earth.

He was roasted by a German newspaper which went with the headline 'Earth to Trump - f**k you!' after he pulled out of the Paris climate change accord

German Chancellor Angela Merkel said the decision of the US President to withdraw from the Paris Climate Agreement is "very regrettable", she said, adding "and I'm expressing myself in a very reserved way when I say that."

The diplomatic gloves are off. World leaders are not used to being barged out of the way, or having their arms wrenched out of their sockets by a man-child intent on making every handshake an infantile battle of dominance.

Angela Merkel is so angry she's fit to burst her lederhosen. She said, 'To everyone for whom the future of our planet is important, I say let's continue going down this path so we're successful for our Mother Earth,'

That's hilarious - "To everyone for whom the future of the planet is important"!

That's akin to taking off her lederhosen and waving her giant Teutonic bottom in his face.

Practically every other leader of a country that you have heard of lined up to pour scorn, disappointment and ridicule on the man who seems to be doing whatever his donors in the fossil fuel industries told him to say.

It is weird that the world's most powerful man is so old and stuck in his ways that he wants to retreat to some Norman Rockwell ideal of 1950s Americana when Pop went to work in the coal mine and Mom stayed at home making babies and apple pie.

The newly minted French President Emmanuel Macron looks and talks like he's from the future by comparison.

He crushed the US President's backward looking stance just as he beat him in Trump's own hand-yanking dance when they met at the G7 summit.

He said, "Wherever we live, whoever we are, we all share the same responsibility. Make our planet great again."

Put THAT on a baseball hat.

Speaking directly to the camera in English, Macron said, 'If we do nothing, our children will know a world of migrations, of wars, of shortage. A dangerous world. It is not a future we want for ourselves. It is not a future we want for our children. It is not a future we want for our world.'

He even speaks English better than Trump.

Apart from world leaders, business people also expressed their dismay - even some from the oil industry.

Exxon, America's largest oil company, urged Trump to back the climate change initiative, as did BlackRock, the world's largest asset manager.

These are companies Trump would have expected applause from. It's the thing he craves the most, but outside one of his staged rallies, applause has been in short supply.

Big names from the world of business quit Trump's advisory council over the Paris Accord decision. Among them was Bob Iger, the CEO of Disney.

Even Mickey Mouse thinks he's goofy.

04.06.17

Anything we can do, they can do better

In less than 50 years, artificial intelligence will be able to beat humans at everything we do.

There isn't a single thing we can do now that won't be done better by a robot within most of our lifetimes.

The future is racing towards us and it's being driven by an android who is coming to terminate our jobs.

A new study from researchers at Oxford University's Future of Humanity Institute, Yale University, and AI Impacts suggests that even having a giant brain and working for Oxford or Yale University won't save you.

They say that within the next ten years alone, AI will outperform humans in language translation and delivery driving.

The first seems an obvious job for automation, the second we have been hearing about for a while.

In the near future, white vans will automatically swerve lanes without indicating and drive themselves right up to your tail lights and flash you to get out of the way for doing 30 in a 30 zone.

No human driver required.

What is less expected is that artificial intelligence will be able to write school essays better than we can and they won't need to copy them off the internet.

Computers will be able to do this in nine years according to the researchers who asked 352 experts for their predictions.

They say machines could be writing bestselling books by 2049. The next Jeffrey Archer will be an electronic box in a cupboard.

The experts, all leaders in their field, say that even shop staff will be collecting their P45s
inside 20 years. In retail, robots will be able to replicate the human

touch.

In the future, you will be efficiently ignored by two cyborgs servers talking to each other, as you stand expectantly at the counter, waiting to pay.

They say that there is a 50 percent chance that artificial intelligence will outperform humans in all tasks in just 45 years and that it is just as likely that there will be absolutely nothing for us meat sacks to do any more by 2140.

If there's anything we have learned from the advance of AI, it is that the seemingly impossible can become reality really quickly, and becomes essential almost immediately it appears.

Smart phones are only ten years old. The first iPhone came out in 2007.

Most people who have one now have only owned one for a few short years but we are now completely addicted to them.

We will probably be similarly enamoured of the robots that are coming to replace people's jobs. All of them except the ones coming to replace our own jobs.

Those down the food chain are likely to lose theirs first. The less you earn, the more likely you are to lose out. That seems to be the way of the world.

That is going to be a bad outcome for millions of people but a bad outcome for humankind in general is less likely.

Computer calculations show only a 5% probability of the advance of AI resulting in the sort of doomsday scenario depicted in the Terminator films.

But that could be just what the robots want us to believe!

09.06.17

The Sun Goes Down

After the biggest sustained assault on anything since Dresden, the right-wing press failed to turn the country against Uncle Jezza.

Just the reverse, it would appear.

It is almost as though we have decided we do not like being told what to do by off-shore billionaires who have only their own interests at heart.

The headlines screamed from the front pages of the usual papers in the run up to the election saying that Corbyn is not strong or stable.

And the polls showed him doing better.

So they ramped it up a bit - Jeremy Corbyn is a friend to the terrorists and he has a suspect device hidden in his beard.

And the polls showed him doing better.

You could sense the papers rolling up their sleeves, as though to say: "Right!" - Jeremy Corbyn feasts on babies and he wants yours as a snack that he can eat between meals without ruining his appetite.

And the polls showed him doing better!

The papers must have thought: these people are not doing what they're told. Like Scottie out of Star Trek, they thought, "Were giving it all we can Captain, but we cannae lose him"

Corbyn dogged Mrs M like a bad smell.

Actually the bad smell wasn't him, it was the Tories' campaign slogan about "strong and stable versus a coalition of chaos".

When I first heard it, I thought it was quite cute - clever, almost.

The second time I thought cute will only get you so far and the fiftieth time I heard it I wanted to put my head through my television just to make it stop.

The Conservatives hugged themselves when they said it - strong and stable...coalition of chaos... They acted as though it was the best use of the English language since Shakespeare.

One smug MP after another took turns at saying it over and over, delighting in it again and again.

Repetition did not improve it. As a political slogan, Nixon's "I am not a crook" was better.

On top of the grating irritant that was that parroted catchphrase, the Tories were guilty of believing their own press.

They thought Corbyn was such a calamity that they could send out a lightly grilled pile of doggy-do and it would beat him, so they didn't really try that hard. Unless that WAS them trying really hard, in which case we're all in big trouble.

The Donald factor might have had something to do with the result as well. Cosying up to a lying, unstable, infantile, climate change denying egomaniac didn't do Mrs M any good at all.

Most people in this country, away from the pull of Fox News, can see what a scary buffoon is Donald Trump, young people especially, and that appears to have been the key - the youth vote.

Brexit and Trump seems to have awakened an interest in politics among the under 24's that has lain dormant since Thatcher.

The generation derided as tear-stained snowflakes, who are only interested in sharing pictures of their personal areas and staring into their phones all day, rose and spoke out in huge numbers.

The Sun was so afraid of their participation, and what it would do to the result, that it printed a comical guide for its older readers on How to Stop Your Kids from Voting.

If that did anything, it will have shown their offspring which newspaper to avoid buying, should they ever get the urge to look at the dead-tree press.

They probably won't, of course. The newspaper industry is in terminal decline.

The traditional press is in danger of losing its power.

Social media has taken its place among the young and the Conservatives were relatively absent on-line, in the run up to the election, whereas Labour engaged quite heavily on Twitter and Facebook.

Labour encouraged social media users to register to vote, the

Conservatives did not, apparently preferring their friendly papers to do their canvassing for them.

Over a quarter of a million under-25s registered to vote on the last possible day. The evidence suggests they did not vote Conservative.

Times have changed.

It is no longer The Sun wot will win it.

10.06.17

Dinosaurs Roar.

In the run up to the election, Britons became very familiar with the phrase "coalition of chaos".

What we did not expect was that the coalition would be between the Conservatives and another party, least of all The Democratic Unionist Party.

We heard time and again that Jeremy Corbyn is a friend to terrorists, what we did not expect was that Theresa May would place herself in the position of being a friend to those that are friends to terrorists, but that is the unexpectedly desperate position she finds herself in.

If Mrs May was a teenager, she would be referred to a shrink for self-harming and her parents would take her computer away.

The day after the election, many people woke to the news that the Tories would be in bed with the DUP and thought: what's the DUP?

Good question. A better one is: what do they believe in?

In a nutshell, the DUP want to party like it is 599.

They are religious. Very religious. This is not unusual for Northern Ireland, which has lagged behind the rest of the country in embracing the modern world for that very reason.

Religion is also the superficial cause of the "Troubles" as they are benignly referred to.

The DUP does not like the gays, of course.

This is the standard default position of religionists.

My personal religious belief is that being gay is anathema to believers because the union of same sex couples does not produce more potential converts to the cause.

There won't be the patter of tiny feet swelling the ranks of the faithful if two men or women get together.

I think the same reasoning applies to birth control.

The DUP are not shy about expressing their distaste of the LGBTTQUI's (I hope that is a fully inclusive set of initials).

The founder of the party was the shouty Ian Paisley, a reverend. His son said that homosexuality was "immoral, offensive and obnoxious".

He called them repulsive, presumably because that's what Jesus would say!

The DUP are also against abortion, causing those women of Northern Ireland that want or need one to leave the country to find help.

This is also standard practice for those that think they possess the final word on What God Wants.

More alarming is the party's attitude to science: they don't believe in it.

Just as Donald Trump has done in his cabinet of chaos, the DUP appointed the climate change denier Sammy Wilson as Environment Minister.

Wilson said it was a con to suggest that humans had changed weather patterns and that cows were more to blame.

If that's their plan, it's a good job we eat so many of them.

The DUP's religiosity goes deep. A significant number of their senior members believe in creationism. That is, they are firmly of the belief that the earth is a mere 4,000 years old and that, therefore, Man used to run with dinosaurs, like in Jurassic Park, but without the music.

Some of their members want this to be taught to children in schools, so that it might counter evolutionary teaching, which is just a theory that does not appear in the Bible, so it can't be true.

Many of their beliefs seem from a different age, and now they will be part of shaping the current one.

If all that sounds like the basis of a strong and stable government, rather than a coalition of chaos, I'm a brachiosaurus.

17.06.17

Here we go again (again)

Labour's Shadow Chancellor John McDonnell has a dream.

His dream is that the union-organised march on Parliament next month will turn into a mass protest of a million people on the streets for the purposes of ousting the Maybot.

It just keeps getting worse doesn't it Mrs M?

How's that whole snap election turning out for you?

John McDonnell believes that direct action is needed to engineer the Government's downfall.

I'm not sure about that.

The government seem to be doing a pretty good job of organising their own downfall.

The Conservatives feigned outrage at the mention of a march. They called the notion undemocratic and accused him of trying to gain power through mob rule.

Apparently that is much worse than trying to keep a grip on power by cosying up to terrorist sympathising, religious fundamentalists who managed just 0.3% of the national vote.

McDonnell called for a 'national demonstration' in support of Labour's manifesto.

He will be lucky. Like all manifestos, no-one read it. I bet the people that wrote it didn't read it.

I bet if I offered you a million pounds you wouldn't be able to tell me what is in it off the top of your head.

There will be an anti-austerity event on July 1, weather permitting.

It is planned to end with a march on Parliament, and should get there just moments before our hard working law makers break from their travails for the Summer Recess, which takes in much of July, all of August and a good deal of September.

Labour's John MacDonald has cleared his schedule of all shouting engagements and is going to be there. He wants you to be there too, to 'keep the momentum going' to force an early election.

Another election!

Don't tell Brenda from Bristol, she'll have a cow.

The Tories are in a bind because they do not have an overall majority. They used to, but then Mrs M had her wizard election idea and that went up in smoke.

Labour, expecting to get a drubbing, emerged simultaneously the losers and the winners, which is a neat trick to pull off, even though they can't claim much credit as it was Mother Theresa that failed, rather than Uncle Jezza that succeeded. He just sounded good by comparison.

It is that result that has emboldened John McDonnell to say,'The Labour Party should have the same right to put policies forward in Parliament, to be properly debated and voted upon and to legislate as well.'

That seems fair - the British people did not vote for the Democratic Unionist Party, so their wishes should not be agreed to ahead of the wishes of the 60% of the population that did not vote either Tory or the DUP.

The Conservatives polled 42.4% of the votes, the DUP 0.3%.

Labour polled 40%, their happy bedfellows might be the SNP, Lib Dems, Plaid Cymru and the Greenies who together polled 52.5%.

McDonald said, 'We need people doing everything they can to ensure the election comes as early as possible.'

What a prospect.

I don't mind the actual voting part, it gets you out the house. It's all the politicking that precedes it that I can't stand.

I wonder what catchphrase the geniuses at Tory high command are going to come up with next time.

Can we say we are sick of hearing it now, to save time later?

18.07.17

The Empire strikes back

The Prime Minister has been overtaken in the popularity stakes by the pool of mystery liquid in the bottom of your bin.

I made that up.

The Prime Minister has actually been overtaken in the popularity stakes by Jeremy Corbyn, who you might think is the most unpopular person that has ever existed, if you read the Mail, the Sun, the Express, the Telegraph or the Times.

Despite the combined firepower of the right-wing press, their darling, Theresa May, is now as unpopular as the smell of a teenager's trainers.

She is almost as unpopular as Jeremy Corbyn was before the start of the election campaign, when the Conservative lead over Labour was more than 20 points.

What has lead us to this place is a combination of a diabolical Tory campaign and people actually hearing what the bearded weirdo from the Socialist Republic of Islington had to say, rather than reading what he is like in the rabid right wing press.

According to YouGov, Mrs M's favourability rating has fallen from +10 to -34,

Meanwhile - great news Jezza - the Labour leader's popularity has soared from -42 to an overall rating of 0.

Jeremy Corbyn is a zero. For him, it must be like Christmas and birthday all come at once.

The joy is unconfined over at Labour head office; Jeremy Corbyn is a big fat nothing.

I bet they've never been so pleased. The British public are totally non committal about him.

They have no strong opinion.

That is a pretty amazing achievement after the massive wave of bile that he had to swim through, in the run up to the election.

The British public have given a pretty big slap in the face to the media barons who told us and cajoled us and threatened us and tried to scare us into voting against him and for Theresa.

The British people gave them a traditional British two fingered salute.

They will have just about been able to see that from the tax havens they inhabit.

Whatever your political persuasions, even if the result did not go your way, I think there is something utterly heartening and commendable about that.

The Murdochs and the Rothermeres, the Barclays and the Desmonds of this world do NOT always get their own way and the British public are not to be dictated to by a bunch of non-dom, tax efficient, off shore fat cats.

It fair makes you proud to be a resident, tax paying, on-shore Brit.

24.06.17

Affray At The Races.

I drove past Ascot racecourse on Ladies Day and outside all was calm and ordered.

Inside, all Hell was being let loose.

Underneath the shade of a thousand silly hats, vast amounts of alcohol were being consumed in the afternoon heatwave.

What could possibly go wrong, apart from what usually goes wrong when Britons are encouraged to drink before they have had their dinner?

The scenes were reminiscent of the crowd at a boxing match, who go to see a fight and decide, all things considered, that they would rather provide their own violent entertainment and start throwing chairs at each other.

A man, naked from the waist up was filmed flailing about, knocking over drinks, people and fencing as he attempted to demonstrate what a big boy he is by acting like a toddler.

It could have been worse. At least he was fully clothed from the waist down.

Not to be outdone, women were soon slapping at each other as well. It was Ladies Day after all.

At Royal Ascot! Isn't that absolutely shocking?

No, of course it isn't. It would be shocking if the day had gone peacefully.

The shirtless man, who was bald as a bowling ball, engaged in a fight with another punter and careened about shouting 'let's finish it off' as he rampaged through the crowd, knocking things and people over like skittles.

This all happened in the Queen Anne Enclosure, which sounds a lot classier than it is.

Racegoers in their dressing-up-box Sunday best screamed as the hairless pugilist and another man shouted earthy abuse at one another as though they were on a building site.

They were not. They were in fact in the presence of Her Majesty the Queen, who had been through enough that day, what with the dull speech she had to rattle through in parliament before hot-footing it to the races.

Around shoeless women passed out on the ground, guests could be be heard shouting 'f****** idiot' and 'f*** off you coward' as the violent man lurched about, fists clenched like the baddie in a Charlie Chaplin film.

A woman cried, 'Where's security? Where the f*** are they?'

They were probably shielding the Queen from what was going on in the Queen Anne Enclosure.

Women joined in the melee because many hands make light work of embarrassing the nation in front of the world's press.

The fight started at about 5pm, which was probably five hours after the main participants had started drinking.

One witness said it started out of nowhere.

No it didn't, it erupted out of people not being able to control their alcohol intake. And it started out of stupidity. There's a lot of that about.

It was reported that the bald man was spotted earlier in the day at the Cobham Services off the M25.

He was apparently shirtless even then, but he was wearing a tie, because, you know, that's classy.

As the events unfolded, Her Majesty was presenting the Gold Cup to the winner Big Orange

But all the coverage went to the big lemon.

25.06.17

Blond bombshell bides his time

It is a rule learned from the television programme Yes Minister that something in politics is only true when it is officially denied.

Boris Johnson has ruled out challenging Theresa May for the leadership.

He has officially denied that he has any ambition in that matter.

Specifically, Bozo of the FO said that he would not challenge Mrs M for the post until Brexit is delivered.

The negotiations will probably be so fraught that it will cause any leader's hair to fall out, and Boris is too fond of his own artfully distressed mop to risk it.

After Brexit has sucked the life out of the Prime Minister and reduced her to a grey husk, Boris will step heavily over her carcass and accede to the position he has always sought: Ruler of the Universe.

He will have to share it with the other clown with silly hair who currently resides in the Whitehouse and whichever of his golf courses he wants to advertise at the American people's expense.

The Foreign Secretary has been hotly tipped to take the top job since David Cameron peed in the political pool by ordering a referendum and sauntered off to spend more time perusing the Boden catalogue.

In fact, Boris has hotly tipped himself to take Number 10 since he was in shorts. He had the exact same hairstyle then as now, and the ambition is also unchanged.

He is tipped to squeeze his size twelves into Mother Theresa's strappy, leopard-print sling-backs as soon as she takes them off.

Sensibly, he has ruled himself out of a challenge for the leadership until the Brexit has stopped hitting the fan.

Publicly, he insists that Mrs M has no immediate fear of his attack because the public wants 'calm and stability'.

I think he means 'strength and stability'.

Maybe he didn't get the memo. Everybody else did, as we know from its endless repetition.

He was asked by Channel 4 News if he was ruling out standing for the leadership until Brexit was delivered in 2019, he said: 'Yes, we have got to get on and deliver on the priorities of the people.'

Well, the priorities of the people seem to be changing on an hourly basis.

A YouGov poll for the Times revealed that 'The People' do not want Mrs M as their PM any longer.

More of them want Jeremy Corbyn to be the leader of the nation than want the current PM to stay in her role.

This is an amazing turnaround, considering that just a few weeks ago, the vast majority thought that Jeremy Corbyn would be only be good for laying on the floor by the kitchen door as a draught excluder.

In other news, rather than the hard Brexit that Mrs M is pushing for, 58% said that they want free trade over closed borders.

Is that one of the 'priorities of the people' that Boris is talking of delivering?

Perhaps the mop-topped minister is not quite ready to steer the nation.

Asked on the radio about the social ills that Theresa May insists she wants to tackle, and what action the government intends to take, our chief diplomat said, 'There are measures I believe in the bill on the courts which I think is supposed to address some of those issues and I think one thing in particular we are looking at is, um, measures to…hang on a second...' (a loud rustling of papers)... 'There are all sorts of measures that we want to take to ensure that we do not discriminate against everybody and, urr, I think you'll find that the Prime Minister has been strong on that ...'

That makes as much sense as a man who wears the same hairstyle at fifty as he did at five.

30.06.17

Wanted: A Change of Heart.

Organ donation is one of those things that people do not like to think about, like how they came to be conceived.

Most people want to believe that their mother knitted them out of some DNA she had lying about the place, while their father was mowing the lawn.

Anything is better than thinking about what actually happened.

People also do not want to think that they will ever require someone else's organ to keep them going.

This has led to a lack of available organs for those that find themselves in need.

The government is tentatively considering addressing this. They may be about to overhaul donation rules from a scheme that encourages people to opt in, to a system where you are assumed to be a willing donor unless you opt out.

This is controversial because no one wants to think of having their organs ripped out of them while they are still warm on the slab.

In their darkest imaginings, people conjure up horror film scenarios, having a tug of war with a keen physician trying to take their liver while they are not quite finished with it.

And because it is controversial, I would expect Mrs M to put it on the back burner that fox hunting is currently bubbling away on.

While England dithers, Scotland is joining Wales which already allows medical professionals to presume consent for organ donation.

They must be medical professionals, that is the rule. They can't be any old professionals.

You wouldn't want your bank manager to make that kind of decision, as they would probably take all of your organs while you are still living and help themselves to the contents of your wallet while they are at it.

The problem with getting public approval is that no-one wants to think about dying but there is no doubt that switching from an opt-in to an opt-out system will provide massively more organs from the dead to donate to the living.

Attitudes change, of course, when those who object to being a donor find they themselves are in want of a kidney, for instance. They probably would not object to an opt-out system if they would die without it.

And it is a big problem - about three people die every day wanting a donor organ.

Wales changed its system in 2015 and Scotland is preparing to make the change, and all No 10 said was that the Government would closely monitor the system.

That means that they don't want to say anything that might upset the aged voters of the Conservative Party because they are in enough trouble as it is.

Theresa May's spokeswoman said: 'We are keeping a close eye on how the changes in Wales and Scotland are affecting donation rates in considering whether we would change our policy.'

That kind of political cowardice and intransigence means that more people are going to die.

You should remember that when you hear the government say that the safety of the public is their utmost concern.

The chair of the BMA's medical ethics committee said: 'As a doctor, it is difficult to see your patients dying and suffering when their lives could be saved or dramatically improved by a transplant.

'It is even more difficult when we know that lives are being lost unnecessarily because of poor organisation, lack of funding or because people who are willing to donate organs after their death simply never get around to making their views known."

That could change, and all it would take is a change of heart from the government.

But they would need a transplant for that, and there's such a long waiting list.

01.07.17

History Repeating.

Did you hear the one about the England v Germany football match?

No, not that one, the one they played last week?

I know what you are thinking. You're thinking what England v Germany football match?

You probably thought that footballists were safely on a break from falling to the ground feigning injury and spitting when they miss a shot on goal, or spitting when they accidentally pass the ball to the opposing side, or spitting when they come off worse in a tackle, or spitting for any other reason whatsoever, all of the time. It must be exhausting for them.

You probably thought that they were on what seems like the brief six day holiday between the end of the last season and the start of the next.

You might have imagined that they would be getting a tattoo top-up, having discovered, while posing for selfies, a part of their anatomy that doesn't have any ink on it.

You might think they would be busy selecting some phony Celtic scribble or misspelled Latin phrase to get stabbed into them that they think means "win at all costs" but actually says "shop at Costco"

You probably thought that footballists were busy boinking a selection of bubble headed, blond, tanned and desperate lovelies at a hotel in Dubai before uploading the footage they have taken of their efforts onto YouTube.

But no - there was an actual international football tournament going on this month. The reason you didn't hear about it is because it is the UEFA Euro Under 21 tournament. That's not an under 21 IQ tournament, it refers to their age.

Guess what is the average age of the England Under 21 football team....go on, guess, I double dare you.

If you said 20, that would be the smart guess. Twenty is the oldest that a player could be and still be under 21, so it makes sense that the team would be made up of the oldest and most experienced players available.

But their average age is not 20 - no, the average age of the England Under 21 football team is...22.

That's actually true - I am not making that up.

And so this week, the 22 year old England team actually reached the semi-finals of the Euro Under 21 competition, which is a great achievement.

They probably got that far because they did not have to play any serious competition until they reached the semi-final stage, when, as though history is stuck like a needle in a record, they had to face Germany.

And even if you do not know the score, you will probably be preparing yourself to be sick as a parrot.

Yes, it went to penalties, and yes they bloomin' well beat us AGAIN.

The England manager announced that he was gutted.

"I'm absolutely gutted", said Aidy Boothroyd, who is the real manager of the Under 21 team, and not just a comedy northern name I made up

He used to manage Watford, so he knows a lot about losing football matches.

Aidy explained that not only was he gutted, but that he was also sick, which is medically not possible.

Germany will, of course, play Spain in the final on the 30th of June, and all eyes in this country will be firmly looking at something else. Anything else.

We would rather look at the Parliament Channel than see our twin nemeses share in the glory of another major football tournament final without us, dammit.

7.07.17

A lot of hot air

Mrs May arrived in Hamburg for the prestigious G-20 Summit And Street Riot.

This meeting sees the leaders of the top 20 nations, as voted for by the readers of What Country magazine, to fly in to Hamburg on their enormous, highly polluting, taxpayer funded planes, at great cost to the environment with the kind of entourage that the rapper Diddy Diddy Puff Dog would expect, to discuss very important things that they presumably can't talk about for nothing over the phone.

It is a good job that they are not going there to discuss climate change, because that would be ridiculous.

In other news: they ARE going there to talk about climate change!

Mrs M flew into the north German city of sin, along with her husband Phillip, and her chancellor, Phillip Hammond.

I get that she took her chancellor; he would have important things to say to people who only speak English as a foreign language but are fully conversant with the international language of money.

But why did the husband have to tag along?

He's going to get stuck with the wives and sent to look at displays on traditional German bratwurst production and taken on shopping trips for Teutonic knick-knacks.

Mr M is a city insider and executive at a financial institution that controls £1.4 trillion in assets.

The other male spouse of the assembled world leaders is Mr Angela Merkel, who is a professor of quantum chemistry, whatever that means.

What are they going to have in common with Melania Trump, apart from not wanting to sleep with Donald?

Why do they get the spouses to come along to an international business meeting, like WAGS to a football tournament?

The chief executive of a company doesn't take their other half to a work conference.

They are expected to able to cope for a day without them. Plus why hire a totally hot secretary when you are dragging the spouse along for the trip?

And if you pictured that as a male boss availing himself of his lovely female secretary, that is on you, because I was at great pains not to mention gender in that scenario, because women can be manipulative sexist pigs too, you know.

At the meeting, Theresa May said would be championing free trade. She said that with a straight face, which must have taken some doing, even for a robot.

The woman who wants to extricate us, with great vengeance, from the biggest free trade bloc on earth wants to champion free trade.

If I had made that up, you wouldn't have believed me.

The other thing she said that she wanted to push for was tougher action on terrorism.

This is also odd coming from a person that has just given a billion pounds to a political party with connections to terrorism in Northern Ireland, and who signs massive arms deals with Saudi Arabia, the place that has terrorism as one of its two greatest exports.

Over here, the British press are helpfully describing the PM as a wounded animal and a diminished figure on the world stage.

Asked if she thought other leaders would pay attention to her, given that a vet would have put her out of her misery weeks ago, the Premier said: 'Yes. We will be playing our absolute full part and I will be playing my full part.'

So, nothing robotic about that then.

She said that we will playing our absolute full part and she will be playing her full part absolutely, her part will be absolute and full and she will absolutely be playing her part fully and absolutely.

She then went into stand-by mode to conserve her batteries.

08.07.17

Orange Harbinger of Doom

Mrs May attended the G20 summit and our helpful and supportive press made a point of describing her cutting an out of place and forlorn figure on the world stage.

This is because, after Brexit, Britain has been demoted from the top table, despite us having nukes and a new warship and everything.

Donald Trump was also there, but outside of the states that he holds his rallies in, he is regarded as a big orange gorilla of limited intelligence that you have to pacify with flattery in case he gets angry and pulls your arms off.

That left the field wide open for the rock star politicians. It was the

Canadian Justin Trudeau and French Emanuel Macron show, with a German Angela Merkel sandwich filling.

Donald Trump doesn't like shade, however, so he tried to steal the limelight with one of his apocalyptic speeches about everything being a disaster, which he read out in Poland.

He warned that the future of Western civilisation is at stake and the West must decide if it has the 'will to survive'.

Er ist ein Buzzkill.

He lashed out at hostile forces, ranging from Islamic terrorism to Russia and the breakfast show hosts on CNN.

When he said Russia was a hostile force, he winked so hard he sprained his forehead.

The whole speech was greeted with enthusiasm bordering on ecstasy by his Polish audience.

During his address, he delighted in taking long pauses as he listened to chants of 'Donald Trump'.

It is his favourite sound.

The reason the crowd was so appreciative was that the supportive Polish authorities had bused in large numbers of people who were given US flags and banners and instructed to cheer.

Posters and adverts were put up by the Polish government to encourage people to cram the square where the event was to take place.

Trump's people knew that their man was to be showered with praise. It is one of the things that Trump likes to be showered with the most.

He basked in the attention and could not resist glorying in it before it had even happened when he boasted about the number of supporters he was about to thrill with his talk of imminent Armageddon.

"I hear we have a big crowd", he said, before taking to the stage.

The fellow with the small hands is still on about crowd size.

That man needs a therapist.

15.07.17

They are coming for our money

There is a part of our society that wants to get rid of cash.

That sounds like the kind of thing that hippies wanted to do in the 1960s. It sounds like the sort of thing that hippies still want to do today.

They are the type that used to go to Glastonbury before it went corporate, and who looked like they lived that kind of life all year, rather than just visited it for the weekend.

They probably would rather barter their way through life. If you live in a loose collective, you could trade your skills as a grower of vegetables for someone else's ability to crochet hats.

If you have an affinity with animals, you might be able to coax a chicken to slough off its feathers and hop into a boiling pot of water for someone else's knack of fixing the engine on a Volkswagen split-screen van like the one that Scooby-Doo used to travel about in.

But it is not the poor and unwashed that want to get rid of money. It is the very clean and stupendously rich.

It seems odd, but the organisation that is working to bring about the death of cash is one that deals in so much currency that it made $2bn of it in clear profit in just three months last year.

It is a credit card company. Just as the number of people defaulting on their credit card payments are rising at the fastest rate since the start of the last recession, those same companies want to force us to use their cards even more and are actively working to make that happen.

The problem with cash, as they see it, is that they do not get a cut of any transaction we make with notes and coins.

As usual in the world of finance, making an absolute fortune is not the goal. The goal is making an even bigger fortune. No amount is sufficient.

A profit made at the rate of $8bn a year is not what they call success, it is what they call not nearly enough.

To make more, Visa is paying small and medium sized businesses in America $10,000 to refuse to take cash from their customers.

Visa wants all transactions to be made via itself, so that it can get a piece of all of the action. They are actively working to bring an end to real money and to make everything on-screen, on-line and under their control.

And what happens in America happens here too.

Visa, said: "With 70 per cent of the world, or more than 5 billion people, connected via mobile devices by 2020, we have an incredible opportunity to educate merchants and consumers alike on the effectiveness of going cashless."

They want to "educate" us!

The revolution has been coming ever since those contactless payments were brought in and we fell under the spell of tapping and going.

With tap-and-go, everything seems to be free. There is no money proffered, no change offered. You don't even have to put in your PIN number.

It is so easy and quick that it does not feel as though you are exchanging money when you pay that way.

It is insidious. The amounts you are spending creep up without the old cues of running out of cash and having to go to get more.

They are like the food companies that engineer their snacks to eliminate the feeling of fullness, to make you keep eating.

This is the way the credit card companies like it. They want you to spend money you don't have because then you won't be able to pay off the full amount of the bill at the end of the month.

The evidence suggests that is exactly what's happening. Personal unsecured debt is as high as the record breaking amount we set just before the last financial crash.

And when you don't pay off the bill in full, then the fun starts, as the card companies start to charge you the sort of interest rates that would make the Mafia blush.

The game is to get you under a perpetual cloud of debt that you can't get out from under. You become trapped, working ever harder to pay the interest on the debt you can't afford to pay off. If that sounds like slavery, it pretty much is.

And it is entirely our fault. We have become addicted to the high of spending, to the rush of feel-good chemicals that flood our brain when we buy something.

The companies that deal in credit are like drug dealers, except they make much more money and it is all completely legal.

The only way to break free is to go cold turkey. Cut up your cards, reign back your spending and pay off your debts.

Small steps can make a big difference.

Maybe you buy a coffee every day you go to work and you don't think anything of it because you touch and go and, after all, it's just £2.50 and it is nicer than the stuff they have in the office.

Say you work 50 weeks a year, five days a week. That £2.50 a day frothy coffee habit costs you £625 a year. Would you drink the work's coffee if I gave you £625? It doesn't taste that bad does it?

We can break free of the tyranny of perpetual debt but we are going to have to give up a few inconsequential, immediate highs to achieve long term happiness and some good nights' sleep.

And if a shop suddenly starts to refuse your payment in cash, tell them that you are suddenly put off shopping there.

The prospect of earning less money will stop the cashless revolution in its tracks.

16.07.17

The NHS is great and terrible

Despite what you may have heard and in spite what you may have experienced, the NHS is the tip-toppest health service in all the world, so there.

The Commonwealth Fund has looked into it and that's what they say. They do not have anything to do with the actual Commonwealth; they are a private American think tank, born of oil money that purports to work for the advancement of health outcomes, specifically for the poor.

They rated eleven countries for the standard of their health services and found that America was the worst, especially for the poor.

This is not surprising. American health care for the poor consists mostly of being refused admission to hospital and being invited to die in the car park. This is called "choice" by the Republicans.

Their thinking is that America's poor have chosen not be rich and so their option is to have no health care at all.

Considering the battering it gets, it is surprising is that of those carefully selected eleven countries, our own NHS was considered the best.

Australia, the Netherlands, Norway, New Zealand, Sweden, Switzerland, Germany, Canada and France were the countries that occupied the positions between The UK and the USA, in that order.

They looked at eleven categories and we came top in four of them, securing our number one position.

Only Ed Sheeran has had such chart success.

We came first in safest care, care processes, affordability and equity.

Two of the four categories we shone in were down to our free-at-the-point-of-use policy.

Of course we are more affordable than the others, because you don't get a bill when you leave an NHS hospital, and of course we won on the most equity of our care because you do not get screened for wealth or insurance before they treat you.

This was all reported with great fanfare by our press which used it to bludgeon the complainers who say that the NHS is in crisis.

They failed to note the irony that it is mostly the press that has been doing the complaining.

The one small fly in the ointment that they failed to put in their headlines was the NHS score for health outcomes.

This is the measure of how successful is the treatment we get from our health service. On that score we were second bottom.

The five year survival rates for breast and bowel cancer and deaths among people admitted to hospital after a stroke, for instance, are very poor compared to those other countries on the list.

That seems to be something of a problem when it comes to rating our health care as excellent.

When you are ill, our NHS will treat you commendably fairly but you might not survive long enough to celebrate that fact.

But it is not as bad as that. It's worse.

The Legatum Institute, a London-based research institute released its 10th annual global Prosperity Index in November, 2016, a huge survey that ranks the most prosperous countries in the world.

One of the big components of the ranking is how healthy are a country's people, measured by three key components: a country's basic mental and physical health, health infrastructure, and the availability of preventative care.

Guess where we were in their list of the top 16 performing countries?

That's right: nowhere.

We came in at a lowly 20th place for health, behind all of the countries we supposedly beat in the Commonwealth Fund's list.

This is doubly disappointing as the relative wealth of each country is factored in, and as we are continuously told, we are the fifth richest economy on earth.

The US, again, came way down the list at number 32.

The lesson is, if you get sick, you should do so in the world that the Commonwealth Fund inhabits but don't expect to make it your next birthday.

Actually, the real lesson is don't get sick in America.

22.07.17

Not getting away with murder

You would think that with hundreds of episodes of Columbo and countless other crime dramas constantly playing on television that people would have got the hang of getting away with murder.

Fortunately for the rest of us, criminals don't seem to have learned a thing.

Murderers leave clues behind them like breadcrumbs in Hansel and Gretel.

According to the murder mysteries I've seen, the most obvious perpetrator is the victim's spouse.

You don't need to be Miss Marple to figure out whodunnit, you just need access to the marriage register.

In Michigan in the USA, a woman called Glenna Durham was found guilty of murdering her husband.

It did not go well from the start. She shot her husband five times then turned the gun on herself in what was described as an attempted suicide.

The word "attempted" is important. She conspired to hit her husband five times, apparently she then managed to miss herself. Maybe she was a moving target.

The thing that gave her away was the observer she overlooked when clearing up the crime scene.

Martin Duram's pet parrot, Bud, was the only witness to the murder.

His ex-wife, Christina Keller, took Bud in after the murder. The parrot then did what parrots are famed for doing - it repeated the last thing it heard.

Unfortunately for Glenna Durham, the last thing it heard was her husband pleading for his life before being shot.

In his new home, Bud repeatedly said, 'Don't f***ing shoot' while mimicking his former owner's voice.

Martin's parents said "That bird picks up everything and anything, and it's got the filthiest mouth around".

Glenna Duram will be sentenced in August and faces life in prison.

And the moral of the story is...if you absolutely, positively have to kill your husband, don't forget to shoot the parrot.

23.07.17

Out with the new, in the with the old

The outgoing leader of the Liberal Democrat Party, Tim Farron, explained his departure by saying that the party needed a fresh start.

They have just crowned Sir Vince Cable as leader. This fresh start is over 130 years old.

He's fresh like last year's bread.

The new leader of the Lib Dems has cardigans that are as old as the man he's replacing.

The reason the Lib Dems have a man as ancient as the exhibits in the Natural History Museum as their new leader is because the previous leader said he could not square heading the party with his Christian faith.

Would it be possible, in future, to have a few fewer political leaders who want to be guided by a book written thousands of years ago by persons unknown?

Would it be too much to ask that they be guided more by what has happened in the past decade, for instance?

Uncle Vince used his first speech as leader to demand an 'exit from Brexit'

He wants to thwart Britain's departure from the EU, and in case you are wondering, that is the only allowable use of the word "thwart" in the English language.

You can thwart Brexit, and no other thing.

Sir Vince said Labour and the Tories had 'abandoned' the mainstream and he intended to fill it.

He said, "It will soon become clear that the Government can't deliver the painless Brexit it promised. So, we need to prepare for an exit from Brexit."

"Exit from Brexit" - that's a cute phrase. The reaction he will get to that idea will be anything but.

It is not the only controversial subject he has tackled lately. He waded into the student fees debate, which is very brave considering the Lib Dem's collapse in popularity is directly associated with the U-turn that a previous leader of the party made on the issue when in power.

Vince thinks that it would be a good idea to pay students to go to university.

Perhaps it would. Many of our direct competitor countries do exactly that. We used to do it ourselves in England. In Scotland they still do.

But for a Lib Dem leader to announce that idea unbidden seems rash.

He said: "Under my leadership the Liberal Democrats will be at the centre of political life: a credible, effective party of national government."

Steady on Vince. Small steps. It seems like a long time away that Britons could credibly be looking at a Liberal Democrat government, but stranger things have happened.

After all, they've got a bright orange game show host with the intelligence of a shower curtain in the White House.

Sir Vince said, "I will serve for as long as I need to. I'm not here for the short term."

Unless there is a dramatic breakthrough, I'm not sure that medical science would agree with him.

But those in the centre ground wish him well.

The best of luck Sir Vince, you are going to need it.

And he's going to need help getting out of that chair and remembering where he parked the car, too.

29.07.17

Don't ask the public what they think, they might tell you.

Biologist, professor, author and keen controversialist Richard Dawkins said that David Cameron's decision to hold a referendum on Brexit was a bad an idea.

He said it was as bad an idea as the former PM walking on a public beach with his top off where children could see him.

He said that once seen, that image could not be unseen.

He didn't say that, I made that up, but he did criticise Cameron's referendum decision because it allowed people to make a "hugely complicated" decision on Brexit "on a whim".

A whim is defined as a freakish fancy based on impulse. That is no way to decide the future of a country.

Dawkins was adamant the decision should never have been left in the hands of the general public.

I have met members of the general public and I can confirm that many of them should not be allowed to put their own socks on without supervision.

Dawkins said that the decision was enormously complicated and could not be boiled down to a simple 50-50 vote.

The huge ramifications and Byzantine consequences of the vote made it such that the electorate were unequipped to make such a momentous decision on the future direction of the nation.

He said, "These are not matters that should be voted on a whim, on an impulse, by day-by-day people."

Us day-by-day people might not like it, but he's right.

You would not want the general public to make decisions about any forthcoming surgery you might have to get, or what car you should buy, so they should not be asked their opinion on matters that are too complicated for them to understand.

Economists with brains the size of planets find it hard to divine the correct course for a country to take. The man picking his nose on the Clapham omnibus has as much chance of making the right decision for the benefit of Britain as he has of finding gold up his nostrils.

Professor Dawkins said there was a "great opportunity for emotion" in the referendum, which "clouded" the judgement of voters.

He said "It should have been done by people with sober reasoning, by people who had really looked into the evidence both ways."

As opposed to people who had looked at an ad on the side of a bus.

There is some evidence that the decision was over the heads of the general public.

Just last year - the Telegraph reported that the traditional 'three Rs' are on the decline in this country, with over a quarter of adults having literacy levels so low that they may struggle to read a train timetable or a wage slip.

The average reading age of the UK population is 9 years – that is, they have achieved the reading ability normally expected of a 9 year old.

The Sun is written to accommodate a reading age of 8, so they understood that all right.

According to government figures, 28 per cent of adults have a standard of literacy of level 1 or below, the equivalent of GCSE grades D-G, which used to be called a fail.

For numeracy, 29 per cent of adults scored the level 1 or below.

Around one in 20 adults have the literacy or numeracy levels of a five-year-old.

They could just about get through the Beano, but that's about their limit.

These are the people whose expert opinions David Cameron sought to determine the future course of the country.

Due to our poor education system, we the public might not be too bright, but he appears to be a stupid idiot.

If I were his parents, I would want my Eton money back.

30.07.17

Health tip - don't breath in

The government is going to do something about the appalling air quality in our cities.

They decided that something ought to be done when they couldn't see their beer through the smog on the river-side terrace at the Palace of Westminster.

They have sprung into action and decided to ban the sale of fossil fuel driven vehicles from the year 2040.

They might as well have said they will do it by 2140 – we'll all be dead by then too.

The car manufacturers are already setting themselves more challenging targets than that.

Volvo has said all its products will be electric or hybrid by 2019.

The mayors of Paris, Madrid, Athens and Mexico City will ban the most polluting cars by 2025, the same year that Norway will ban all diesel and petrol cars.

In Britain, 40,000 people have their lives cut short and children next to areas of high pollution have their health dramatically affected by the cars and lorries that thunder by.

The poor air quality actually stunts the growth of children's lungs, and the government is so blasé about it that the target they have set for doing something is 23 years from now.

If you could get high from traffic fumes, they would illegal right now, but you can only get dead, so no rush.

In a comically weak response to such a serious problem the government has announced that in order to cut pollution, lorry drivers will be trained to drive less aggressively.

Good luck with that.

The Department for Transport is to subsidise training for 10,000 commercial drivers this year, as part of government plans to make it look like they are doing something to improve air quality.

The eco-driving courses will teach truckers to cause less pollution by accelerating slowly away from the lights.

If all goes well, they will graduate from their training just in time to be replaced by a robot.

The government say they believe that pollution is caused by poor driving techniques.

It is our fault, rather than the result of successive administrations' supine capitulation to whatever the car giants have demanded to site their factories here.

To educate drivers, and shift the blame, they are going to throw £2.8m at the problem, a sum that is also known as a drop in the acidified ocean.

They will spend more than £2.8m on the carpeting for their offices in the newly refurbished Houses of Parliament, the place they call work.

They should order some highly expensive, top of the range air purifiers for themselves while they are at it.

After all, they need to protect themselves from the air outside and they know not to wait for the government to do anything about it.

05.08.17

It'll be all left on the night

The Daily Mail reports that Labour's 'hard-left' Momentum group has launched a so-called 'decapitation strategy' aimed at taking out Boris Johnson, Amber Rudd and other senior Tories at the next election.

They needn't bother. If they leave them for long enough, they'll decapitate each other.

The Tories are fighting like contestants on Love Island. The only people they hate more than Labour are themselves.

The Mail writes this up as though it is an extraordinary and sinister development. I thought that's what politicking was all about: campaigning to oust the opposition and put your own people in their place.

To that end, Momentum is reportedly putting its supporters on a permanent war footing in preparation for a possible snap election.

Another one? Surely Mrs M isn't that desperate?

The PM forced the electorate to undergo weeks of unnecessary debating and feuding and it got her precisely nowhere. She would have to be one trek short of a walking holiday to put us through all that again.

Momentum do not want to get caught out for lack of preparation though.

It has given notice that it will target senior Tories in marginal seats, and has embarked on a training regime to ensure it is fit for the fight ahead.

They are going to train activists in the dark arts of knocking on peoples' doors and asking them if they are going to vote Labour. They will also teach them to make videos about the cause and how to stick them up the internet.

That is the twisted evil plan that the Mail are warning their readers about.

The brain behind this is a woman with the un-left-wing sounding name of Beth Foster-Ogg.

Ms F-O said, "we want to skill up the hundreds of thousands of new Labour party members so they can be better, more effective campaigners when the next election comes".

The reason the Mail is so upset is that next time, Labour might actually win, and the prospect of a bearded man in a 1970's Open University jacket as Prime Minister is keeping them up all night in a cold sweat.

This permanent election campaigning that Momentum are proposing sounds a lot like the left are learning the lessons from the right.

About time too.

As with much of our politics these days, the idea has come from the United States of America.

Over there, the right organise themselves with military doggedness.

They get their people phone calling and sending out mailshots and knocking on doors and putting up posters.

And they get their people out to vote. No matter what the weather or how long the queues, the right-wing are out there ready to put their cross next to anyone's name that is Republican.

It has won them two elections in recent memory, despite the fact that they did not accrue the most votes.

Both Hilary Clinton and Al Gore won more votes than the men they fought against but they were beaten to the Whitehouse anyway.

That was the result of targeted campaigning - the appliance of science.

Voters in key marginal areas were carpet bombed with messages of love and foreboding to get them to vote Republican. They did, and the less popular candidate overall won both elections.

The same technique was applied to the Brexit vote in this country. Offices full of workers bombarded the social media feeds of target demographics to ensure that they would both go out to vote and vote out.

They relied on the fact that pensioners are more likely to be right-wing and are also much more likely to vote than the young, who are more likely to be left-wing.

The techniques the Americans have honed also include the repetition of simple slogans that they pound home loudly and often.

The Conservatives attempted to copy that with their "strong and stable versus a coalition of chaos" line that was too clunky and irritating and annoying but they still won.

What they really needed was a catchy three or four word slogan, like "take our country back" or "make America great again".

Perhaps the Tories thought that would be too brash, too modern but this is how you win an election these days.

Yet the Mail is writing this up as though it is underhand of Momentum to be trying it.

It's OK when the right do it, but it is sinister if the left catch on that's how you win an election - get a simple message and repeat it often.

Be vague about promises - basically do a Trump - just say that everything is going to be great and tremendous.

It is what people want to hear.

Momentum should stroke their hair like mummy used to do and tell them it is going to be all right.

Or in their case, all left.

06.08.17

It's tougher at the top.

Do not envy the top 1%, they are having a particularly hard time of it lately.

The pay packets of FTSE 100 chief executives fell by almost a fifth in the financial year to 2016.

They are tightening their Gucci belts and trying to get by on a remuneration of just £4.5m.

That is why what they get is called 'remuneration', by the way - it is a very long word to denote a very large sum...and that is why what you get is called 'pay', for the same reason.

Britain's average worker's salary is £28,000. It would take them 160 years to make what a top boss makes in one year.

The CEOs get paid that much because they sit on each other's remuneration committees and award people like themselves stupendous amounts so as to set a benchmark for their own pay when their remuneration committee sits.

It's a circle of executive back scratching - I'll set your pay and you can set mine.

Once the standard is set, they pretty much get to award themselves so much in bonuses and benefits that their performance in the job bears no relation to their income. They're safe no matter how cack-handed and inept they are at their job.

The worse that could happen is that they suffer a pay cut to £4.5m a year, or they get fired and given a cheque so big you could cover a football field with it.

This remuneration inflation is infecting other organisations too.

An Oxford University bursar has slammed the 'grossly excessive' pay packet of his own vice-chancellor.

New College bursar David Palfreyman said it was hard to see a 'value for money return' for the escalating pay of Oxford's leaders or any 'improvement in governance'.

Oxford's vice-chancellor Louise Richardson earns around £410,000 including pension.

Now we know why student fees are so huge and will rise to £9,250 a year next month.

If the people running universities were paid handsomely, as they used to be, and not stratospherically, as they are now, maybe students would not have to graduate with average debts of £50,000 hanging over their heads.

Supporters of university chancellors insist that they are modestly paid when compared with the UK's top bankers.

But they're not bankers...and they're not footballers or film stars either, for that matter.

Celebrities can get paid a lot because they make more money for their employers than they cost.

And bankers get paid the way they do because they deal in money for a living. If they were bakers, they'd come home covered in flour but they're bankers so they come home covered in cash.

Plus, there has to be some compensation for doing the world's most dull job.

The vice-chancellor of the University of Bolton, George Holmes, defended his £222,000 salary saying university bosses are not paid enough compared to those in other countries.

Not paid enough?

It's amazing what you get used to straight away - you get used to a massive TV pretty much the moment you replace your old tiny one, and you get used to the comfort of first class the moment you turn left on the plane and you get used to earning 10 times the average salary as soon as it goes into your bank account.

Because if you have wangled it, you must be worth it.

By the way - the Federation of Small Businesses has announced that the forthcoming rises to the National Living Wage may need to be delayed.

It's all to do with the sluggishness and uncertainty in the economy caused by you-know-what.

The wage is currently scheduled to rise to £8.75 an hour by 2020.

But it said the National Living Wage should rise from £7.50 an hour to no more than £7.85 next year.

A whole £2.45 extra per day for our lowest paid workers over 25 years old to lavish on themselves.

Workers younger than that are paid the National Minimum Wage, which is £3.50 an hour for an apprentice.

To bridge the wealth gap, all the low paid worker needs to do is to make an effort and become one of those CEO's.

But as they've just had a pay cut of 20%, down to only £4.5m a year, it hardly seems worth the effort.

12.08.17

Fury from the fairway.

Donald Trump is on a break from his hectic schedule of visiting his country club in Florida.

For a holiday, he has decided to spend time in his country club in New Jersey instead.

He took a brief sojourn from cheating at golf to threaten to go to war with two different countries, on two different continents, at the same time.

The leader of Venezuela has irked His Orangeness because of, among other things, a crack down on the freedom of the press in that

South American country.

Trump announced this to the North American press that he has been trying to silence since he started his campaign.

Donny doesn't get irony. Irony better watch out because it is next on his list.

First, he has to deal with Kim Jong-Un, the other finalist in the World's Worst Haircut Contest.

The American presidents before him have treated the ruling Kim family by meeting with them, containing their aggression and making sure that they do not lose face publicly, which might cause them to lash out.

Trump has approached the problem by trying to out-shout them.

He is now locked in an escalating contest to see who is crazier, in which neither can back down without looking weak.

Whatever you would define as diplomacy, this is the opposite.

Sitting around a dining table at his golf club, Trump said he would rain down fire and fury if the North Korean leader "utters one overt threat against the US".

Kim Jong-Un then issued just such a threat, making Trump look like a chump.

The problem is that Trump does not think before he speaks, and he does not pass his thoughts by any supervising grown-ups before saying them out loud.

Having been caught out lying about pretty much everything he has ever uttered, the tendency is not to take him seriously.

How can we believe anything he says when it becomes apparent that he is so vainglorious that he lied about receiving a phone call from the Boy Scouts of America, praising the extended rant he performed in front of them?

The Boy Scouts had to issue a statement saying that they never made any such call.

Who lies about getting praise from boy scouts?

He also lied about having consulted his generals about the ban on transgender personnel serving in the military. His own commanders had to issue guidance that no ban was in place.

The first they had heard of it was seeing his Tweet on the news.

That is the problem with Trump trying to frighten an opposition that knows he did not follow through on his first promise to retaliate to an "overt threat".

The assumption could be made that everything he says can be ignored.

The people around Trump are reportedly ignoring him all the time.

The military, his defence chiefs, the leader of the Republican Party and the Secretary of State have all contradicted him openly.

Indeed, Trump contradicts himself all the time. He changes his mind like the direction of the wind.

Unfortunately, he knows that everyone on Earth is paying close attention to him, and attention is what he craves the most.

China have specifically said that they will stop any American aggression, if they judge the US to have attacked first.

We could slide into nuclear war just because Trump likes to see his face on the TV news.

The rest of the world can barely believe that the stable and consistent party in this spat is Kim Jong-Un.

Truly we live in interesting times.

17.08.17

Hey buddy, can you spare £1.3m?

Amazon, the company, was given a tax credit by Her Majesty's Government of £1.3m last year.

Considering Amazon's earnings, we might as well have thrown that £1.3m in the actual Amazon, for all the difference it made to them.

It is the kind of money that Amazon founder Jeff Bezos spends on Ray Bans and leather jackets.

In total, Amazon paid just £15 million in tax on European sales of £19.5 billion last year.

The figure was based on pre-tax profits of £53.5m. That is the amount that the company declared through its headquarters that are in Luxembourg.

They chose that location for their head offices because:

a) it is such a vibrant and exciting place

b) it is the established centre of business for internet companies

or because

c) that entire country is just one giant, well scrubbed tax haven.

We in the UK recognise Luxembourg's business model, as it is one of the few tax havens that is not run by us.

Amazon saw its UK corporation tax bill halve from £15.8m in 2015 to £7.4m last year.

You might imagine that is because it is doing very badly. If so, I will assume that you are not an expert on international taxation.

Of course it is not doing badly. While its tax bill halved, its turnover doubled.

So naturally, it deserved a tax break, and it got one, receiving a £1.3m tax credit from the Government.

That is the same government that takes almost all of the money you make and deducts it from your wages before you get them, to spend on vital necessities like weapons of mass destruction and tarting up the Queen's palaces with carpets so deep you would need snow shoes to traverse them.

£1.3m of the money we paid in tax last year went straight into the organisation that Barclay's said is on track to being the first company valued at $1 trillion.

The whole world's gone insane.

The Liberal Democrat's leader Vince Cable said companies like Amazon of 'taking the Government for a ride'.

Save your breath Uncle Vince.

The government aren't acquiescing under protest - they are begging to be ridden.

Some light sleuthing finds that American documents reveal that the amount Amazon received last year from the UK citizens buying things we don't need with money we haven't got was actually £7.3bn.

On a revenue of £7.3bn, we paid them a tax rebate of £1.3m, and I know what they will say - all such companies say the same thing, as though they have the same accountants - they'll say that that they pay all the taxes that are required by every country in which they operate.

Amazon stated that 'We've invested over €20bn in Europe since 2010, and expect to hire 15,000 new employees this year, bringing our total permanent European workforce to over 65,000 people.'

The implication being that they're doing us a favour by investing and employing people, as though they could do business any other way.

They should stop doing us so many favours - we can't afford it.

The founder of Amazon, Jeff Bezos, was named the world's richest person for a while this year, with a net worth of more than £69bn, and to be fair, he is using some of that money to good effect by running The Washington Post, which might be the best newspaper in the world at the moment.

But try as I might, I couldn't find coverage of this story anywhere in its pages.

19.08.17

Buzz Lightyear, UKIP candidate.

Our elected representatives might be on a Summer break that also takes in much of Spring and Autumn but they are not entirely idle.

On sun loungers from Tuscany to Torquay they are plotting the overthrow of the person that is hindering the fruition of their burning ambition – the leader of their party.

Theresa May has been looking in the rear view mirror to see who will stab her in the back ever since she called that snap election to bury Jeremy Corbyn and the Labour Party once and for all.

The pollsters were certain, her ministers were urging her on. It looked like the easiest of political assassinations but somehow, the weird-fest that is the year 2017 conspired to work against her.

She won but by the smallest of margins, which was actually a loss. The man who came second claimed victory. That's how strange things have got.

Another poll, this time by ConservativeHome, has found the most popular successor to the Prime Minister is the candidate called None Of The Above.

Apart from A.N. Other, which was the preferred choice of 34% of respondents, David Davis was second on on 20%. His poll rating was down 4 points in one month.

He's not waving, he's drowning. Brexit is pushing him under.

He will be happy to learn that while he is doing very badly with the grass-roots, Bozo of the FO is faring even worse.

Boris Johnson went from 19 per cent last month to just nine per cent in this poll.

Justice Minister Dominic Raab was in fourth with eight per cent support among Conservatives who expressed a preference.

Chancellor Philip Hammond is down in equal fifth on just five per cent, alongside Home Secretary Amber Rudd.

It is a party that has a fatally weakened leader, that doesn't know where it is going with Brexit and doesn't have a viable candidate to rally the troops come the inevitable changing of the guard.

And all this because Theresa May went to the polls and came a cropper when it looked like she had it in the bag.

Still, it could be worse – they could be UKIP.

Paul Nuttall quit as leader of UKIP and now the party is looking for another nuttall to take his place.

They have a lot to choose from.

Senior UKIP leaders seem to spend most of their time distancing themselves from their own people.

One leadership candidate has suggested that British dual-nationals could be paid up to £9,000 to leave the UK.

John Rees-Evans said that such a scheme would help reach a goal of reducing net migration to minus 1 million a year.

The former soldier said "It's not going to be fascist. I'm not interested in using eugenics or any evil things like that". So that's OK then.

Rees-Evans' name might sound familiar. You may remember that he was the fellow that claimed a gay donkey tried to rape his horse.

I am not making that up. He actually said that.

He is not the only candidate vying to take over the sinking ship that is the SS UKIP.

Aiden Powlesland is another. He is known for arguing in favour of slashing taxes, cutting welfare and, as a post-Brexit development opportunity, mining the asteroid belt and the moons of Jupiter and Saturn.

He wants to start drilling within nine years.

He also wants the UK to invest £100m on an interstellar colony space ship.

This makes as much sense as anything else we have heard this year.

Voting opens on 1 September, with the result announced at UKIP's annual conference at the end of the month.

If he wins, we could be headed to infinity and beyond.

Conservative Campaign Headquarters have already booked a seat for Theresa May.

20.08.17

Re-evaluating Boris.

Boris Johnson's tenure as Mayor of London was notable for the amount of time that his self-promotion coincided with his promotion of the city he was representing.

He flew from zip wires, stuffed himself into a kiddy's go-cart, rode bicycles with Arnold Schwarzenegger, slammed an innocent ten year old into the ground in a "friendly" rugby game, gurned with Chinese dragons, did the Mo-bot and appeared on the television more often than Fiona Bruce.

You could say that he was spreading the name of London to the world but the world knew about London already.

More likely he was spreading the name of Boris Johnson.

Apart from his vaunting ambition, cleverly cloaked in that bumbling dip-stick act he has perfected, Boris became known for his Grand Projects.

It was French President François Mitterrand who instituted an architectural programme to build modern monuments to delight Parisians in the 1980's.

His *Grands Projets* include the Louvre Pyramid and the Arche de la Defense.

The buildings and renovations were mostly controversial at the time of construction but have become well loved by residents and tourists alike.

Boris wanted to make his mark in the same vein.

What is the point of being the Mayor if you can't do something grand and visionary?

The most recent of those plans was the building of a garden bridge over the River Thames. It was to be on a stretch of the river that was already well served by crossings but getting from one side to the other was not the point.

The bridge was to be a destination, not a method of linking banks.

The world's hottest designer was brought in to imagine the scheme. Thomas Heatherwick was the man behind the Olympic cauldron for the London Games.

His vision was for a fully planted, traffic-free retreat from the city, right in the heart of the West-End. A place to linger and enjoy some of the great urban views of the world.

The idea has been scrapped by the new mayor Sadiq Khan, citing cost overruns and high maintenance expenses.

This seems a shame. It also makes little sense that something so life-enhancing for the people and visitors to London should be shelved due to money considerations when we think nothing of blowing £167bn on submarine-based weapons of mass destruction.

We have no cash when it comes to improving life but the cheque book is open when it comes to funding the ability to extinguish it.

Boris is currently being criticised for many of the things he tried during his tenure as Mayor.

The replacement for the iconic Routemaster bus came in for much sniping when it had teething problems with air-conditioning and cost more than the double-deckers that are the alternative.

They were a Thomas Heatherwick project as well, and are the only buses designed so far that come close to being as pleasing on the eye as the old ones they are replacing.

That is the problem with making things that look good – they are usually more expensive than those that don't.

Those buses were cancelled by the new Mayor of London as well. Now we can look forward to ever more of those unlovely red boxes that are cheaper but have no art to their design at all.

The most ambitious of Boris' plans was to close Heathrow Airport and site a new airport for London to the East of the city.

Putting it there, in a place only frequented by passing birds and the odd newt, would mean that 650 planes a day would not have to fly over one of the most populated places on earth, with all the pollution and noise and danger that entails.

That was cancelled on cost grounds too.

When the richest woman in the land wants repairs to one of her palaces, no amount of money is too much. When Londoners would like a good night's sleep and would prefer not to die an early death from breathing foul air, then nothing can be done.

Boris Johnson may be a carefully dishevelled galumphing great buffoon with a carefully created cartoon personality but he was right about the airport and he was right about the buses and he was right about the bridge.

It is a shame that the greatest city in the world, in the fifth richest country on earth can't find the money to improve the lives of its citizens.

All of those things would have happened in more enlightened places run by more determined and resourceful people.

For his part, the current mayor, Sadiq Khan, has instituted a scheme to charge Londoners for only one ticket if they take two bus trips within the same hour.

All that after only 15 months in charge.

26.08.17

Threatening us with what we want.

North Korea has warned the United Kingdom faces a 'miserable end' if it joins Donald Trump in menacing the country.

This is not much of a threat. We like miserable ends. All of our soap operas end miserably every week and practically half the country watches at least one of them.

We enjoy being steeped in misery. We actively seek out anguish and despair. Watching our fellow country-people suffering in torment and grief is how we like to spend our spare time.

Lil' Fat Kim can blow it out of his hat. We can take all the woe he can send. It's like catnip to us. Despondency is our default setting.

He doesn't know this, of course. He imagines that threatening us with imminent doom will help us make our minds up about joining the Tangerine Scream in the Whitehouse in his bellicose cage-rattling.

The truth is that both leaders, the dictator and the wannabe, are playing to their own people when they are shouting at foreign governments. They are both engaged in a show of strength.

They are like two doughy kids in the playground that are goading each other to throw the first punch. Neither actually wants to fight but they have a crowd around them now and the more they threaten, the harder it will be to back down without losing face.

That is where the rest of us come in, because in a playground, only the two combatants might get hurt. With these two leaders of nations, the reverse is true. Everyone outside their nuclear bomb-proof shelters are going to be the ones that suffer.

Kim will be fine in his underground lair. He will have a lifetime supply of cake and a fluffy white cat to stroke.

Donald Trump will have his bunker fully mirrored so that he might gaze on his presidential magnificence and tell himself that he is doing a fantastic job. Probably the best President of all time.

Everybody says so.

Kim Jong-un is running a country full of people that may have some idea that the world outside their domain is a better place than the one they inhabit.

They probably imagine that those over the border are better fed and might have more in the way of amusements than watching Kim's relatives getting executed by being tied across the business end of a canon.

By keeping his country on a permanent war footing, and stoking the paranoia of everything foreign, Kim is maintaining his grip on power.

Even if his people do not get the news, Kim must have seen the statues of toppled despots being pulled down with the help of the USA.

He needs to promote conflict with external enemies to stay in power. Unfortunately, so does Donald Trump.

His approval ratings at home are lower than those for herpes. He has achieved almost nothing and is stymied at every turn, often by members of his own party. A good way out would be to have a nice little war to get the country and the media on-side, even for a short while.

This bank holiday Monday, a military exercise led by the US begins just south of the North Korean border. That is one reason for the heightened tension in the region.

The Korean Central News Agency said: 'We solemnly warn not only the US...but also satellites, including the UK and Australia, which are taking advantage of the present war manoeuvres against the North.'

State media showed Lil' Fat Kim standing next to a diagram of an intercontinental ballistic missile more powerful than any it has previously tested .

Either they plan to bomb America with a diagram, or they are pursuing the ability to strike at any place on the American mainland.

Can I recommend Florida? It's too hot and there's mosquitoes there the size of Volkswagens.

North Korea's military said there will be 'merciless retaliation and unsparing punishment' on the United States over the drills that begin on Monday for an 11-day run.

Those exercises were planned long in advance but are coming at the worst time for international relations and, potentially, the survival of Mankind.

And just when it seemed to be going in the right direction, after Trump claimed Kim was starting to 'respect' him and that Trump respected anyone that respects him.

Things looked positive for a brief moment before the North Korean response.

They said Trump was 'weird'.

Maybe they do get the news there after all.

27.08.17

Things you would rather not hear.

There are some things you just don't want to hear, like the announcement of another television show about people making cakes.

Sadly, the BBC is about to make another cake baking show but with the very important twist that it is going to be a family doing the cooking.

That stroke of genius must be worth the Licence Fee all on its own.

It starts imminently and will join the 86,000 other highly original programmes on TV that centre on the oven and what comes out of it.

Another thing that you might prefer not to hear is that a weather event might deliver an alligator to your front door.

That is what the residents of a Texas town were told before Hurricane Harvey hit them this week.

The heavy flooding could force wild and dangerous animals to migrate to within close contact of humans, the local Sheriff's office announced.

You could have a ravenous prehistoric monster with a huge mouth full of teeth preventing you from leaving your house.

Unfortunately, the same storm is likely to bring out highly deadly water moccasin snakes that could take shelter inside your house, which might make you want to leave in a hurry.

Also on the list of things you would rather not know is that there has been a mass delivery of anti-sarin and VX epipens to front line emergency staff in Great Britain.

Sarin is a military grade poison that attacks the body's nervous system and causes death in the manner of drowning on dry land within minutes of being exposed to it.

VX, on the other hand is similar in effect, it is just 150 times more toxic. The 'V' stands for venom.

According to an alarming report, a national programme is under way to provide hospitals, emergency responders and support staff with large stocks of nerve agent antidote kits, in case of an attack by the Women's Institute, or ISIS.

Probably ISIS.

Naturally, the government says that there is nothing to worry about, which is reason enough to start worrying.

Security chiefs declare that Islamic fundamentalists will have no compunction about using such a weapon.

A couple of buckets of that stuff and a child's flying drone should be enough to please their god and quiet the voices they hear inside their heads.

VX was the weapon that did for Kim Jong-un's half-brother in the airport in Kuala Lumpur in February.

His half-brother is now completely dead.

The stuff is classed as a weapon of mass destruction by the United Nations because of its toxicity and the horrible way that it causes death.

Apparently, the gas it gives off is even more poisonous than the liquid, making it very attractive to terrorists and the leader of North Korea.

You might be wondering which pariah country could come up with such an evil product.

Which disgraced nation could be so monstrous as to invent such a hideous and evil substance?

Well, that was us, that was. It was invented in jolly old England.

And now we are preparing for it coming back home.

01.09.17

Donny to the rescue.

There is an enormous rock hurtling through the inky void of space that has been given the inappropriately benign name of Florence.

Florence was the name of the little girl in the Magic Roundabout that used to hang out with a stoned rabbit, a talking dog and a weird old man on a spring who wanted to get her into bed.

That is what children used to watch on TV with the full collusion of their parents, who, on reflection, ought to be prosecuted for corrupting the morals of minors.

Florence is also a city of great beauty and artistic importance that is celebrated the world over.

It will be a smouldering pile of bricks and broken statues if the space rock called Florence were to hit it.

Assuming that the giant asteroid that is heading right at us misses us completely, or strikes somewhere that no-one will miss, like Southend, then the biggest story of the year so far, in a year that has been packed with big stories, is the great deluge.

Heavy rains have caused the worst floods in years and the casualty numbers continue to increase.

More than 1,200 people have died, with 40 million affected by the devastation which has also destroyed or damaged 18,000 schools, meaning that about 1.8 million children cannot go to classes.

The effects of the floods will be felt for generations if those children are denied the education the need to make a better life for themselves and for their own offspring in the future.

The charity Save the Children warned that hundreds of thousands of youngsters could fall permanently out of the school system unless the relief efforts concentrate on getting them back into the classroom.

The area is poor enough as it is. This is the last thing they need.

On top of that, the floods have been causing landslides which damage roads and pull down electricity pylons, denying the residents the power that they would need to run their homes if those homes hadn't been swept away by the floods.

The waters have covered vast areas of farmland and have affected about 20 million people and destroyed about a million houses.

If you are wondering why you haven't heard of this, it is because it happened in India and Nepal.

Meanwhile, everyone in the news media was concentrating on whether English-speaking people were getting wet.

Forty people died and 100,000 homes were affected in Houston, while thousands died and a million homes were destroyed in Asia.

From the coverage in the press, you'd have though it was the other way round.

I suppose the misery of some humans is more newsworthy than the misery of others.

Journalists at the scene in Texas have been reporting, in hushed tones, that many of the victims in Texas do not have flood insurance.

How many in India would even know what that was?

Millions in Asia are cut off with no food and water.

In Houston, the residents are not likely to starve to death and they are not dependent on flooded farm land for survival.

Furthermore, Donald Trump isn't going to come to their rescue with a very public show of charity for the people of India, because nobody there has bought one of his hats.

By the way – that offer of a nice round million dollars for the people of Texas and Louisiana that Trump announced and then had his people reiterate on television, to make sure that everyone knew, is the same as someone on an average salary donating £70 of their annual earnings.

Unless he's lying about the amount of money he makes.

He wouldn't do that would he?

02.09.17

L'addition s'il vous plait.

Britain's Brexit chief, David Davis, declared himself determinedly optimistic about Brexit.

He said that as his opposite number in Brussels, Michel Barnier, announced he was steadfastly despondent about the very same thing.

David Davis declared that the UK is committed to being outward looking and playing an 'instrumental role' in the world.

He's hopped off to America to address the US Chamber of Commerce.

Presumably he couldn't just send them an email.

He had to get on a plane with all his entourage, sit in first class no doubt, stay in the finest establishments known to man, at vast expense to us the taxpayer, to remind America that we still exist.

There's good value for money – at least we don't waste cash like they do in the EU.

He skipped out of the country after the third round of Brexit talks ended in deadlock because of the divorce bill.

The EU is insisting Britain agrees to pay the bill before they can move on to trade talks.

They have been saying that since March.

The British position has been to put its fingers in its ears and say we're not listening.

The Europeans are standing tough and the British are standing tough and they're all posturing for the cameras and it all seems like such a lot of pretence.

We'll pay the bill, we'll carry on accepting their rules and regulations and we'll keep having those immigrants coming in because without them we're sunk.

We will do that because, despite the tough-guy approach, we really do need to keep trading with Europe as we do now.

The banking racket will up sticks and swan off if we don't, because they will lose some money if they don't retain their ability to defraud people across borders without impediment.

Banks hate losing money and as our economy has become dependent on them, what they want is what they will get.

It all seems rather pointless.

All this pain and suffering just so the people that believed what they read on the side of a bus can glory in "getting their country back", whatever that means.

In a speech in Washington, David Davis said Britain is determined to carry on playing a strong international role.

After all, where would all those dictators and despots hide the money they stole from their people and buy the weapons to keep them in check if we turned our back on them?

That's what we do for a living. It's too late to learn some new skills now. We might as well stick to what we're good at.

The International Trade Secretary Liam Fox said Brussels must not be allowed to blackmail Britain by demanding the Brexit divorce bill is settled before trade talks can start.

That word "blackmail" is harsh. It would be appropriate if it were commonly used in a restaurant to refer to the amount that you have to pay before you are allowed to leave.

You don't ask the waiter for the blackmail, you ask for the bill.

Michel Barnier revealed details of some of the projects that bill would help to cover.

It includes money for foreign aid, green projects and refugee programmes.

We are refusing to pay for things like that.

The Prime Minister, Theresa May, is another of those politicians that proclaim she is guided by her faith.

Apparently, we are refusing to help our European friends save the planet and give succour to the poor because we are a Christian nation and that is what Jesus would do.

09.09.17

When is a shoe not a shoe?

It's back to school time, so that must mean it's back to stories about parents freaking out because their little darling has been reprimanded for not wearing the school uniform.

Right on cue, one father has vowed to pull his son out of school until teachers accept that the 12-year-old's new Nike Air Force 1's comply with uniform rules.

The people that drew up the rules say that they don't. You might have thought that would be an end to it, but that would be to ignore the zeitgeist, which is: "it's my right, I can do what I want".

The father said to the school: 'I'll teach him at home if I have to'.

And the school said "wa'eva". I made that up - they didn't say that, at least not in so many words.

Noah Stott, 12, has been given a detention three days in a row this week at Treviglas College, Newquay, Cornwall, because school management say he's wearing trainers.

He arrived in the same shoes three days in a row and was punished every time, because if at first you don't succeed, keep doing the same thing over and over again. That'll work.

His father Phil insisted the black pair of Nike Air Force 1s, which retail at £74.95, are shoes and not trainers.

Isn't that incredible? Can you believe it - that a pair of plastic shoes for a 12 year old cost 75 quid?

Noah has been informed that by standing up for his human rights to ignore instructions, he will have to go to detention every day until he changes his footwear.

This seems clear enough, unless you are not listening, in which case you will argue that the trainers are not trainers, they are shoes, which is exactly what the dad did.

He could have spared his son all this grief, but he thinks he has right on his side so he is engaged in a stand-off about footwear.

Mr Stott, said: 'We bought a pair of shoes on the Nike website, which are clearly classed as men's shoes. They wouldn't advertise something that wasn't meant to be.'

The second part doesn't seem to make sense but he is correct about the first bit. Every item of footwear that Nike sell is described as a shoe, including ones that are so colourfully bright that you can't look at them with the naked eye.

You would need those glasses that people use to view an eclipse to peer at some of the offerings on the Nike website.

They have footwear on there that they describe as shoes that look like ET's moccasins.

They are clearly trainers, and while trainers are a subset of the category shoes, they are expressly forbidden by the school rules, which must be obeyed, lest you get a story written about you in the press which paints you in an unflattering light.

It happens all the time. A correspondent shows up at the door of a complainant and asks to take a photograph of the individuals to illustrate the story. They will say something like: 'Hold the shoes up and look sad'.

These people have clearly never read the British press, or they do not believe that they will be made to appear as fools because they can't see past their own righteous fury to appreciate how silly it all is.

To add to the indignity, the feature will be commented on by people who should not be left alone in case they start a fight with themselves.

Here is a random example from the helpful and kind people who have taken time out of their busy day to post a comment on this story on MailOnline:

'If the father is stupid enough to buy trainers when told not to how on earth will he have the intelligence to home school his son? Pathetic!'

I can't believe I am about to say this, but a commenter on the Daily Mail website has a point.

The dad said 'As soon as he went in on Tuesday wearing the shoes, he was given a detention.

'So I phoned the school and told them that I'd pick him up and withdraw him.

'He was given another detention on Wednesday and again on Thursday so I've taken him out again.

'I'll keep on withdrawing him until it's sorted out, or at least until I go back to work on September 18.'

Take THAT school rules – he'll keep his child at home for ever, or for the next ten days, whichever comes first.

The father said the shoes matched a pair which were included in the 'acceptable shoes' section of the school's official uniform guide, which to be fair has pictures of shoes that are quite similar and others that are MUCH more ugly than those he bought for his child.

Ian Dury called them "shoes like dead pigs' noses".

I had a pair that matched that exact description, in brown and black, which was just the very thing in the mid-1970s, but not at school.

The father may have inadvertently caused a further problem down the road by alerting the school to their inaction over what I assume is another infraction of the rules by highlighting their lack of response to the child's hair.

He said, 'they've said nothing about his hair, which is blonde at the top.' And it is, sort of – it is black on the sides and yellow on top.

As soon as the school has finished giving him detention for his shoes, they'll most likely give it to him for his multi-coloured mop.

The boy's father said 'School is difficult enough for the kids without being presented with these hurdles all the time.'

Correct Mr Stott – but you ARE a hurdle – just get him a pair of regulation ugly shoes and he can get on with what he is supposed to be doing at school, which is learning maths, not learning how to take a pointless stand against an organisation that you can't beat.

The head teacher said, 'Most of our young people have returned to school looking incredibly smart and ready to learn.'

Well, steady on Miss, I used to be a school boy who used to have to wear a uniform and I would say that the last thing we looked was smart, but at least we didn't waste our days debating the definition of the word "shoe".

10.09.17

Taking the biscuit.

The chief of the University of Bath has claimed £8,000 for laundry and housekeeping on expenses.

How much laundry can one person go through – is she dry cleaning her towels?

Dame Glynis Breakwell claimed more than £18,000 in total during the last academic year.

And you might think that's about right for someone who is a teacher.

But on top of the 18 grand, she also earns £450,000-a-year and lives rent-free in a £1.6million home.

Along with the £8,000 on washing, ironing and all that other stuff that a busy administrator would rather have someone else do, the university spent about £5000 on gas and electricity and £3,082 on council tax.

The vice chancellor also billed them £279 for cleaning products.

Her house is so clean, surgeons could operate in her kitchen.

As you would expect, there is a huge gulf between the salaries of ordinary staff and those of management at the university.

If everyone was paid as handsomely as the vice chancellor, students would have to stump up much more than the £9,250 a year for tuition that they are charged now.

It would be hard to fill the places as the only people who could afford to go would probably want to study somewhere more glamorous than Bath.

Still, over £9,000 a year does seem quite steep.

That's why education costs so much kids – it is so that you might be treated to excellence in management

The local Labour councillor Joe Rayment said 'While ordinary working people in this city have seen rent and bills rise at a much faster rate than their wages, Glynis Breakwell has seen her salary skyrocket and her rent and bills stay static at £0.'

Ordinary working people do not get to pay £0 for their bills because they have not taken the precaution of becoming a Dame.

This is not the first time that Dame Glynis Breakwell has come to our attention.

Last year we found that she claimed £20,000 in expenses over 12 months on top of her eye watering salary and free house.

She even claimed £2 for biscuits.

In February, Bath's University Court swung into action. It is a body which says it 'does not take part in the day-to-day oversight of the University's affairs or in the decision-taking process but provides a forum where members of Court can raise any matters concerning the University'.

And they did.

They met to discuss a motion censuring the remuneration committee for allowing Dame Glynis's pay to escalate.

A censure! That would teach 'em.

After a debate, the court voted by 33 to 30 not to censure the committee.

You might not be altogether surprised that the vice chancellor and members of the remuneration committee took part in the vote themselves.

That is your first lesson in Politics 101.

That'll be £2 please, the chancellor wants a Hobnob.

16.09.17

Keep on keeping on.

As usual when there is a terrorist attack, politicians form a disorderly queue to go on television to tell us to remain calm.

There cannot be a much more alarming sight than people with looks of grave concern telling us that there is nothing to worry about.

The London Mayor Sadiq Khan said that 'we have got to be calm'.

Boris Johnson the Foreign Secretary said that Londoners should 'keep calm and go about their normal lives'.

Prime Minister Theresa May said that we should remain 'strong and stable'. No she didn't. I made that last one up.

The PM actually said that the threat level would not change in reaction to the attack in Parsons Green, of that she was absolutely certain.

She said this just moments before the threat level was raised to its most alarming category.

It went from 'Oh no' to 'PANIC!'

Presumably she was distracted by having to criticise President Donald Trump for his tweets about the incident, while taking care to appear as though she was not criticising him, so as not to make him grumpy and sad.

What she meant to say was 'keep calm and carry on'.

Well, here is the news: we do not need to be told that. We have 'Keep calm and carry on' coffee mugs and T-shirts to remind us of that.

Keeping calm and carrying on is what defines us as British people - stiff upper lip, don't make a fuss and all that.

It is as meaningless a thing to say as 'all of our thoughts and prayers are with the victims'.

No they aren't. Which politician that has ever said that actually kneels down with their palms pressed together and beseeches God to take care of various strangers that they have never met?

It is one of those nonsense things that people in the public eye mutter because they think it is expected of them, and they can't think of anything else to say.

They also urge us to get on with our lives otherwise the terrorists will have won.

What else are we going to do, abandon everyone we know and shelter up a damp hill in Wales?

Are they worried that we might give up our jobs to stay indoors all day where it is safe?

A thousand people die every year falling down their stairs. We would be safer out in the streets of Baghdad.

We have no option but to carry on, unless we are so rich that money means nothing to us.

If we gave up our lives, how would we pay for our frothy coffee fix and our Sky TV?

Like it or not, we are stuck travelling the tube and the bus and congregating where other people are because if we didn't we wouldn't be able to afford the roof over our heads and we wouldn't be able to go to the football or the cinema or the shops.

Keeping calm and carrying on is our default position. It would be even if we had get to work by picking our way over the smouldering ruins of a North Korean missile attack.

At moments like this, politicians seem locked in a bout of competitive empathising. They feel the need to rush to the nearest camera to assure us that they are in charge and if we put our faith in them, we have nothing to worry about.

Unfortunately, the government's reaction often looks like they are trying to prevent the attack that has just happened.

Since the Shoe Bomber, we all have to take our footwear off to board a plane, since the bridge attacks in London they have erected bollards to stop vehicles mounting the pavement.

All this means is that the would-be attacker uses exploding underwear, or drives over the bridge to mount the pavement on the other side.

The PM announced that extra armed police and army personnel would be patrolling the streets this weekend but as we have one of the only police forces in the world that are not routinely armed, come Monday we will return to being protected by coppers with whistles.

Or, more accurately, no coppers at all.

Apparently, police and MI5 are running 500 investigations involving 3,000 individuals at any one time, while also keeping tabs on 20,000 former 'subjects of interest' all while operating on a budget that has had more cuts than a butcher's window.

Which probably goes some way to explaining why the police won't come to your house if you are being burgled even when you have the assailants on video and have their licence plate number and their passports and a signed confession.

The press will not be interested in covering your break-in, so the politicians will not be interested in addressing it on TV.

You will just have to decide to keep calm and carry on all by yourself.

17.09.17

Part time parliamentarians.

Politicians have a hard time of it.

No sooner are they back from a gruelling seven week holiday than they have to endure another five weeks off from work.

The summer recess started on the 20th of July. That was a Thursday, so let us assume that they did little of any import from Monday to Wednesday, just as we did little learning on the last few days of a school term.

The holidays really started for them on the previous Friday, which was July the 14th.

The House returned on September the 5th.

That makes it seven weeks and a day for them to lounge about trying to come up with some old flannel about how it wasn't really a holiday at all and that they were working hard for their constituents.

Oddly, September 5th is a Tuesday. Which means that they didn't really get back to doing anything 'till Wednesday, and really, why bother to come back early for a short week, so they were really back at it on the following Monday.

That gave them a full three days at the office before the commencement of their next holiday, which they call 'Conference'.

Conference recess runs from the 14th September for over three weeks during which time the main parties have their away-days.

The attendees will be forced to rough it in five-star hotels and live with the very real possibility that their mini-bar might run dry.

Conference season involves much drunken debauchery and the sight of elderly men trying to avail themselves of the delights of their carefully selected youthful assistants.

They say that politics is show business for ugly people and that may be true but a brief tour of the Palace of Westminster impressed upon me that the politicians' young staff seem to be unusually gifted in the looks department.

They will come into their own while staying away with their masters at their various conferences.

They will all be highly qualified, or willing to occupy a connecting room.

The country is going through probably the most testing time since the Second World War, and our elected representatives are enjoying more breaks from activity than a nursery school toddler.

We have it constantly impressed upon us that this is a time of great uncertainty, what with Brexit and ISIS and the threats coming from North Korea but our lawmakers are always out to lunch.

Judith Chalmers never took so many holidays.

The Liberal Democrat conference is first up and begins next week in Bournemouth.

This is followed by Labour's jolly in Brighton and lastly the Tories go mad in Manchester. This last one starts on the 1st of October, a full two weeks after the parliamentary recess begins.

As they are the party that is supposed to be running the country at the moment, would it be too much to ask that they forgo the extra break and get on with their jobs in the meantime?

It is not as though they do not have anything pressing to do.

The Brexit negotiations need constant fine tuning and a delicate touch, ISIS require the close attention of the Prime Minister and her security personnel and that Kim Jong-un isn't going to topple himself.

He is a human Weeble – he may wobble but he won't fall down.

Still, the problems of the nation will have their complete focus when parliament returns on the 9th of October, when there will be just one short week of holiday left for them to take before they swan of for another three weeks over Christmas.

And to think, they only charge us £76,000 a year plus expenses for their service.

Imagine what they would cost if they were full time.

23.09.17

Uber and out?

The Mayor Who Likes To Say No and Transport for London have decreed that the taxi firm Uber has delighted us enough.

Teenagers all over London are coming to terms with riding the bus or walking back from their nightly shenanigans.

Grown-ups are quite put out too. As I write this, 531,420 people have registered their dismay that their favourite way of getting around will be denied them in a few weeks' time.

Its 40,000 drivers are none too pleased either.

TfL announced that Uber was not "fit and proper" to hold a licence. It accused the company of "a lack of corporate responsibility in relation to a number of issues which have potential public safety and security implications".

The regulator is unsatisfied with the way it reports criminal offences, its handling of drivers' background checks and the use of software allegedly designed to evade regulators.

It is also accused of adding to London's congestion, ruining the business model of the existing taxi services and treating its drivers poorly.

London has consulted its ethical moral compass and found Uber wanting.

This seems strange, because for every case against Uber, there are a myriad of organisations that are at least as guilty, if not more so, and they seem to be immune to regulation or retribution of any meaningful kind whatsoever.

If the authorities plan on putting out of business companies that mishandle criminal offences, then we will have to go back to hiding our money under the mattress because there wouldn't be a single bank left operating in the country.

I challenge you to name one bank that has not had billions of pounds of fines for laundering money for drug cartels or ripping off their customers or rigging the game for their own benefit.

They all have form in that regard and they paid staggering amounts in fines, which hurt them not one bit, and they just carried on regardless. They are still at it now.

If we're suddenly concerned about disruptive technologies, then Amazon should be put out of business for decimating the high street.

The public used to buy their stuff in shops but now they use physical bricks and mortar outlets to finger the goods they are thinking of buying, then return home to purchase them from Amazon because they'll save ten pence.

If it is extra traffic we are troubled by, what about all those delivery vans bringing all that stuff we bought to our door?

If we were to apply the same standards that are being used to evaluate Uber, it would mean Amazon should be run out of business twice.

And if we're uneasy about background checks, then there is a certain organised religion that should have been put out of operation years ago.

How much evidence do you need? Ten thousand abused children? Twenty thousand?

How many is too many? Despite the abuse and then the cover-ups, not only has the church survived pretty much unscathed, it has kept its place at the moral high table, retained its status as a charity and gets to run schools!

Can you imagine if a world-wide burger chain had been as guilty of systematic child abuse? There wouldn't be a branch left in any town on earth.

Uber stands accused of mistreating its staff. If we're distressed about that, we will have to examine every business in the country.

Most companies treat their staff as badly as they think they can get away with.

How many go out of their way to treat their workers better than they think they have to for their own benefit?

If companies treated their staff better, wages would not have stagnated in real terms since the 1980's and the spoils of the workers' efforts would not have been divided up among the top 1%.

If it is public safety that we are bothered about, then why have we not banned from our shores the car manufacturers that lied about how polluting their vehicles were in order to make more money?

And if it is swerving regulations that troubles us, we will have to shut ourselves down.

We are pre-eminent in that – the whole of the City of London is geared to saving tax for billionaires and multinationals – practically every company you have ever heard of is guilty of some form of tax evasion, despite their chorus of protestations of innocence.

We have heard it so many times we can say it along with them: "we pay all the relevant tax that is applicable according to the regulations in every area in which we operate."

Sure they do.

If everything in Britain was assessed by the criteria that Uber has been judged by, the whole country would have a closed sign on its door.

Just one thing though - it won't stand.

Uber will continue because there are too many people who like using it and who can't afford the alternative, the black cab, which is a luxury product.

40,000 people won't get chucked on the dole because of this - it's too many.

What would they do for a living?

The fact that the company's ethos is to undercut the competition and put them out of business is not unique.

What company on earth doesn't want a monopoly?

Uber found a huge gap in the market, just like Apple and Google and Starbucks and Pret a Manger did before them.

They have all hurt existing businesses that catered to the market they entered into.

It doesn't mean that they should be stopped.

That's survival of the fittest. That's life. Things change.

It's not fair but then what is?

24.09.17

Going ape.

Japan's defence minister Itsunori Onodera warned his countrymen to buckle up, it's going to be a bumpy ride.

The leader of North Korea seems intent on testing an intercontinental ballistic missile by flying it over Japan to land somewhere in the sea.

This is why the President of the USA, Ancient Orange, called him "Rocket Man" when delivering one of his doom laden speeches, this time to the United Nations.

As an insult, it is not that great. In fact it sounds like quite a cool thing to be. Both Elton John and David Bowie wrote songs about rocket men. Who wouldn't want to have those two sing about them?

After Donald Chump acted the tough guy, North Korea's foreign minister, said Pyongyang could respond by testing a powerful nuclear weapon in the Pacific.

Kim is acting this aggressively because he feels threatened. Only a fool would shout at an unstable person with nukes at their disposal.

Unfortunately, a fool is running the most powerful nation on earth.

He's going to get us all killed with his desperate need to be popular and to appear like a strong man and his propensity to yell at anyone that doesn't do what he wants, like a toddler having a tantrum.

L'il Fat Kim is like a cornered cat – he's going to strike out because he feels he has no other options for survival.

If you stop threatening a cornered animal, they stop spitting and scratching but diplomacy won't make Donald feel like a manly man, which he seems to want desperately.

He surrounds himself with military men and dons military attire and throws out threats to whoever hasn't told him how handsome and smart he is.

That sort of thing might get you somewhere in business, if you aren't very good at business, but it is a terrible quality for someone running a country

At this point, to affect a regime change, I don't know if it would better to invade North Korea or North America.

Because of these two tyrants, we are in greater danger of nuclear war than at any time in history – at least when the Americans dropped the two nukes on Japan, nobody else had them...now they are more numerous than TV shows about people making dinner.

Kim called Trump "mentally deranged".

That was also the conclusion of a group of psychiatrists in the US that spoke out for fear that if they didn't, they would feel culpable for whatever he did next.

On November 29, 2016, three distinguished Professors of Psychiatry from Harvard and The University of California decided to defy "The Goldwater Rule", which states that they should not publicly evaluate the mental capacity of someone they have not had direct experience of, to publicly diagnose Donald Trump and to warn about what they saw as his severe personality disorders and mental incapacities.

Kim drew a critical comparison between Trump and his predecessors in the White House, calling him unfit to hold the position of Commander in Chief.

Kim said, "Far from making remarks of any persuasive power that can be viewed to be helpful to defuse tension, he made unprecedented rude nonsense one has never heard from any of his predecessors."

He said, "the unethical will to 'totally destroy' a sovereign state … makes even those with normal thinking faculty think about discretion and composure."

It comes to something when Kim Jong-un is the voice of reason and sanity.

Kim finished with a flourish, saying: "I will surely and definitely tame the mentally deranged US dotard with fire."

That is a new one on me.

The Oxford English Dictionary defines the word dotard as "an old person, especially one who has become weak and senile".

The Korean term used by Kim translates literally as "old lunatic".

Meanwhile, world-renowned primatologist Dame Jane Goodall has likened Donald Trump's behaviour to that of a chimpanzee.

The British monkey expert has studied primates for more than 50 years. She brought all that experience to make this insight, saying "In many ways the performances of Donald Trump remind me of male chimpanzees and their dominance rituals,"

"In order to impress rivals, males seeking to rise in the dominance hierarchy perform spectacular displays: Stamping, slapping the ground, dragging branches, throwing rocks."

That works well if you have hair on your palms, you sit in trees all day and all you are in charge of is throwing around your own poop but it is behaviour less well suited to being the leader of a whole country.

Dame Jane's opinion has since been echoed by psychologist Professor Dan McAdams.

Describing what he called a male chimpanzee's "charging display" in an article in The Guardian, Professor Adams, of Northwestern University, said: "The top male essentially goes berserk and starts screaming, hooting, and gesticulating wildly as he charges toward other males nearby."

He said: "Trump's incendiary tweets are the human equivalent of a charging display: designed to intimidate his foes and rally his submissive base, these verbal outbursts reinforce the President's dominance by reminding everybody of his wrath and his force."

He's like a great big ape.

Except a real ape usually has an orange bottom, not an orange face.

30.09.17

Safety first

Here comes another train strike.

You could set your watch by them.

This time it is the turn of the Tube drivers, who are concerned that their working conditions are not to their satisfaction, which is to say that they actually have to come in for work.

The Underground shutdown will begin at midnight on Thursday and last for 24 hours by which time it will be midnight on Friday, so that's a long weekend for all those lucky drivers who are not rostered 'till Monday.

This action, we are assured, is the first salvo in a forthcoming 'Autumn of Discontent', which sounds like the name of a film that Nicole Kidman would get an Oscar for.

In addition to the walkout on the Tube, we can look forward to strikes planned on buses and trains which will not be limited to London, so that the rest of the country does not feel left out.

As the entire Tube network will shut down next Thursday, commuters have been told that they are better off walking to their jobs or staying in to work at home.

"Working at home" is not what people will do if they stay in.

Not those who normally have to get up with an alarm clock set just far enough away that they have to get out of bed to turn it off.

Just because they don't have to squeeze themselves into a carriage or bus or sit in traffic sweating, it does not mean that they will use that freed-up time to put in a full shift.

"Working at home" actually means "taking the day off", or doing the absolute minimum required to make it look like they are not slacking.

There will be a luxurious lie-in, followed by a late breakfast, television shows that must be watched, followed by lunch and a nap, after which it will time to open a bottle of wine, because it's bound to be five o'clock somewhere.

The cost to the economy will be huge, business will suffer and that is why the Tube drivers are some of the most highly paid unskilled workers on earth – they have the welfare of millions to use as leverage to get what they want.

And what they want includes, but is not limited to: a 32 hour 4 day week, holidays, sick leave and pensions that are 100% of salary, longer holidays and retirement at 55 in a list of demands that is as long as the terms and conditions on an iTunes contract.

If the strike goes ahead, Tube trains will be scarce and buses will be packed, and the traffic will be a nightmare.

Nigel Holness, director of network operations for London Underground, said: 'Should the planned strike action go ahead, there will be substantial disruption.'

They don't pay him the big money for nothing.

Transport for London warns that road journeys will take longer than normal and that people are advised not to drive into central London unless "absolutely necessary".

As opposed to normally, when people drive into central London just for the thrill of the open road!

Bus controllers have joined rail workers and tube drivers in announcing strikes in the coming weeks - they're falling out of work like leaves off a tree.

In the short term, members of the Rail, Maritime and Transport union at Southern, Merseyrail, Arriva Rail North and Greater Anglia will walk out on October 3 and 5.

The Southern dispute seems to have been going on for aeons.

That one is supposed to be about their safety concerns over driverless trains.

The problem, they say, is that if the driver has to close the doors of the train, without the assistance of a guard, there will be safety implications.

It looks like they are more concerned with the employment implications of doing away with the dedicated button pusher at the back.

Still, if all the trains are safely parked in sidings, imagine how safe they will be then.

31.09.17

Fruit? Stuff that!

Parents in Yorkshire are fighting a school ban on sausage rolls and pork pies in lunch-boxes.

This is similar to a fight that took place in the same county eleven years ago when parents pushed bags of crisps and chips through school railings to feed their cow-sized children who were denied their favourite way to a short, wheezing existence because some health Nazi at school wanted to save their lives.

Parents weren't having any of that. Jamie Oliver can take his healthy eating initiative and shove it.

Shirley Manor Primary Academy, in Wyke, West Yorkshire is the new battle ground in the war to save stupid people from themselves.

The school imposed a pastry ban to promote healthy eating.

The policy has faced a backlash – you would be surprised if it hadn't.

Outrage ensued after the school went so far as to introduce a 'Whole School Food and Drink Policy' which they say is to ensure children eat well.

It said it and wants to work with parents to achieve this. Best of luck with that.

Parents are pulling in the opposite direction, explaining in the modern manner that, "it's my right, I can do what I want!"

The school said: 'Pork pies, sausage rolls, pepperoni sticks should not be included in a pupil's packed lunch-box.

'Desserts, cakes, biscuits and crisps: these foods are high in saturated fat, sugar and salt - too much of these foods can be harmful to health. If a pupil has more than one of these items in their lunch-box they will be removed by staff and returned to the child at the end of the day.'

There is a similar policy on squash and fizzy drinks.

This is to promote the idea that inside the doughy rolls of fat that sit around the playground, there is a healthy child that wants to get out, if only their dopey parents would stop sticking fried beige food in their mouths.

And if you thought that no one would actually fight for the right to make their kids fat, you don't know people much do you?

Parents queued up to express their fury to reporters who arrived at the scene.

They typically claimed that their child was fussy about what they eat and that they don't like that new-fangled fruit and vegetable stuff and that they don't send them to school to get healthy, they send them there so their parents can watch Jeremy Kyle in peace.

They whined that it is hard when they have a child that is a picky eater.

This is true. But the reason that their child is a picky eater is because their parents have caved in to their offspring's demands because they want to be considered their friend, not their guardian.

Whatever happened to "you'll sit there 'till you've eaten it?"

Here is the news mummy: your child does not want you as a mate – they don't even want to be your friend on Facebook.

The job of a parent is to make decisions in their best interests, which might sometimes not be what they want.

Stupid parents insist on stuffing their stupid kids with things that their grandparents wouldn't recognise as food and the result is that families are so wide they have to wobble in single file down the pavement of the high street.

Childhood obesity is up 40% in 4 years, and 19% of children leave primary school obese.

But let's not get carried away and insist that those of little brain should regulate their kids' food intake and deny them their sausage roll treats.

It's no biggie - just life times of ill health and lot of early deaths

What's that against the taste of a cold, congealed blob of mystery meat in a soggy lard tube?

07.10.17

Stay tuned...

Donald Trump might as well have been teasing across an advertising break on the US version of The Apprentice: "Come back after this to find out who we'll be at war with next."

The president surrounded himself with military staff, called in the press and said on Thursday night that it was the "calm before the storm".

"What storm?" was the question from the press, and Trump said "You'll see".

Isn't it exciting? Who will we be joining America to bomb next? Will it be North Korea, China, Iran, Puerto Rico, CNN?

Outside of his fans with the Tiki torches and straight arm salutes, he is about as popular at home as doggy-doo on the carpet and as ratings seem to be the most important thing to him outside of money, he is likely do the only thing he can think of to boost his numbers, which is start a war.

A real war, not the phoney, well thought out war with black American footballers, or the one with women who want birth control.

They were just pre-planned distractions aimed at keeping the press off guard and his fans sending in the money (his supposedly off-the-cuff remarks about NFL owners firing those players that take a knee during the National Anthem were followed by adverts made by wealthy donors asking those that agree to turn off the game).

No, this will be the real thing and the unlucky recipient of his plan to get re-elected might be Iran.

Trump is supposed to be giving one of his apocalyptic speeches in a few days' time and he's already rated his performance as A+.

It will be the greatest speech by an American president or anybody else, I can tell you that, everybody says so, even though it hasn't happened yet.

On October 12, it is expected that he will blame Iran for fuelling terrorism and causing instability throughout the Middle East.

But you know what he's like, he could see something sad on TV and declare war on Disneyland for allowing Bambi's mother to get shot.

He is warming us up for war, saying that Iran had not lived up to the spirit of the nuclear deal.

This is interesting because just a few months ago, that very same Donald Trump was forced to admit that Iran WAS living up to the spirit of the nuclear deal which, by the way, was brokered by six countries, one of which was us.

The deal was that Iran should get rid of most of its nuclear fuel and infrastructure and submit to intensive monitoring to ensure it doesn't cheat.

The United Nations nuclear watchdog, the International Atomic Energy Agency, has repeatedly said Iran is complying with the accord. The U.S. Energy Department has said the same but that doesn't give Donny a chance to strut about on stage with a military backdrop and play John Wayne for the day.

The excuse Trump gave for increasing sanctions was that Iran is accused of human rights abuses and they support militant groups.

If that is the criteria for sanctions and sabre rattling, then Saudi Arabia had better batten down the hatches, just as soon as they run out of cash and natural resources.

It was not Iran that the terrorists of 9/11 came from, it was Saudi Arabia. It was not Iran that Osama Bin Laden came from, it was Saudi Arabia.

Iran is not bombing children in Yemen, it's Saudi Arabia but they live on a lake of oil and they have a pile of money you could see from space, so they get a pass.

It couldn't be that the deal was brokered by Obak Arama, could it?

Trump seems desperate to rescind everything that Obama ever did.

I'm not saying he has a problem with black people but he really seems to have a problem with black people.

Maybe it is just that the Iran deal was not made by Trump himself, and every deal he did not make is the worst deal ever, a hugely bad deal, nobody ever saw such a bad deal.

The White House press secretary, said: "The president is going to make an announcement about the decision that he's made on a comprehensive strategy that his team supports, and we'll do that in the coming days."

Would that include the part of his team that thinks he is a "moron"?

Is anyone else just ever so slightly alarmed that a bright orange narcissistic buffoon off the telly with an ego as fragile as a Fabergé egg and a brain as small as a lark's is the one who is going to make decisions that could take us all to war, or is it just me?

08.10.17

Friends in strange places

The world awaits, agog for the news that Donald Trump is expected to release on October the 12th about who he is keen to start a war with as a new diversion to get the press to stop following the collusion with Russia story.

Iran looks like it is in the cross-hairs.

Trump says that Iran is not complying with the nuclear deal that limits their ability to make bombs.

Germany says he is wrong, and France, the whole of the EU and Great Britain too.

Rex Tillerson is Trump's Secretary of State, or at least he was this afternoon when I checked last.

He said that Iran was complying with the deal but that did not change the president's mind, it just made him grumpy and cross.

He's like a toddler that has been told he can't have another rusk.

Trump is making up reasons to attack Iran because that was one of the things he promised at his rallies before the election.

He said it because he knew a bit of Arab bashing would go down well with the yokels from the ding-a-ling states.

He hasn't been able to do any of the other daft things he promised: he won't build a wall and Mexico won't pay for it; he can't repeal

Obamacare; he didn't lock Hillary up, so now he is left with attacking Iran just to get another cheer from his fans.

The British, French, German and European Union ambassadors to the US went to Washington to say please don't do it Donny.

Boris Johnson urged him to have faith in the potential of the deal to create a more open Iran.

Boris said "we in the UK feel that Iran – a country of 80 million people, many of them young and potentially liberal – could be won over. I think it is important they see there are benefits from the nuclear agreement, so we in the UK want that alive,"

I can't believe I am about to say this...but Boris Johnson is right.

That is one of the more sensible things that he has ever said, alongside "I think Donald Trump is clearly out of his mind".

When you see Iran on the TV, it is always some baying crowd burning US flags.

Where they keep getting them from, nobody knows, but that is not Iran, any more than the Las Vegas shooter is America.

I know for a fact that there is a liberal side to Iran because my sister-in-law is Iranian.

I have an idea of what life is like in Iran for young people and it's not what you see on the news.

Don't just take my word for it.

As long ago as 2009, a World Public Opinion poll found that 51 percent of Iranians hold a favourable opinion of Americans. Other polls have said the same thing.

Even US allies like India aren't that supportive.

Americans are more widely liked in Iran than anywhere else in the Middle East.

Why would anyone want to destroy that?

There was a report in the Business Insider online newspaper a few years ago that said that "to travel as a Westerner in Iran is to be routinely stopped on the street and welcomed by curious and generous strangers.

"A clear majority of Iranians want the nuclear talks to succeed. If talks fail, many expect that moderates like the current president would lose power to religious hardliners."

Who would benefit from that other than a US president that wants to shore up his support by acting tough on the world stage and the weapons manufacturers who donated such a lot of money to get him elected?

The more you look at Iran, the better it seems.

Unlike in Saudi Arabia, a close ally of the US and the UK, women in Iran have long had the right to vote, drive, and travel alone. Women have served in parliament and in cabinet, and they get to go to universities.

And apparently Iran has the second highest rate of gender realignment surgery in the world, which is not the sort of thing you would expect of a country that you only get to see portrayed on television as a group of furious beardies shouting "death to America!".

On International Women's Day, Donald Trump spoke out against sex discrimination.

He winked so hard his comb-over nearly fell off.

It comes to something that the president of Iran can speak more authoritatively on gender equality than the president of the United States.

There is another Iran to the one you think you know. More than half the population is under 24 years old.

They don't want war, they want Game of Thrones.

14.10.17

Planet of the Dopes.

Natural selection has come to an end for human beings. We have peaked as a species.

Look around, this is as good as we are going to get.

Advances in medical science and our tendency to care for those who are least able to care for themselves is both our salvation and destructor.

Cancer treatment, for instance, is allowing survivors to pass on the genes that cause tumours.

Before modern medicine found a way around it, those people sick with cancer would have died and those cancer genes would have been naturally selected out of the gene pool.

That is not happening any more. Now you can live on a diet of cigarettes and turpentine and you can mainline cake right into your arm and modern medicine will keep you alive long enough to have 15 kids who will be parents themselves a few years after going on to solid foods.

A study from the University of Adelaide, which is an actual institution and not something I made up, concluded that besides the good things that medical science has brought us, the unintended consequence is that the gene pool is being degraded because those with illnesses that natural selection would have killed off are able to survive and pass those illnesses to the next generation.

People are being born with ill health because their sick parents were kept alive by medicine.

This is also true of stupidity.

Stupidity used to be an impediment to reproduction. It used to be a factor that made you unfit.

Chimpanzees of limited intelligence do not use tools and do not hunt in packs and so do not get the chance to reproduce because they are less fit for their surroundings than more intelligent chimps.

They make less attractive mates. The more adapted and advanced an individual is, the more likely they are to pass on their genes, making the whole species fitter over time.

That equation is broken in the human race.

You must watch a film called Idiocracy. It used to be a comedy about the future, now it is a documentary about the present.

It's about a time when through medical advances and social aid, the stupids out-reproduce the smarts and they get a leader that has barely enough sense to tie his own tie.

See? It is happening already.

The Australian study concluded that natural selection is broken for humans because of the quality of our healthcare.

Say what you like about the NHS, it is better than relying on leeches and prayers to extend our lives.

This broken order has allowed genetic mutations that would have been selected out to be passed on and to flourish.

And the better the healthcare, the worse the effect. Poor countries do not have the levels of cancer in their people as advanced Western nations.

Similarly, the better the social care, the more it is likely that those with the intelligence of a mealworm will be able to have multiple children, all cared for by the state.

The study suggested that cancer patients should consider undergoing genetic engineering to 'turn off' their tumour-causing genes and prevent them being passed on to future generations'.

And so should stupid people. Life should be like one of those roller-coasters at Disneyland – you must be at least this smart to go on this ride. Everyone else gets terminated.

That's not a controversial thing to say is it?

The researchers noted that 150 years ago, only half the population was fit enough to be able to pass on their genes. These days, everyone can regardless of the quality of those genes.

And the result is: The Jeremy Kyle Show, your neighbours, the audience in a cinema and everyone else on the road.

15.10.17

Mayor Canute

Uber has launched its appeal against Transport for London's decision to deny it a new operating licence in the capital.

Uber is appealing. There are about 20,000 black cab drivers that would beg to disagree.

For the customer, nothing has changed so far. Your Uber car will continue to be an app-tap away until all legal avenues are exhausted.

Lawyers in London are so happy they can hardly count.

It could take more than a year of legal wrangling, plenty of time for Transport for London and the Mayor-Who-Likes-To-Say-No to back down.

They refused to renew the firm's licence last month on the grounds of 'public safety and security implications'.

Which, considering that 10,000 people a year die an early death in London alone due to the poison in the air caused in large part by buses and lorries and black cabs, is pretty rich.

Uber's new chief executive is Dara Khosrowshahi, which is very nearly an anagram of "Oh, a shark's word".

He met transport commissioner Mike Brown last week to discuss the firm's future in the capital.

The talks were described by both sides as 'constructive'.

Maybe he should be doing the negotiations on Brexit for us, because so far, no one would call them constructive.

The concerns that TfL and the Mayor WLTSN have concerning Uber are reportedly over the safety of the public and allegations of illegality.

If those really are the issues that concerned them, then it is curious that they allow those pedal cabs to operate, those that careen round the roads in central London at night full of drunken squealing kids, hurtling the wrong way down one way roads and through red lights.

If they were worried about the public's safety, those things would have been drummed off the roads years ago.

If it was safety that the London mayor was concerned about, street traders that sell mystery meat from stinking wagons would have been rounded up and sent through a crusher - the wagons, not the sellers.

If they were really worried about people earning money outside the law and avoiding enforcement officials, they would have cleared the streets of all those floating Yodas and the bands that set up PA systems and blast their versions of All Along the Watchtower to Trafalgar Square at 10 o'clock at night.

There's a man that regularly sets up his own disco in front of the National Gallery - turntables, lights, dance floor, the lot – how is that allowed by a mayor who is worried about the letter of the law?

It sounds more like the authorities are trying to turn back the tide of a disruptive industry, or to make it seem like they are, to appease the black cab drivers.

If the status quo had been successful in stemming the march of change in the past, we would not have electric lights, or industrialised farming and we wouldn't have solar power or mobile phones and we wouldn't have frozen decaf half-fat salted caramel mocha frappuccinos.

We'd have tea, or nothing.

There is a reason that the Uber ban won't stand - 3.5 million passengers and 40,000 drivers use the service in London, and 850,000 people have now signed an online petition to keep Uber in the capital, and every one of them has the vote and London mayor Sadiq Khan is reliant on votes to maintain the position to which he has become accustomed.

Plus, the new boss of Uber has apologised for 'the mistakes they've made'

He said "sorry".

There you are, that sounds sincere.

What more could you want?

21.10.17

<u>Warning of twisted tongues</u>

The Organisation for Economic Cooperation and Development is a real tongue twister.

Any telephonist working there should get danger money for answering the phones.

If you had to say that name every time someone called, you'd tie your tonsils in a knot.

The OECD is an intergovernmental economic organisation, which is even harder to pronounce.

It was founded in 1960 with the single aim of making the average reader of the Daily Mail lapse into a fury that you could see through walls.

This week, they announced that a second referendum that reverses the Brexit vote would have a positive and significant impact on the UK economy.

When they read that, the Leaver half of the country made positive and significant impacts on the tables in front of them with their fists.

The OECD warned that a disorderly Brexit could cause adverse reactions in the finance markets, the pound would tank, consumption would go down and investment would stall.

That sounds like yesterday's news.

All that has happened already. The exchange rate is about Euro 1.10 to the pound. We used to be able to get nearly Euro 1.50. No wonder European tourists now see Britain as a cheap holiday destination - comin' over 'ere, cloggin' up the place, askin', "*ou est Madame Tussauds?*"

It's cheap for them but not for us. Prices are shooting up at the fastest rate in more than five years. The inflation rate in Britain is now 3.3%. In non-Grexit Germany it is 1.8%. In non-Frexit France it is only 1%.

And as you would expect, wages in this country are not keeping pace with inflation. Not for the have-nots, anyway. We are mostly all poorer than we were before we voted out.

The supermarket price war is probably making things look a little rosier than they actually are.

The big retailers are trying not to pass on higher prices to their customers, so they are squeezing their suppliers. That is a dam that will eventually break. Businesses will go bust or be swallowed up by bigger corporations that will have more muscle in setting prices with the supermarkets.

At the moment, food price increases are lagging slightly behind the overall inflation rate but probably not for long.

Expect your weekly shop to become much less affordable.

The OECD was sounding an alarm for a fire that we already know about but they weren't finished there.

They chided us for our lack of productivity, particularly outside the South-East and highlighted the difference in skill sets and education between the regions.

In truth, it is worse than that. The whole country needs to stay back for extra homework.

Fortunately, the government has been spending a huge amount of money on education to put things right. Unfortunately, it has made absolutely no difference whatsoever.

We poured cash into it and we went nowhere.

Sounds like the mission statement of Southern Rail.

Last year, the Pisa rankings that compare the educational achievement at age 15 between nations put us at 27th in the world for maths and 22nd for reading.

It's a good job we don't read or understand maths very well, considering how depressing those statistics would make us if we had the ability to comprehend them.

22.10.17

Married to the Moron

Here's a sentence that has been rarely uttered: Ed Miliband is right.

He said the President of the United States of America is an absolute moron.

We have Donald Trump to thank for turning the normally reserved and taciturn ex-Labour leader into a Twitter troll.

Ancient Orange saw a report on his favourite Fox TV news show, which took a moment between singing hymns of praise to the President to alert its readers that Britainland was experiencing a rise in crime.

Armed with no further information of any kind whatsoever, Trump went straight to his phone to Tweet that it was all the fault of Islamic extremists.

Trump just lobs these bones out of the window so that the press will keep what he says at the top of the bulletins and concentrate less on his abject failure in the job.

It is a simple plan that is working wonders. I bet that he gets re-elected simply on the basis that he is a giant distraction machine.

Like a street mugger he waves one tiny hand in front of your face while picking your pocket with the other, all the while keeping up a stream of inane verbosity that could turn a windmill.

Other British politicians took turns to pause from their busy schedule to heap scorn on a man that only accepts praise and flattery and vows vengeance on those that do not deliver it.

There goes the special relationship. It was not going to last under his administration. The most special relationship Trump has is with the beautiful orange god he sees in the mirror.

From the looks of it, he doesn't even seem to have much of a relationship with his current wife.

She flicks his hand away, shows little affection, remains emotionless in his presence and spends just enough time by his side to make it look like a contractual obligation.

Or does she?

Conspiracy theorists are suggesting that Melania Trump has a body double who appears alongside the President in public.

The evidence they used was footage of Trump last week as he addressed the media about hurricane relief for Puerto Rico, or as he pronounced it: Poo-rey-tow Reeee-co.

The First Lady stood at his shoulder, silent and unmoving, her stiff features hidden by a pair of enormous black sunglasses.

They were so big you could have used them as a windscreen on a bus.

Despite the fact that she was standing right there, Trump pointed out her presence as though it needed confirming.

He said, "This really is my wife, she's not barricaded in her room, refusing to come out. She's a tremendous wife, she's the best wife in the world, I can tell you that, at least until someone better comes along, which should be any day by my count – how old are you now dear?"

That is fake news, I made that up. He actually referred to 'My wife,

Melania, who happens to be right here', as though she would have been invisible had he not pointed her out.

Conspiracy theorists based their theory of a First Lady stand-in on the apparent differences in the shape of the supposed imposter's nose.

So, the question is: Is Melania using a body double?

And the correct (fake) answer is: only in bed.

28 10 17

Fraternising with the enemy

We do not like banks very much. We have billions of good reasons not to.

Unfortunately, we are in the invidious position of resenting them for everything they have done to us, yet being completely dependent on them.

And there is the very real feeling that they have not exactly mended their wicked ways.

Banks' contribution to the UK's public finances climbed 3.5pc to £35.4bn last year. That pace of growth is far higher than pretty much any industry that is not associated with medicating an ageing population, or dealing in illegal drugs.

Banking is so highly paid that it provides employment for only 1.6pc of the UK's workforce but it generates 7.2pc of all employment tax receipts.

We might hate those money-grubbing swindlers but we'll miss them when they're gone.

Whether they will stay here and continue to pay taxes and employ people is rather up to whatever deal we get on leaving the EU.

Banks are not going to stay out of loyalty. They will get out their enormous calculators – the ones that go to 14 digits – and they will find out where they can maximise their income and that is where they will go.

They will leave London and decamp to some dull European or Asian backwater to save a few pennies because in banking circles there is no such thing as enough money.

This is especially true of foreign banks. They contributed £17.3bn to the exchequer last year, almost half of the entire contribution from banking.

According to research by the accounting and services firm PwC, foreign banks also represent a majority of payroll taxes in the sector.

That means they either pay their staff more than British banks or they employ more people than British banks.

Either way, we really can't afford to be without them, and they are already siphoning off some jobs because of their concerns over Brexit.

Last week Goldman Sachs boss Lloyd Blankfein suggested the investment bank could move some of its operations to Germany post-Brexit.

Billionaire financial media mogul Michael Bloomberg said that Brexit was the "single stupidest thing any country has ever done" apart from electing Donald Trump!

Bank of England governor Mark Carney has been warning of the risks to the economy should financial services firms encounter barriers to defrauding customers across borders.

He didn't put it quite like that, but you get the idea.

Of course, Mark Carney is an expert, so no one is interested, and as he is saying that a no deal Brexit might be bad for the economy there has been all sorts of preening ninnies calling him an enemy of Brexit and a remoaner and all that other infantile playground nonsense.

It is somewhat irritating that we are being held to ransom by an industry that has inveigled its way into our lives to such an extent that we would be ruined without it.

Banking is like the ivy that is holding up an old wall. It is the thing that has ruined the structure but take it away and the whole lot falls down.

I am not the only person that thinks that the banking business is based on criminality.

American senator and ex-presidential candidate Bernie Sanders repeatedly argued that "the business model of Wall Street is fraud".

In February of last year, The Financial Times noted that many of the big firms in the sector had been in trouble for price fixing, bid rigging, market manipulation, money laundering, document forgery, lying to investors, sanctions-evading, and tax dodging.

It concluded that there is an essential truth in what Sanders said.

Unlike most businesses though, banks engage in the kind of fraud that you can get away with even if you are caught.

At most, the punishment will be to return some of the money they took.

What a racket.

They are what the Mafia would look like if they dressed better and left their guns at home.

It is a bit like being a victim of Stockholm syndrome. Our economy is so dependent on them it is like we have been taken hostage and have fallen in love with our captors.

In this case, it is our captor's money that we have fallen in love with.

And what does that make us?

29 10 17

Who are you calling uncivil?!

President Donald Trump says he is not 'uncivil'.

He said, "I am not an uncivil person, I can tell you that, everybody says how not uncivil I am, I get tremendous calls from every country from great people who say Donald Trump is a hugely civil person, probably the most civil person who ever lived, apart from the great Abe Lincoln, believe me when I tell you", or something like that.

If you have somehow gained the impression that he lacks civility, it is the fault of the press who are presenting a distorted image of him by taking down what he says and repeating it verbatim.

He said 'People don't understand. I went to an Ivy League college, I was a nice student, I did very well. I'm a very intelligent person.'

That is the thing with intelligent persons – they always have to remind everyone how intelligent they are.

Darwin and Newton were notorious for handing out leaflets explaining how smart they were and Einstein never stopped shouting about his vast IQ.

Trump said, "I really believe, I think the press creates a different image of Donald Trump than the real person.'

There he is talking about himself in the third person again – and to think people say he's a colossal egomaniac. Where do they get that impression?

He was responding to complaints that he'd been uncivil to the widow of a decorated soldier.

She says he was disrespectful in a condolence call, that he could not recall the deceased soldier's name and told his widow that his fate is what he signed up for when he went into the military.

He said that to her on the 'phone while she was in a car on the way to pick up his body.

What's uncivil about that?

Trump explained that he did not forget to say her husband's name. Pointing to his head for the cameras, he said, 'One of the great memories of all time'.

There is no level of self-aggrandisement that is over the top for Donny.

And no fight will go un-picked.

He justified attacking the wife of the dead soldier saying, 'When somebody says something about you that's false, I think it's always okay to counterpunch or to fight back,'

He's counterpunching widows now.

I thought he was great with women – he told us so himself.

Others have said the same, it is just that those others may have also been Donald Trump in disguise.

A letter supposedly written by Trump's secretary in 1992 has been unearthed by New York Magazine and published as part of their 50th anniversary edition.

The letter rebuts an article of the time that apparently suggested that Trump does not treat women well, which was written by a journalist called Julie Baumgold.

The letter, signed by Carolin Gallego, who claimed to be his secretary, reads:

"Based on the fact that I work for Donald Trump as his secretary—and therefore know him well—I think he treats women with great respect, contrary to what Julie Baumgold implied in her article … I do not believe any man in America gets more calls from women wanting to see him, meet him, or go out with him. The most beautiful women, the most successful women—all women love Donald Trump."

Various publications have searched in vain for a Trump employee called Carolin Gallego. She appears not to have existed.

It certainly reads like something that Donald Trump would write about Donald Trump.

He finds anything but constant praise difficult to take, so if it is not forthcoming from external sources, he will manufacture it himself.

Whining to the press this week about his coverage, he said 'Everybody has said unbelievable, good things about me, but you never report that,'

Everybody has said good things about him?

He's right – that is unbelievable.

04.11.17

Right message, wrong messenger

Prince William has warned that the future of wildlife is under threat.

He said, 'In my lifetime, we have seen global wildlife populations decline by over half, many of which were personally shot by members of my family.'

No he didn't, he said that the root of the problem is rapid population growth.

People are having too many children and he wanted to explain that to us before he has to take some time off to help choose a nanny for his 3rd child.

The Having Kids organisation campaigns for smaller families for the benefit of the children and the Earth.

They wrote to the royal couple urging them to forgo having a third child. Two is a more sustainable number, they argued.

But when you have a guaranteed income of unimaginable riches without having to do anything for it, and pretty much everything you want is provided free, any number of children is sustainable, so they went ahead and planned for a third one anyway.

He is following the typical 'don't do as I do, do as I say' routine.

Wills said, 'We are going to have to work much harder and think much deeper, if we are to ensure that human beings and the other species of animal with which we share this planet can continue to co-exist.'

Sorry to be the bearer of bad news your worship, but we can't coexist.

Humans will eat anything they like the taste of and kill off anything they don't like the look of.

Members of the animal kingdom had better be tasty or cute, because that's all we'll have room for after we do as we have done in London and concrete over the planet to build high rise executive flatlets for the international criminal super-rich to launder all the money they nicked.

In the future, maybe we will create android animals to remind ourselves of the good old days when David Attenborough had something to point a camera at.

The prince said 'Africa's rapidly growing human population is predicted to more than double by 2050, a staggering increase of three and a half million people per month.'

If the current sex scandals can do anything to arrest that rate of multiplication by making flirting unacceptable, then at least there will have been something positive come out of it.

Wills said, 'Urbanisation, infrastructure development, cultivation— all good things in themselves, but they will have a terrible impact unless we begin to plan and to take measures now.'

Again, sorry about this but here is the bad news: we won't plan or take measures until after the point at which it's too late.

Planning and taking measures in good time is not what we do.

At best, humans employ the just-in-time principle.

Politicians almost always work on the basis that doing something now for the long term will cost them in the short term, so they cross their fingers, do nothing and hope it doesn't all go belly up while they are in office.

The prince was right about much of what he said. It just seems a bit rich coming from a member of one of the most profligate and wasteful families on earth.

His grandmother has eight vast homes to choose from, three of which are castles and all of which are permanently cleaned and heated and maintained to her exact specifications.

His father has five homes and travels about on his own personal train.

If they want to go to lunch, the family members take a helicopter.

There is nothing sustainable about them.

If the whole world lived the life of the royal family, we'd run out of resources on this planet pretty soon and I'm not sure there would be enough planets in the solar system to provide for us.

We would have to go searching for land in the next galaxy.

And that's far, far away.

In the meantime, it is probably better to be satisfied with a simpler life and just two kids for the benefit of the one planet that we don't have to commute a billion miles to get to.

05.11.17

The sound of silence.

An employee deactivated Donald Trump's Twitter account on their last day of work.

Some say that person should be recommended for the Nobel Peace Prize.

It certainly was peaceful online.

For a brief period, the internet became a safe space for people that do not wear a Make America Great Again hat and do not think that Captain Chaos in the Whitehouse is best president ever ever ever.

The BS stream dried up, the number of Tweets of self-congratulation went way down, and some bile was drained from the swamp.

The president's @realdonaldtrump account was down for 11 minutes.

Best. Eleven. Minutes. Ever.

Eleven whole minutes of peace and calm before the one-man garden hose of self-love and rage started to spray again.

It only took 11 minutes for Twitter to turn the stupid back on.

During the brief period of downtime, anyone going to the Trump Twitter page would see the message "Sorry, that page doesn't exist!"

They might have thought: "Well, maybe it WAS all just a bad dream...I mean no one in their right mind would think that a bright orange narcissistic old con man off the telly could actually fool enough people to become the leader of the free world...how ridiculous would THAT be?"

And then it all came rushing back.

Twitter initially said the account had been inadvertently deactivated "due to human error by a Twitter employee".

Doesn't seem like an error to me. Sounds more like correcting one.

Twitter said, "The account was down for 11 minutes, and has since been restored. We are continuing to investigate and are taking steps to prevent this from happening again,"

What…to prevent it from being *restored* again?

They should definitely investigate how to prevent that.

Why is he still allowed to be on there? Trump must have broken every rule in Twitter's terms and conditions.

It is hard to know because like every Twitter user, I've never read the terms and conditions despite legally stating that I have.

He must have transgressed at least some rules. He's a giant troll for a start.

Everything he tweets is offensive and rude and childish.

Mind you, if they kicked off every Twitter user that was guilty of that, they'd have no business left.

The company finally admitted that the outage was due to an employee's action on their final day in the job.

Trump, of course, managed to make it into another thing that underlines the glory that is Donald.

He said that the incident meant that his tweeting was "having an impact":

Yes – like a plane flying into a mountain has an impact.

There were rumours that Trump had been hacked, because despite all that fury he vented about Hilary Clinton and her unsecured email account, Trump actually uses an old, unsecured Android phone instead of trading it for an encrypted device supplied by the Secret Service.

Like a rock star that likes to use his old beaten up guitar despite being able to afford a new shiny one, Trump's old phone is what he wrote his most offensive messages to women on.

He can't get rid of that - it's got sentimental value.

11.11.17

<u>Bouncing into trouble.</u>

A family faces eviction from their home in Blackpool, after a dispute with elderly neighbours over Dylan, their 13-year-old son, using a trampoline in the garden.

The term "garden" is a bit misleading. It looks more like a desolate concrete patch where you might put a broken washing machine to disintegrate in the rain.

Not only is the family liable to be chucked out of their house, the mother also faces the threat of a £20,000 fine if Dylan continues to bounce outside their house.

The noise it makes has annoyed the neighbours so much that the council has had to step in just six weeks after they moved in.

Margaret is the pensioner next door neighbour and she has begged for 'peace and quiet' but begging don't get you much these days, not when set against the right to do anything you want, which seems to be the credo of the Jeremy Kyle world we are living in.

Margaret says the 10ft trampoline was pushed up against her wall and has made her life 'hellish', damaged a light fitting in her home and allowed youngsters to peer through her stairs landing window.

Presumably they are peering in the window in half second bursts, at the apex of their bounce.

Unusually, council bosses are doing something about it.

They said that after exhausting all other options, they have given the family an official warning. And if that doesn't work they will slap then with an admonishment – that'll teach 'em.

No need! Dylan's mum Amanda has agreed to restrain her child, get rid of the trampoline and has vowed to be a good neighbour from this moment on.

Just kidding, she invited the Mail along expecting them to be on her side.

Perhaps she has never read the Daily Mail.

They did what they usually do in such circumstances and asked her to pose next to the trampoline with the council letter and look folorn.

She said, 'I'm sure this is not right. My own child cannot play in his own garden. It has upset me. I can't stop crying. All he's doing is bouncing on the trampoline with his friends.'

And that's the problem – trampolines increase the vocal level of children to supersonic jet take-off volume – they scream and they scream and they scream but parents seem to have selective deafness when it comes to their own children making a noise.

This can become annoying to anyone else with functioning ears.

For some reason, every other house in the country has one of these bloomin' things in their back yard. The only thing that makes children scream louder is a swimming pool.

Don't buy a house next to one.

Old lady Margaret said that not only does she have to put up with the racket of kids bouncing and yelling, she has also had eggs thrown at her home and has been on the end of lewd and abusive comments.

Does that sound like the actions of a 13 year old who is in a pupil referral unit, an establishment that houses children excluded from normal schools?

Of course not. It was bound to have been another, unrelated child.

The mother Amanda said the legal letter from the council had left her son Dylan too scared to go back on the trampoline.

I think I speak for all people who have neighbours when I say: good – that's the idea.

12.11.17

Little people of the world unite!

There has been another release of papers from a firm that caters for the super-rich by organising their finances so as to maximise their efficiency, or whatever is the phrase these people use to justify what your average non-expert person in the street might think should put you in jail.

The New York billionaire Leona Helmsley once famously said "We don't pay taxes, only the little people pay taxes".

She was shortly afterwards found guilty of tax evasion among other things and was sentenced to 16 years in prison.

However, after the court realised she was a rich white person, she only served 19 months.

Only the little people serve time too.

That was in 1994 in America but the same kind of people are still doing the same kind of things and getting away with it.

They use arrangements set up by genius accountants and legal professionals that are so mind-bogglingly complex that Einstein would have had to sit down with a cold compress on his brow if he had ever tried to figure one of them out.

Mostly these schemes are kept secret from us. Secrecy is the key to their success.

That way, for instance, people can use off-shore money that has been hidden from the taxman to influence politicians and governments and steer the country in a direction of their choosing.

The old notion that there is one rule for the rich and another for the rest of us is not just conspiracy theory nonsense.

The Paradise Papers follow the Panama Papers and the Luxembourg Leaks and show to what lengths the international super-rich will go to avoid paying what a reasonable person might describe as "their fair share".

The guilty trotted out the exact same excuse they always give – we've heard the same thing word for word whenever one of these individuals or companies gets found out – "we pay the full amount of tax applicable in every jurisdiction in which we operate and we arrange our affairs completely within the law".

That translates as: we ply one country off against another and strong arm them to change laws and we pay huge amounts to accounting and legal firms to comb through the regulations and find ever more opaque and clandestine ways of skipping round the rules without actually breaking any of them.

They can only do this because no one in authority ever had the imagination to dream up such tactics, so they never thought to outlaw them.

I mean, who would think that someone could give all their earnings away to a company in the Cayman Islands that exists only in name, then appoint themselves as the sole financial advisor for that fake company and then tell that company that the best way to spend its money is to pay for houses and sports cars and holidays for the person that gave that company the money in the first place?

By using this method of sending their earnings on a 14,000 mile round trip, the person does not pay any tax on their earnings, because, on the face of it, they have given them away.

Technically, that's not illegal because nobody in authority ever had the foresight to predict that anyone would dream up such a scheme.

The Cayman Islands are one of the many tax havens that operate under the British flag. We are the pre-eminent nation on earth for the rich and shameless to hide their wealth and launder their money.

Our own head of state got caught up in this latest scandal. A great chunk of the Queen's half a billion pound personal fortune is invested in tax havens.

When that little nugget came out, the usual royal hem-sniffers leapt into action to defend her.

They said it was disgraceful that the good name of her majesty had been sullied by association with such schemes and that she could not possibly have known and etc. and so on.

These are the same apologists who will tell us of how well informed is her majesty on all matters and what a tight grip she has on the purse strings, right up to the point at which she is tainted by scandal and then she magically morphs into a dotty old lady who doesn't know where her money is.

The same trick is pulled by business people who will speak glowingly of their ability to make millions from their titanic acumen and genius and, when found out to have been cheating the tax man, then claim to be clueless dupes of dodgy financial advisors.

The one thing that seems certain is that this latest revelation of how the rich avoid paying tax will have no effect whatsoever.

The public will quickly grow bored of reading the same story and will seek out other amusements like the John Lewis Christmas TV ad or whatever Princess Whatsit wore to glad-hand toothless flag wavers at some royal walkabout.

We little people will continue to be the ones that pay taxes because they are taken from our wages before we get our money.

And if you have ever wondered why so much tax is taken from your earnings and yet the NHS is in crisis and the police are so understaffed they can't investigate your break-in and the pot holes in the roads don't get fixed, just remember that all the tax that is avoided on the £6 trillion kept off-shore has to be made up by you.

You are subsidising the lifestyles of the haves and the have-mores.

They would say that they are grateful but I imagine they are too busy laughing.

17.11.17

Ape attacks lion.

Just when you though he couldn't go any lower – Donald Trump found a way.

The world's most powerful man has declared war on animals.

He is blowing off steam by killing things vicariously through big game hunters.

Lions and tigers are his *amuse-bouche* before the main course which will be World War III.

That will start when he hears a translation of Kim Jong-un calling his hair fat.

Trump has reversed a ban on importing trophies from big game hunted for sport that was brought in after Cecil the lion was killed.

Cecil was killed in a dentist related incident, in that he was shot by one.

That happened in 2015 and when we heard the news, the whole world to reach for its hankies and the previous president, Obak Arama, instigated a ban on importing the parts of recently shot rare animals into America where they would be hung on the wall in some rich man's snug.

Coincidentally, two of those rich men just happen to be the sons of one D. Trump.

There are pictures all over the internet of Tweedle Dumb and Tweedle Dumber posing with the animals they bravely killed from an off road vehicle, surrounded by armed wardens and security guards.

They courageously used high powered rifles, fired from so far away that the animals did not even know they were there before the shots rang out.

It's as though those two were getting back at nature for everything it has done to them.

They shot all fauna that moved, quite a lot that was stationary and probably didn't spare the flora either.

They have sprayed more ammunition around Africa than Robert Mugabe, but for a few frustrating years they have been unable to bring back the prize parts of the beautiful beasts they so heroically dispatched.

And if you happened to be on a killing holiday while the import ban was in place and you were unable to return with your quarry, Trump has made his new directive to be applied retroactively.

This will please that most cruelly overlooked and downtrodden of demographics: rich white men with guns.

It is not only big cat trophies that Trump announced he will allow.

Elephants are also back in the cross-hairs. Their tusks are highly prized because they are phallic-shaped and there is nothing that manly men like to collect more than things that are longer than they are wide.

Orange apes are not on the kill list, in case his sons start preparing for a hostile takeover of their father's business.

Trumpists say that hunting wildlife brings in big money in tourism for countries that need it but most tourists want to see the animals while they are still alive and not being kneeled on in a pool of blood by a millionaire for a Facebook snap.

A hundred years ago there were estimated to be four to five million African elephants and 100,000 Asian elephants in the wild.

There are now one tenth of that remaining on the African savannah, and in Asia there are only about 35,000 left.

They are being killed by poachers at a rate of 100 a day.

This seems a shame as, unlike the billion animals we chew through a year for our dinner in Britain, these trophy animals are rare. David Attenborough is not likely to want to point his camera at a herd of cows or a barn full of chickens and we wouldn't watch it if he did.

There is also the issue of intelligence.

We would frown on someone who hired a boat to go shooting dolphins, yet elephants are among the smartest animals on earth.

They haven't fallen for the £1000 iPhone for a start. They're brighter than a lot of humans.

The locals think that each live elephant is worth over £1 million in terms of tourism revenues it brings in for hard-up countries.

For the US president, that appears to be nothing compared to the momentary thrill and lifetime of bragging rights for millionaires who like killing things on their holidays.

*Update:

After a day in which the whole world expressed its anger at this lifting of the ban on the import of big game trophies into America, Trump reacted to that outrage and tweeted, in the manner of Tarzan communicating to Jane: "Put big game trophy decision on hold until such time as I review all conservation facts".

Facts? Reacting to outrage? Maybe he is not as slow witted as he sounds. He might even be as bright as that squirrel he keeps on his head.

18.11.17

We need houses but not round this way

The Communities Secretary, Sajid Javid, who is in charge of housing policy, attacked the over-60s for the chronic housing shortage.

It is the NIMBY problem – not in my back yard, not in my village, not in my town and definitely nowhere near me, we're full up.

He said older people had 'no understanding' of the problems and were 'living in a different world'.

And they are.

They are living in the good old days, a world of houses so cheap they were giving them away free with a carton of cigarettes, when a house had room to move about in and actually came with cupboards, when a person could retire at 55 and still earn as much as they brought in before they got the gold watch.

In the modern world, houses are as out of reach as the moon and young people will not retire at all.

The young seem to have been screwed over by the generation we call the Baby Boomers, those people born after the Second World War and before the Beatles took off.

They grew up in a place that was less dirty, less crowded, less unequal and less expensive. The changes that have occurred since then were caused in great part by that older generation and are unduly affecting the younger generations.

Sajid Javid said it was time to deliver 'moral justice' for the young.

Part of that plan is to stop older people standing in the way of a massive house building drive.

That sound you hear is older people getting ready to dig their heels in.

Mr Javid said that he still hears from those who say that there isn't a problem with housing, that affordability is only a problem for millennials that "spend too much on nights out and smashed avocados."

The NIMBYs say that if the young just cut down on their cappuccino habit, they'd bound to be able to afford a house.

Theresa May has echoed some of Sajid's thoughts.

She has promised to fix what she called "the broken housing market"

She can put that on the list of broken things that need mending, starting with her own party.

As you would expect, the problem has been caused by short-termism. Successive governments have ignored the issue, hoping that it will go away.

In some years since World War II, while Germany has been steadily building 250,000 homes a year, we have managed just 5,000.

There has been some movement on the issue. The number of new homes in England rose by nearly 220,000 last year.

In London 40,000 new homes came to market. Unfortunately, they came to market in Malaysia, Hong Kong and Saudi Arabia.

You may have seen the forest of cranes on London's skyline that have been putting up those 40,000 new homes. They are almost all executive flatlets in towers, priced at a million pounds for a studio and sold off plan to foreigners who are diversifying their assets and have no intention of living in them.

Why would they? If you had a million pounds to spend on somewhere to live, would you choose to reside in a tiny flat with nowhere to put your stuff, with a living room the size of a kitchen, that has a kitchen in it?

The towers that have ruined the look of London are not for Londoners. They have not addressed the problem of the housing shortage, they have addressed the problem of where the rich can park their money in a safe asset.

The average age of a first-time buyer in this country is now 32. This should worry the Tories.

Middle aged people with no houses to protect and no pensions to rely on are unlikely to stop their youthful dalliance with Labour and start voting Conservative.

If you don't have anything, you don't need to vote for the party that will most likely allow you to keep it.

Unfortunately, there is no magic money tree for the building of truly affordable homes and council houses.

If only homes could vote in the Commons, there would be. If the DUP's experience is anything to go by, the going rate is £1bn per ten votes.

That would be enough to build some pretty exciting starter homes.

They might even come with cupboards.

25.11.17

<u>Inept, inefficient, in trouble.</u>

The reason that nothing appears to work in this country is that we are being run by incompetents.

We have a government that is disorganised and disjointed, like a pile of broken Meccano bits.

And our ministers are mediocre.

But that's not me saying that, it's the people we are engaged with in the tricky task of extricating ourselves from the European Union, without actually parting company on bad terms.

A confidential internal Irish government document demonstrates the true feelings of top European officials who described Boris Johnson, the Foreign Secretary, as "unimpressive" and our Government's performance in the Brexit negotiations as "chaotic and incoherent".

Mrs M's unhappy gang chaotic? Bozo of the F.O. unimpressive? Surely not.

We were never supposed to see that paper. That's why they wrote what they thought.

As any jobbing plumber would say: thank goodness for leaks.

The super-secret, but now highly public document also says that EU officials bemoan "the quality of politicians in Westminster".

Oh no – bemoaners!

Irish embassies across Europe at the start of November shared their thoughts and experiences on how Brexit was going.

They wrote those thoughts down and now we know that the Czech deputy minister for foreign affairs told officials "he felt sorry for British ambassadors around the EU trying to communicate a coherent message when there is political confusion at home".

OK, this is getting embarrassing. Now the Czechs are feeling sorry for us. Pretty soon Zimbabweans will be sending us care packages and advice on forming a capable government.

Those Irish documents also illuminate what goes on when our top Brexiteer goes on his travels.

It said that Brexit was barely mentioned during a recent meeting between David Davis and French ministers.

Barely mentioned? What do they talk about? What wine to have with lunch?

And which language are they talking it in? I bet David Davis doesn't do French.

Like a typical Brit abroad, I bet he walks up to Jonny foreigner and starts talking English at them, loudly, expecting them to switch from their own language because we're British, damn it, and we don't talk foreign.

Still, I'm sure that everything will work out for the best because regardless of how the negotiations go, we will still boast some of the most highly skilled workers in the world.

The Organisation for Economic Co-operation and Development said so.

It would be great if they had stopped there, but they then said that we are highly skilled in all the wrong things.

We may ace our exams and have enough diplomas to wallpaper a gymnasium but the skills we possess do not match the positions available.

They said that as many as 40pc of workers are either over-skilled or under-qualified for their jobs,

I know the government is not run by people who are over-skilled, and if we can agree that they are not perfectly suited to their task, that leaves us with just one other possibility.

Now we know.

26.11.17

Lazy and fat like a cat

The man who is responsible for promoting British business abroad says that Britain's businesses are fat and lazy.

With promoters like that, who needs enemies?

Liam Fox, The International Trade Secretary, accused companies of not wanting to export their goods abroad because they can't be bovvered.

He said the reason we are trailing behind our main competitors is that the people running Britain plc are not looking up past their bellies to foreign markets.

"Must do better" is the mark on our report card.

One reason that we lag behind our colleagues in Europe, the Far East and America is that we are terrible at spending money on the future.

Our research and development budget is paltry compared to the amount of money our businesses have at their disposal.

I suspect that short-termism is to blame here, as it is with much else that ails us.

British companies put too little effort into training workers in the right skills, because companies aren't interested in investing in long term gain – they are more interested in investing in the fabulous lifestyles of the people that run them in the short term.

The amount we spend on research and development puts us 14th on the list of countries in Europe. Not 14th on the list of countries in the world, in Europe!

According to the 2015 Eurostat year book, going by gross domestic expenditure by country, the fifth largest economy on earth is only the 14th most forward thinking country on this continent.

Where do our workers lack skills? Well, nothing important, just verbal, cognitive reasoning, social and complex problem-solving skills, and maths, sciences, technology and engineering.

Which sounds like everything.

And the problem is getting worse as companies cut back their already meagre training budgets.

They will not, of course, be cutting their management remunerations, because they're worth it!

The Organisation for Economic Cooperation and Development said: "Skills mismatch is very high in the UK compared with other countries."

They said that it is the responsibility of employers to train their workers in the skills they need.

But if CEO's and MD's spend money training their workers, or planning for the long term, that's less that they can award themselves in bonuses in the short term.

This is all highly alarming because in a very short period of time, a robot is probably going to take your job, so you will need to be highly skilled for the jobs of the future, because simple jobs and some quite complicated ones will be terminated by a computer chip.

The OECD insist that this is not a new problem.

They said "We could be talking about these issues 30 or 40 years ago, and if you want to be really pessimistic you can go back to the 1890s when people were talking about the same sorts of issues in the UK."

British business has had over 120 years to address this problem. Perhaps management has been busy.

Busy flipping through What Yacht magazine.

01.12.17

High time the law changed.

The government is dead set against recreational drugs, which makes it odd that they have just legalised a previously proscribed recreational drug for purchase over the counter at the chemist.

They did this after a public consultation which found that many people were buying it illegally online and from drug dealers.

This meant that they did not know what they were taking until they took it. There is no quality control in the domain of the drug dealer and clearly the situation was a danger to the public.

How refreshing and sensible to finally be treating marijuana this way, you might think.

And you would be wrong. It wasn't marijuana that the government relaxed the law on, it was Viagra.

The erectile dysfunction pill is a recreational drug in that it is not essential for health and it is not used for work, you use it recreationally. If you use it at work, you are either a sex worker in the wrong job, or a celebrity about to get fired under a blaze of publicity.

You used to have to go to the GP to get a prescription, which was embarrassing and time consuming, especially if you were in throes of passion and you found you were in need of one.

It was impractical to ask your paramour to wait 'till you could get an appointment at the surgery and dash to Boots. The likelihood is that the moment will have gone.

Now you can stock up for a night in without the two week wait for the doctor to OK it.

Officials hope that this new convenience will steer people away from illicit sources of the drug, with all the dangers that are involved with buying mystery pills from unknown sources.

There are a lot of forgeries about - £50m worth confiscated in the UK in the past five years alone.

That is £50m that could have gone to the powerful and influential pharmaceutical giants. The government had to act, and now those legal producers of the drug are going to get a lot more money.

They are so happy they can hardly count.

The reason that the government is liberalising the law on erectile dysfunction (ED) pills and not marijuana is that the former is safe and the latter is dangerous.

At least, that's what you would think.

Marijuana is also a popular drug for criminals, of course. The growing and supply of it is completely unregulated and the user has no idea what they are taking until they have taken it.

The government's position is that by continuing to prosecute the war on specific drugs, they will prevent harm.

Unfortunately, that's not true.

Marijuana never killed anybody.

Look at the government's own cause of death statistics for any given year and you will find a zero next to deaths from marijuana.

ED takers have not been so lucky.

In 2014, Psychology Today reported that, in America alone, according to a study of erection medication side effects during the decade from 1998 (the year Viagra was approved) through 2007, Viagra has been implicated in at least 1,824 deaths mostly from heart attacks.

Similar drugs Cialis (approved in 2003) has been linked to 236 deaths, and Levitra (2003) to 121.

In addition, the three medications appear to have caused or significantly contributed to at least 2,500 non-fatal heart attacks and other potentially serious heart problems, and more than 25,000 other potentially serious side effects, among them: mini-strokes, vision loss, and hearing loss.

America's Food and Drug Administration's entire catalogue of adverse event reports for erection medications over 10 years was of 26,451 reports.

That's 220 reports a month.

The little gentleman's helper is implicated in a steady trickle of heart attacks, serious illnesses and death.

It is available at a chemist near you. Marijuana has not been implicated as the cause of any deaths at all and possessing it could put you in jail.

That is the government's considered policy. Maybe they were drunk when they made it.

02.12.17

Scaredy fat cats

The financial giant Morgan Stanley is frightened of Jeremy Corbyn.

They said that Uncle Jezza coming to power would be a bigger threat to investors than Brexit.

They think that he would set about changing the way the free-market economy works.

Why would he do a thing like that? We are all doing so well out of it.

And by "well" I mean "badly".

Multi-national corporations are draining the country of its wealth, decimating traditional, local business and squirrelling that wealth away at the centre of legal labyrinths on Pacific islands where the tax man can't get it.

The result is that where lots of little businesses used to pay tax and the money was used to fund the health service and the police, now we find that mega corporations that have replaced them hold trillions of pounds off-shore where it does no good to anyone except those dozen or so individuals who vie for bragging rights to be the richest person on earth.

Why would a politician elected by the people want to change that?

Corbyn hit back at Morgan Stanley saying that organisations like them are more like gamblers than investors and they are right to regard him as a threat.

He said he wants to transform a rigged economy that profited speculators at the expense of ordinary people.

Ordinary people used to earn about one twentieth the salary of the CEO of the company they worked for.

That was in the 1960's. Today, CEOs earn not 20 times the average person working for them, they earn almost 400 times that amount.

UK bosses of our biggest companies make in two and a half days what it takes the average worker a year to earn.

That's the way the free-market economy has worked for the many – not at all.

The result of that, and the tax avoidance that is endemic to corporate culture, is that the police do not have the money to investigate crimes, the NHS is cancelling operations, schools are asking parents to supply books and the council can't keep the street lights on.

The Institute of Fiscal Studies says that we are looking at 50 years of stagnating living standards since the financial crash caused by the banks.

They produced a report that they say makes grim reading.

Not to the people running the banks it doesn't. They weren't touched by the catastrophe they caused at all. In fact, they prospered. The bumper pay-outs on the top floors of the world's biggest banks remain unchanged since the crash.

The people who run the big banks made $20m a year before the crash and they are making $20m a year today.

Jeremy Corbyn strikes fear into their hearts because he might rebalance the economy to benefit the many.

Which of his manifesto pledges might concern them the most?

Not the increase in the tax rate for those on over £123,000. If you are earning £20m a year it is unlikely that you will be troubled much by tax. That's what the accounting department is there to help you avoid.

It could be the pledge to prevent businesses that pay their top people over 20 times their average worker from bidding for government accounts.

That work is probably easy money, and the banks hate losing easy money.

The thing they are likely to fear the most is the Robin Hood Tax.

The tax on financial transactions would see 0.5 per cent of the value of bonds and derivatives going to the Treasury, which would raise about £26bn.

That is a lot of money, but to put that into perspective, bankers have given themselves over £100bn in bonuses on top of their gargantuan salaries since the financial crisis first hit.

That's not a misprint, it really is over one hundred billion pounds.

Top bankers are crying foul at the thought of that tax happening because if they give back a proportion of their profits to the people that saved them from their greed and stupidity, it would be a little less that they could award themselves as bonuses for a job well done.

They would become ever so slightly less fabulously rich.

I would imagine that frightens them more than anything.

09.12.17

Another presidential slur.

Donald Trump is the most magnificent person to ever hold the office of President of the United States of Amersh.

At least that's how he sounded at the end of a typically unhinged and rambling speech about how fantastic he was and how tremendous is his orange enormity and how huge his hands are.

Oh, and there was the thing about re-annexing Jerusalem for the Israelis, in the interests of peace and stability!

The riots across the world and predictable deaths that followed that announcement were given less prominence than might have been expected because of the way in which he concluded his address.

He said "let's re-think old assumptions and open our minds to possible and possibilities"

That makes as much sense as anything else he has ever said.

But it got worse. Like an automaton on the blink, or a robot running low on batteries, he seemed to slow down and slur his garbled message and only just got to the end without smoke coming out of his ears, the lights in his eyes going out and falling flat on his face to say, "God bless the Unitesh Shtsts".

Some commentators have mused that a plate holding some of his bleached bright-white teeth in place became loose and caused his speech patterns to falter.

Others say it's not a dental problem, it's a mental problem.

There seems to be an upswell of agreement that the President is not well. I mean, even less well than previously assumed.

A Republican Senator called Bob Corker suggested that Whitehouse officials are doing little more than running "an adult day care centre."

The chairman of the Senate Foreign Relations Committee expressed fear that the president's erratic behaviour is putting the United States "on the path to World War III."

The Secretary of State reportedly called the president a "moron."

The National Security Adviser allegedly said Trump has the mind of a "kindergartner."

Republican political campaign manager Steve Schmidt said that "the question of his fitness, of his stability is in the air."

White House insiders tell Vanity Fair that Trump is "unravelling" mentally.

These are his own people.

Theresa May went out on a limb and said that he was "wrong" to re-tweet anti-mulim videos and that recognising Jerusalem as the capital of Israel was "unhelpful".

That is the verbal equivalent of dancing carefully around a grumpy bear, on ice, in stilettos.

American newspapers have not been so circumspect.

The New York Daily News, opined that "the President of the United States is profoundly unstable. He is mad. He is, by any honest layman's definition, mentally unwell and viciously lashing out."

The New York Times described Trump's recent behaviour in nautical terms, saying he is "unmoored."

If he were a boat, he would be clear of the jetty and lurching out to sea over storm tossed waves, listing heavily, with a fire in the engine room.

The White House department of non-fake news explained, "His throat was dry. There's nothing to it."

That might wash if it were an isolated incident but Trump exhibits all the self-control and thoughtfulness of a two year old that's had his lolly yanked out of his mouth.

All this might be amusing if he were not trailed everywhere he goes by a man with a briefcase that holds the key to launching the deadliest weapon that Man has invented, with the ability to destroy all life on earth.

It is the sort of thing that would not be out of character for Trump to do, in a fit of pique, if he overheard someone making fun of his physique.

And if you think that we are safe, far away from targets like North Korea and wherever Hillary Clinton lives, then think again.

During an interview in 2016, the most powerful man on earth refused to rule out using nuclear weapons in Europe.

May God have mercy on ush allssh.

10 12 17

The theatre is no place for it

A man has claimed he was punched during the interval of a production at the Old Vic.

It is a theatre of world renown and a favourite of polite society.

These days, getting punched in such an establishment is known as: par for the course.

A theatre producer called Adam Gale says that he noticed a woman in the audience was using her mobile phone throughout the first act of A Christmas Carol.

He asked her to stop and she immediately agreed and apologised for her embarrassing lack of tact.

Just kidding, she egged on the man she was with to haul Mr Gale from his seat and hit him.

This was probably because of the credo of modern manners which is, "It's my right, I can do what I want".

The couple left during the interval but Mr Gale was left fearful that they would be waiting to attack him outside, which is what you would expect of people that object to being told that using a phone while in the audience of a theatrical production is not the done thing.

Mr Gale said, "Things have escalated from rude audience members to people who assault other people,"

"People are constantly complaining about sitting next to someone horrible, and they say they don't challenge them as they are afraid it will make the situation worse if they ask them to stop."

He's right.

A woman was allegedly assaulted when she took her son to watch Dirty Dancing at Liverpool's Empire Theatre in September.

The victim, in her 50's, claimed she asked another female audience member to be quiet during the show.

Naturally, she was attacked at the end of the performance and left with facial injuries.

There's road rage and trolley rage and escalator rage but you might have thought that the theatre would be the last place that such idiotic, self-centred and boorish behaviour would reach besides a funeral, but it is everywhere now.

Cast members are often interrupting their own performance to tell the audience to turn their phones off or stop taking pictures.

Shakespeare never encountered such a lack of etiquette. That is because the phone had not been invented. If it had, he most certainly would have.

In his day, stage actors were lucky if they got through the play without being hit by flying fruit. The distracted viewers in the balcony were probably having sex.

Since then, the upper classes have striven to distance themselves from the masses by embracing rules of etiquette to make the lower orders feel unwelcome.

Sitting bolt upright and viewing a show in silence, being one of them.

In some things, the good old days have been vastly improved upon.

Let's not go backwards.

If you must eat and fight and tweet your sexual adventures while out of the house, don't go to the theatre to do it.

Go to the cinema like everyone else.

16.12.17

RoboFlop.

The future is here – it arrived shiny and new and white and whizzed about silently on wheels.

In about ten minutes flat, it was a dirty brown, broken and rolling about helplessly on its back.

If you think that police robots only exist in the imagination of Hollywood scriptwriters, you are wrong.

RoboCop isn't science fiction, it is science fact.

It might not come out with witty *apercus* like "Your move creep" but it is out there and patrolling a facility near you, if you live in San Francisco.

The home of the counterculture and the most liberal city in America since the California Gold Rush turned it from a small, sleepy hamlet into a throbbing hive of miscreants and ne'er-do-wells, San Francisco is the unlikely early adopter of a technology that seems at odds with everything it stands for.

The Knightscope K5 security robot is a 400-pound machine that looks like something out of a Star Wars film.

It does not possess guns or lasers (yet) but it does have four cameras to monitor its surroundings, can move its little wheels at up to three miles an hour and is as tall as a small person and as wide as a large one.

It was deployed in San Francisco to deter loitering near a building.

Guess which organisation put it there.

You are probably thinking that it was bound to have been some evil entity like a cigarette company, or a weapons manufacturer.

Perhaps a shady hedge fund wanted to maintain its secrecy?

Would it help if I explained that the purpose of the robot was specifically to stop homeless people from sheltering near the building?

That's right! It was the Society for the Prevention of Cruelty to Animals.

I am not making that up.

The Society for the Prevention of Cruelty to Animals has used all its empathy on our furry, four legged friends and has none left for those earth dwellers that walk upright and do not have a roof to call their own.

They will rush to the scene of a puppy in distress but would rather you did not approach if you are a person in the same predicament.

This did not go down well with the do-gooder hippies in San Francisco.

Instead of getting even, the locals got angry. And then they got even.

The bright white vision of the future had its sensors covered with the first thing to hand, which was barbecue sauce.

San Franciscans never leave the house without a large supply, in case they want to baste a sausage, or teach the future a lesson.

They then knocked it over, like R2D2, and smeared it with faeces. Where they got the faeces from I do not know, but you might want to think twice before annoying anyone from the City by the Bay.

To hide its shame, K9 was then covered with a tarpaulin and left to think about what it had done.

If the Society for the Prevention of Cruelty to Animals had spent the same amount that it took to develop a Homeless Person Deterrent Droid on a shelter for the homeless, then everyone would have been happy, especially the robot, which would still be bright and white and working.

It is not the first time that K5 has been embroiled in controversy.

It knocked a toddler over in Silicon Valley, and fell into a pond in Washington DC after missing a set of stairs.

The future is robots and the robots are drunk.

What could possibly go wrong?

17.12.17

A problem with gas

Britain is one of the lucky first recipients of Russian gas from a £20bn Yamal pipeline from the frozen wastes of Siberia.

In June, Poland halted supply because of the poor quality of the gas, but what is unacceptable to the Poles, is OK for us.

We're desperate.

We know the situation is bad because the British government said that there is nothing to worry about.

We are running on empty because of a perfect storm of a malfunctioning North Sea pipeline, an explosion at a hub in Austria, technical problems in the Norwegian supply and a world-wide massive increase in demand.

Ships fitted with ice-breaker armour will smash their way to us by the end of the month.

It is Vladimir Putin to the rescue.

Just as that was announced, one of our top military brass was busy ripping into the Russians for their meddling.

Air Chief Marshal Sir Stuart William Peach, GBE, KCB, ADC, DL is not just a series of titles and acronyms, he is one of our top military persons.

He was named as NATO Chairman of the Military Committee, the first Briton to hold the position for 25 years.

I have no idea what that position entails but it probably means that he knows his stuff.

In an alarming speech this week he warned that Britain's economy and way of life are at 'catastrophic' risk from Russian submarine drones that can cut underwater cables – the cables that bring us all the delights and conveniences of the internet.

If it had been anyone else saying that, you might have thought that he had been watching too much James Bond.

He said 'Can you imagine a scenario where those cables are cut or disrupted which would immediately, and potentially catastrophically, affect both our economy and other ways of living.'

It is a sobering thought.

It is so sobering it made me want to get drunk just thinking it.

How would we get our feed of puppy dog and pussy cat videos if the internet cables are cut?

Would we have to go back to talking to each other if Facebook and Twitter were not available? It is too awful to contemplate.

The Air Chief Marshall was not alone in sounding the warning bell.

The Defence Secretary Gavin Williamson said Russian submarine activity around Britain's coast has increased tenfold in the last six years.

Last month, Theresa May warned that Russia was meddling in elections and planting fake stories in the media in a bid to 'weaponise information' and sow discord in the West.

That's not the same Russia that we are relying on to send us the gas we need to keep the country going is it?

Can you warn us a little more quietly Mrs M?

I am sure Vlad can hear you.

Still, he doesn't seem the type to hold a grudge. At least that's what his political opponents say from their solitary confinement cells in the very same Siberia we are getting that gas from.

23.12.17

Where there is harmony, may we bring discord?

The relationship between Britain and Russia is at a delicate stage. Not since the Cold War have feelings between the two nations been so precariously balanced.

Distrust and enmity are in the air.

At a time like this, we need to be represented by our most skilled and tactful diplomats; emissaries of sensitive refinement and discretion.

So naturally, we sent Boris Johnson.

He started his tour to Russia by addressing the press and accusing his hosts of being hostile. They replied that they would like to have him say that to their face and would he care to step outside?

It got considerably worse from then on.

To paraphrase and summarise: Boris said that the Russians have smelly pants and the Russians said the British have smelly pants.

If it were in school, teachers would be pulling them apart in the playground.

Bozo of the F.O. accused the Kremlin of interfering in the EU referendum.

This is a pretty odd thing for a born-again Brexiteer to say.

Essentially, by his own admission, we are leaving the EU in part because of Russia meddling in our democratic system.

He tried to assure the people back home that such intrusiveness did not work, but how could he possibly know?

The Russians are also famously on the hook for trying their best to get Ancient Orange into the Oval Office.

The FBI said they did it and the CIA said they did it and the National Security Agency said they did it and MI5 and MI6 and GCHQ and Theresa May said they did it but the Russians said they didn't, and that's good enough for the leader of the free world – case closed, move along please, nothing to see here.

The reason that Trump is so sensitive to claims of Russian help is that if true, it would mean that he did not win the big prize all by himself.

It would tarnish the shine of his orange stupendousness.

Boris is not so sensitive. In fact, he does not appear to have any sense at all.

He flat-out accused the Russians of trying to sway the vote on the EU and of efforts to sow discord and hatred among us British by employing factories of internet trolls to send out messages designed to whip up anger and disharmony.

They are accused of doing this by employing so called sock-puppets.

These are not the amusements of our childhood.

Sooty and Sweep were not involved. They are otherwise engaged.

Sooty is currently on remand for dealing in stolen goods and Sweep is facing historical allegations of abuse, like pretty much every other children's television entertainer of my youth.

These particular sock puppets are people posting on social media, supposedly paid by the Russian state to send out inflammatory messages on both sides of arguments to whip up us locals.

Boris says this had no effect.

I am not so sure. If 2017 was notable for anything, it was for the cacophony of animosity that filled the air.

If that was the Russian's plan, I would say that it was very successful indeed.

24.12.17

A blue, blue, blue Christmas.

Let the joy be unconfined. The nation has an early Christmas present. We can now distance ourselves from the European Union by the colour of our passports.

A gift at this most joyous time of year - it is what Jesus would have wanted.

No longer will we have to spend ten seconds glancing at the burgundy cover of the EU affiliated passport as we proffer it to the person behind the glass after disembarking the plane.

That is a whole ten seconds less of being dictated to by the unelected bureaucrats of the insidious European experiment.

We will have to be patient, of course. The best true-blue things come to those that wait. From October 2019, we will be able to apply through the post for our new blue passports.

These will be sped back to us in only six short weeks, or seven if we are actually planning to leave in six.

For an extra fast return, for those who forgot or who are too eager to endure a delay for the return of their British birth right, an ultra-quick Premium service will be available, at extra cost.

For many, no price is too high for the ability to gaze wistfully at the correct coloured cover before replacing it in the drawer and going on holiday to Clacton, because they don't talk funny there, the food is chips with everything and the tea is strong enough to stand your spoon up in.

True blue Tories have been heralding its imminent return for some time.

Speaking in April, the member for ultra-patriotic, very British Romford, the Conservative MP Andrew Rosindell, said the burgundy EU passport had been a source of national "humiliation".

He said, "The restoration of our own British passport is a clear statement to the world that Britain is back,"

"The humiliation of having a pink European Union passport will now soon be over and the United Kingdom nationals can once again feel pride and self-confidence in their own nationality when travelling."

Just a few points: if you are the sort of person who feels humiliated by the colour of your passport, you probably shouldn't be going abroad in the first place for fear of humiliating the nation, and if you need a specific hue on your official identification document to feel pride in your nationality, then that pride does not run very deep.

That crack about the EU passport being pink was a telling one. It is not pink, it is quite clearly dark red, but pink has certain connotations and we would not want Johnny foreigner to think we were like *that*, do we Mr Rosindell?

They can keep their filthy European perversions to themselves.

He tweeted, 'A great Christmas present for those who care about our national identity - the fanatical Remainers hate it, but the restoration of our own British passport is a powerful symbol that Britain is Back!'

There are fanatics all right, just not the people he is pointing at. And if Britain is back, where have we been? Was it abroad? What was the weather like?

Brandon Lewis, the immigration minister, said: "Leaving the EU gives us a unique opportunity to restore our national identity and forge a new path for ourselves in the world.

"That is why I am delighted to announce that the British passport will be returning to the iconic blue and gold design after we have left the European Union in 2019."

The thing is, we could have had any colour passport we wanted all along. There is no binding EU stipulation as to the shade, hue, tint, tinge or complexion of the travel document.

The government has admitted that it chose to change to the burgundy red of its own volition. It said that to change it back would have previously seemed odd but that it doesn't now.

Put out the bunting – it doesn't seem odd now!

What is odd is to celebrate, in such an effortful patriotic fervour, the release from something that was never a rule in the first place.

Hopefully, the new document will be made from unbendable wood, like the old one, and not fey and pliable, as they are now.

They must be so stiff that you give yourself a slipped disc if you put them in your back pocket and sit on them.

That way we can suffer in silence for our country, like a proper patriot should.

I'd be tickled if they get made in France, on German printers with Italian ink.

24.12.17

Pay back…what's owed to HMRC

Some very rich patriotic Brits bankrolled the Brexit campaign because they wanted the return of British laws for British people.

Now that they are victorious, and Britons will be forever subject to only British laws, made by British politicians and applied by British institutions, they couldn't be happier.

Just kidding, they are still complaining.

That is because they do not like a particular British law.

Not that they are complaining for themselves, you understand, they are doing it on behalf of the massed little people of this great land.

The spectacularly rich men who poured a small percentage of their vast wealth to steer the country on their preferred course, have been notified by Her Majesty's Revenue and Customs that they must pay a tax bill because of their selfless generosity.

You would think they would be glad to pay. It is being requested on behalf of Her Majesty after all.

Instead of being delighted to help the cause, they are whining that it is an obscure tax law, that they weren't expecting the bill and that the government should intervene on their behalf.

The Brexiteer ultras have called this The Revenge of the Establishment. When it happens to us, we call it Receiving Our Tax Bill.

HMRC has cited an inheritance tax law which requires people to pay tax upfront on large gifts.

It is no more obscure than any other tax law – it is written right there in the code.

A law is only obscure if your accountant did not tell you about it when you asked if your donation to the cause would attract a bill from the tax man.

Perhaps they didn't ask their accountant.

Perhaps they forgot in their giddy delight at getting our country back.

Perhaps they would prefer to be subject to the tax laws of the Bahamas.

It is not as though they can't afford the money. They had the cash to write the cheques to fund the campaign to keep Britain British, they should be able to write a smaller one to the government so that it can fund the totally British NHS, for instance.

Midlands entrepreneur Lord Edmiston, banker Peter Cruddas and former UKIP donor Arron Banks have all received tax demands from HM Revenue and Customs in the last fortnight.

How sad. The two that are not a millionaires, are billionaires.

They have been issued demands, in the proper British manor, because in giving money to the leave campaign, they have reduced the value of their estates and hence the amount of inheritance tax that would become due in the unlikely event that any of these saints died.

It would have been all right if they had been donations to political parties, but the leave campaign was not that. It would have been fine if it had been a charity, but was not that either. Not by a long chalk.

The complaint is: it's so unfair!

They say it is specifically unfair that leavers will be hit harder than remainers by the application of this totally British law.

Unfortunately for this argument, remainers who donated to their cause were also hit by tax demands.

This has not stopped supporters of our three heroes from squealing so loud you could hear them through the walls of a concrete fall-out shelter.

They have said that Her Majesty's Revenue and Customs is acting undemocratically and the Chancellor Philip Hammond could come under pressure to intervene.

I bet his phone is red hot.

It should be wet with their tears of gratitude to be subject to the British law they spent so much money reinforcing, or do they only want to obey the laws of that land that suit them?

Lord Edmiston, who made much of his money selling cars, donated £850,000 to the official Vote Leave campaign and £150,000 to an unofficial leave campaign.

He has been politely asked to pay a tax bill of £200,000.

Peter Cruddas, a financial trader who in 2007 was named the richest person in the City of London, gave £900,000 to a leave campaign and has been asked to pay HMRC £180,000.

Arron Banks, the former UKIP leading light, is being asked to pay £2million in inheritance tax on the generously patriotic £8.1million he gave to the Leave.EU campaign.

British rules state that Britons can give away £325,000 in their lifetime before being taxed.

A representative of Her Majesty's tax collectors said, 'Donations to campaign groups don't qualify as exempt gifts to political parties, unless the recipient is a political party meeting the criteria set out in section 24 of the Inheritance Tax Act 1984.

'No special exemption was granted ahead of the 2016 referendum."

Of course, these men could pay these bills with the spare change they keep in the ashtrays of some of the cars they don't use, or in the kitchen drawers of one of their spare homes.

You would think they would delighted to do their bit for Britain and pay the tax as it becomes due.

The rest of us poor dopes have to.

Maybe, if they don't get any joy from Philip Hammond, they could take their case to the EU's Court of Justice?

06.01.18

Imperfect recall

Poor Donny is grumpy. He needs a Farley's Rusk and a rattle.

A nasty man has been saying nasty things and the leader of the free world is in a huff.

If it were just the book Fire and Fury, that looks likely to save struggling book shops the whole world over, it might be bearable.

His side could say that it is simply a collection of tittle-tattle and lies written to make money from the boffo box office that is Donald Trump.

The President could refute the suggestions contained within its pages that he is incompetent and not bright enough for the post by tweeting that he is "like, really smart".

And that is exactly what he did.

He added that his, like, smartness is one of his two greatest assets, the other being his mental stability.

Any suggestion to the contrary was a hoax on the American public and that "the Democrats and their lapdogs, the Fake News Mainstream Media, are taking out the old Ronald Reagan playbook and screaming mental stability and intelligence".

Probably not the best example to highlight. Ronald's own son said that his father had Alzheimer's while in office and Reagan was formally diagnosed with the disease in 1994.

A real, like, smart person would have picked a better example.

Unfortunately for all of us who live in Donny's world, it is not just the ramblings of the current President and the book of the year that suggests we have a problem.

A Yale University psychiatry professor has met with members of Congress to discuss President Donald Trump's mental health.

To paraphrase, she thinks he is out of his tiny orange mind.

Dr Bandy X. Lee, a name I am not making up, believes that the President is 'unravelling' and that he poses a 'public health risk' by being in office.

She is an expert on violence, but there is no proof that Trump is predisposed to aggressive outbursts.

Well, there were the tweet-storms against other world leaders and fellow politicians and celebrities and models and sports people and the threat to punch a dissenter in the face and saying that others should be roughed up, and the time when he told an audience to "knock the crap out of" anyone objecting at his rallies, and that he would pay for the assailant's legal fees, and when said he loved the old days when protesters would be carried out on a stretcher.

But apart from that there's no evidence that he is violent.

In December last year, Dr Lee gave a presentation in Congress on why Trump's presidency was an 'emergency' to a group of Democrats and one Republican senator who was presumably lost and couldn't locate the exit.

She said 'From a medical perspective, when we see someone unravelling like this, it's an emergency.'

Lee told the New York Daily News. 'We've never come so close in my career to this level of catastrophic violence that could be the end of humankind.'

She might have been referring to Trump's boast about his nuclear button, which, like everything else about him, he insists is the biggest.

He has boasted that he has the biggest buildings and big genitals and a big nuclear arsenal and it is the latter that is verifiably true.

America does have the world's biggest nuclear arsenal and Trump can set it off at a moment's notice, for instance in a fit of pique if Melania swats his hand away again.

There is no button on his desk, as he claimed. The launch procedure involves a briefcase called the "football" that is attached to a man who follows the President everywhere he goes.

If Kim Jong-un calls him fatty, Trump can beckon the man over and enter the codes that are delivered to him every day.

These codes are what they call "the biscuit".

Donny has been told not to eat the biscuit.

For security reasons, the biscuit has several fake codes, so the President has to memorise which are the correct ones.

And that is where things get a lot more comfortable for all of us without access to a fall-out shelter.

The chances of him recalling something like that are pretty slim.

We can all relax now.

He probably couldn't remember where he left his giant orange bottom.

-

The A-Z of 2017

This is the list that my listeners came up with during my run of shows over Christmas.

These are the buzzwords, people and events of the year.

Those that pertain to Donald Trump are followed by (T), reflecting his big orange dominance of the news.

A

Died
Gregg Allman, rocker, Allman Brothers Band
Aadvark from Regent's Park Zoo fire
Alessandro Alessandroni, spaghetti western musician
Roger Ailes, Fox News head (T)
Brian Aldiss, author

ABC – last cinema closed
American divorcee to marry British royalty
Austerity (again)
A&E waiting times
Alternative facts (T)
Australia approves same-sex marriage
Jane Austin £10 note
Artificial Intelligence
"Ancient Orange" my name for (T)
Aircraft carrier leaks
Dianne Abbott's arithmetic
Acid attacks
Austria gets a far-right president
Astronomers find half of missing matter in universe
Apple's £1000 phone
Apple's new spaceship campus
Julian Assange
Abortion Act 50th anniversary
Antifa (T)

Alexa
Airlander 10, airship that looks like a giant bottom crashes
Alternative for Germany wins 13% of election vote
Alt-right (T)
Atlas, back flipping robot
Airbags on lampposts, Salzburg smartphone zombies protected
Adele confirms marriage
Affordable housing
America First (T)
Alabama Senate race (T)
Aragog, lookalike spider named after Harry Potter monster
Asthma medication and British cycling
Aung San Suu Kyi, loses shine
Jacinda Ardern wins New Zealand election
Article 50
Aleppo, fall of
Alaska, oil drilling allowed in wildlife refuge (T)
Lord Adonis quits as infrastructure tsar, calls May the voice of UKIP
Asos overtakes M&S as UK's favourite clothing retailer

B

Died
Walter Becker, rocker, Steely Dan
Brucie – Bruce Forsyth, entertainer
Chuck Berry, rock 'n' roller
Rodney Bewes, Likely Lad
Keith Barron, actor
Michael Bond, Paddington Bear author
Ian Brady, Moors murderer
Chuck Barris, Gong Show TV host, CIA assassin (?)
Leon Bernicoff, Goggleboxer
Hywell Bennett, actor
Chester Bennington, rocker, Linkin Park
Roy Barraclough, Coronation Street
Geoffrey Bayldon, Catweazle
Leo Baxendale, cartoonist Bash St Kids
William Peter Blatty, author, Exorcist
Gilbert Baker, artist, rainbow flag

Dee Boyle, rocker, Longpigs
Anthony Booth, actor, Till Death Us Do Part
Rodney Bickerstaffe, trade unionist

Brexit
Brexit "decision could be reversed": David Davis
Blackamoor brooch worn by Princess Michael
Brown cows – 10% of Americans think that's where chocolate milk comes from
Boris Becker bankrupt
Breitbart (T)
Steve Bannon (T)
Burnley FC smallest team in Premiership, seventh at Christmas
Big Ben stops chiming
Borough Market terrorist attack
Boeing v Bombardier
Michel Barnier
Britain First
Bitcoin
Balfour Declaration 100th anniversary
Badger cull
Scott Baldwin pets a lion
Bubonic plague in Madagascar
Bank Levy cut
British Airways' computer meltdown
Brenda from Bristol reacts to snap election
Bumpstock for rifles
Richard Branson caught in hurricane
Richard Branson's Virgin Care sues NHS
Banksy's Walled Off Hotel + identity discovered?
Bathmophobia – Trump afraid of stairs (T)
"Boris bus" scrapped
Bee colony collapse disorder
Blade Runner sequel
Blue passport
Blue Planet II
British Airways IT failure
Beyonce has twins

Brazil nut shortage
Kevin de Bruyne, best midfielder in the world?
Brakeless bike crashes
Alec Baldwin spoofs Trump on SNL (T)
Bowling Green massacre, fiction told by Kellyanne Conway defending Muslim travel ban (T)
Berlin NYE "safe zone" for women
Black Sabbath play last gig
Usain Bolt retires
John Bercow, Speaker of the House opposed to Trump parliamentary address (T)
Henry Bolton new leader of UKIP
Jeff Bezos becomes richest person in the world

C

Died
David Cassidy, singer
Keith Chegwin (Cheggers goes pop)
Glen Cambell, singer
Max Clifford, PR
Holger Czukay, rocker, Can
Chris Cornell, rocker, Soundgarden
Larry Coryell, jazzer
Antonio Carluccio, chef
Eugene Cernan, astronaut, last man on Moon to date
Brian Cant, actor, presenter

Coughing – Theresa May's Conference fiasco
Catalonia independence referendum
Jeremy Corbyn goes to Glastonbury
Cladding on tower blocks
California fires
"Covfefe" (T)
Charlottesville far right rally (T)
Cassini spacecraft crashed into Saturn
Crimewatch axed
Crimes that no longer warrant police response
Peter Capaldi exits Dr Who

Cashless society
Cutbacks
Climate change
Coal free energy day – UK's first since 1880's
"Clean" coal (T)
Cybercrime
Kellyanne Conway (T)
Credit card debt
"Cheesegrater" building sold to Chinese
Cambridge Analytica and Brexit and Trump (T)
Canada 150 years old
Curry button on Indian washing machines
Cadburys replace Fudge bar in selection box
Dany Cotton, first female Commissioner, London Fire Brigade
Chocolate cake, "most beautiful" fed to President Xi while bombing
Syria (T)
Nick Clegg Knighthood announced
Curb Your Enthusiasm returns
James Comey, FBI Director fired (T)
Confederate statues and flags (T)
Jeremy Clarkson catches pneumonia
"Coalition of chaos"
China accused of selling oil to N Korea, despite sanctions
Bill Cosby sex assault case ends in mistrial
Cancer diagnosis scanners in supermarket car parks
Curtsey, Meghan Markle
CNN, constant attacks by (T)
Hayden Cross, UK's first pregnant man
Croydon cat killer
Collusion with Russia (T)
Gemma Collins, TOWIE star falls down hole
Vince Cable new leader of Lib Dems
Cornwall flash flood in Coverack
Chlorine washed chicken

D

Died
Fats Domino, rock and roller

JP Donleavy, writer
Jonathan Demme, director
Liz Dawn, Coronation Street
Danielle Darrieux, French actress
Tam Dalyell, politician
Roy Dotrice, actor

Damian Green's computer
Colin Dexter, author, Inspector Morse
Diesel cars
DUP
Dippy the diplodocus goes on tour
Dairy Milk made in Poland
Seb Dance MEP's "He's lying to you" sign re Farage
Dotard – Kim Jon-un's description of Trump (T)
Domestic abuse - Putin decriminalises it Russia
Cressida Dick Met Police's first female Commissioner
Bob Dylan accepts Nobel Prize
Dr David Dao dragged off United flight
Dumoulin couple found after 75 years missing in melting Swiss glacier
Johnny Depp divorce – loses Pistol and Boo
Dreamers (T)
Drumpf, original family name of (T)
Dunkirk, the film
Dr Who, first female
Deep learning, AI
"Dementia Tax"
Princess Di's death 20th anniversary
"Don't let them in" Tory councillor at Grenfell Tower meeting
Drone lands on HMS Queen Elizabeth
Diesel and petrol cars and vans sale to be banned from 2040
Dennis the Menace loses the menace
Dominica devastated by Hurricane Maria
"Dishonest media" (T)
DeepMind's AlphaZero, AI programme becomes best ever chess player
Vin Diesel, highest grossing actor of the year

Dakota Access Pipeline, Trump v native Americans (T)
Driving test changes include following sat nav
Doklam conflict, China-India border standoff
Doping, release of 2011 survey finds 57% of elite athletes admit to it, 2% caught
Daily intelligence briefings, Trump says he doesn't need them because he is smart (T)

E

Died
Ugo Ehiogu, footballer

Bernie Ecclestone out of F1
Edward Enninful, new editor British Vogue
Eastergate: National Trust
Easter eggs in shops before Christmas
Executive Orders (T)
Elizabeth Line trains start running
England wins U-17 World Cup
England wins U-19 European Championship
England wins U-20 World Cup
Evening Standard new editor George Osborne
Euston Station transformed to feed homeless at Xmas
East Sussex coast chemical haze
European Union
Excitonium, new form of matter discovered
"Exit from Brexit"
Exeter schoolboys protest at hot uniform by wearing skirts
EU Banking Authority moves from London to Paris
EU Medicines Agency moves from London to Amsterdam
Earthquakes upsurge as earth rotation slows
Eclipse of the sun, stared at by (T)
Elephant trophy import permits (T)
Megan Ellis, student fills hot water bottle with cold water & waits
"Exquisite", House Speaker Paul Ryan's description of Trump's leadership (T)
Eminem returns, raps against Trump (T)

Elvis, 40th anniversary of death
Equifax admits massive cyber breach

F

Died
Carmen Franco, Duchess, daughter of Franco

Flat-Earthers
Fox entertainment assets sold to Disney
Floyd Mayweather Jr. vs. Conor McGregor, "the Money Fight"
Fox News taken off Sky in UK
Fidget Spinners
Fake news (T)
Far right, rise of
Faraday FF91: fastest electric vehicle 0-60mph in 2.39sec
Aretha Franklin retires
Tim Farron resigns as leader of Lib Dems
Fluffy McFluff Face – rare penguin named in Norfolk sanctuary
Florence speech - Theresa May
Jayda Fransen, Britain First, retweeted by (T)
Felix the Huddersfield Station Cat, media star
Fatberg, biggest ever, 130 tonnes, Whitechapel
Finland's independence from Russia 100th anniversary
Michael Fallon resigns as Defence Secretary
Fracking banned in Scotland
FTSE 100 record high
Colin Firth becomes Italian citizen following Brexit
Fox and Friends appeals to and watched by (T)
Faecal flora cloudburst, what happens when you flush the loo
French election
Mike Flynn resigns (T)
"Fire and fury like the world has never seen" (T)
Mo Farah wins his final track race
Harrison Ford crashes plane again
Chris Froome wins Tour de France
Chris Froome adverse urine test

"F****** moron" Sec of State Rex Tillerson reportedly describes President (T)

Arlene Foster, DUP leader

Fox and Friends, Trump praising show is Trump's favourite (T)

Food banks

Al Franken, US Senator sexual allegations

FBI, constant attacks by (T)

Funicular, world's steepest opens in Switzerland

Susan J. Fowler, ex-exec's blog reveals toxic culture at UBER

Facebook accused of supporting ethnic cleansing in Myanmar

Facebook accused of publishing child pornography

Facebook accused of publishing content sponsoring terrorism

Facebook shuts down chatbots after they invent own language

Flattery, Whitehouse insiders say it is the way to get Trump's attention (T)

G

Died

Buddy Greco, jazzer

Dick Gregory, comedian

Bob Givens, Bugs Bunny animator

Charlie Gard, subject of court battles

Richard Gordon, surgeon, writer

Stanley Greene, photojournalist

J Geils, rocker

Barry Gibb plays Glastonbury

Garden Bridge scrapped

Kathy Griffin and Trump's severed head (T)

Ariana Grande concert attack

Grenfell Tower fire

Gender neutral

General election

Gravitational waves discovery wins Nobel prize

Barry Gibb at Glastonbury

Sebastian Gorka resigned/fired (T)

Guatemala to move Israeli embassy to Jerusalem (T)

Getlink, new name for Eurotunnel post Brexit

Gold coin, 100kg, stolen from German museaum
Great Repeal Bill
Grammar vigilante corrects mistakes at night in Bristol
Damian Green sacked re. porn found on computer
Philip Green
Greg's sausage roll Jesus
Great Barrier Reef dying/dead
Great British Bake Off moves to C4
Gender identity
Gender neutral language
The Grand Tour, TV
Game of Thrones, TV
Pep Guardiola, Man City manager: special
Guam, Trump promises 10 fold increase in tourism after N Korea nuke threat (T)
Germophobia, Trump's affliction "proves" Russia sex tape not real, (T)
Golf, Trump spends almost one third of presidency at his own clubs (T)
Golf, Trump uses truck to block media filming him playing (T)
Golf, Trump claims he goes to his clubs for meetings but filmed playing (T)
Generation rent
Global warming, Trump tweets we need it because it is cold in winter (T)
Len Goodman retires from Strictly Come Dancing
Prince George kidnap plot
Graydon Carter steps down from editing Vanity Fair
Google v Amazon feud

H

Died
John Hurt, actor
John Heard, actor
Johnny Hallyday, French singer
Hugh Hefner, Playboy
Sean Hughes, comedian
Robert Hardy, actor

Jon Hillerman, actor, Magnum PI
Heather Heyer, activist, Charlottesville
Howard Hodgkin, artist
Darcus Howe, activist
Peter Hall, theatre director
Claire Hollingworth, journalist, first to report outbreak of WWII

Hyperloop
Hull, UK City of Culture
Frankie Hill, 6, sets up homeless campaign
Historical sex crimes
Hunting trophies (T)

Homosexuality decriminalised, 50th anniversary
Homelessness
Tristram Hunt quits politics, new head of V&A
Lewis Hamilton wins F1 championship
Lewis Hamilton and the princess dress
Lewis Hamilton avoids tax on private plane
Prince Harry engaged
Tom Harrison completes London marathon in 6 days in gorilla suit
Hollyweed, Hollywood sign changed
Handshakes, weird (T)
Nikki Hayley, US ambassador threatens UN on Jerusalem (T)
Hand towels on Air Force One not soft enough (T)
Katie Hopkins fired from Mail Online
Michael Hestletine: Brexit worse than Corbyn government
Huntingdon's disease, "groundbreaking" drug found
Hard Brexit
Marcus Hutchins stops WannaCry virus
"Hot Felon", Jeremy Meeks dates Philip Green's daughter
High five, Jeremy Corbyn and Emily Thorberry's goes wrong
HS2
Rolf Harris released from prison
Jeremy Hunt takes on Stephen Hawking on NHS, loses
Heathrow third runway

I

Iran nuclear deal (T)
Iran street protests
Inappropriate behaviour, euphemism for sex assaults
Island of Ireland, border and Brexit
Iceberg water costing £80 a bottle goes on sale
Kazuo Ishiguro, winner of the Nobel prize in literature
Invictus Games
iPhone, 10 years old
International Campaign to Abolish Nuclear Weapons, wins Nobel
Peace Prize
Intercontinental ballistic missile, first test by N Korea
ISIS militarily defeated in Syria and Iraq
Inauguration crowd size (T)
Irma, hurricane, one of strongest in history
Impeachment often discussed (T)
Ivanka claims people will do their taxes on a postcard after tax cuts
(T)
Ivanka, Trump tweets the wrong one (T)
India set to become 5th largest economy
Immigration
Iraq Historical Allegations Team
Insects decline 75% in 30 years, German study
Irish Coast Guard Rescue 116 helicopter crash
Interest rate rise, first in ten years
IKEA switches to snap together furniture
Impact assessments, absence of, on Brexit
Italy fail to qualify for first World Cup in 60 years
IMDB, film website closes message boards

J

Died
Al Jarreau, jazzer
Boris Johnson of the F.O.
Clifton James, Sheriff Pepper, James Bond
Joel Joffe, Mandela defence lawyer
Anthony Armstrong Jones, photographer

Jerusalem – Trump declares capital of Israel (T)
Boris Johnson's Iran gaffe
Boris Johnson's Myanmar gaffe
Boris Johnson's dead bodies in Libya gaffe
Jobs, jobs, jobs (T)
Anthony Joshua beats Wladimir Klitschko
Jogger attack on Putney Bridge
Javanka, Steve Bannon's name for Jared and Ivanka (T)
Judges: "enemies of the people" , Daily Mail front page rant
Jean-Claude Junker
Juno spacecraft pictures of Jupiter
Doug Jones, Democrat wins Alabama Senate seat (T)
Boris Johnson and the non (?) radioactive peach juice
Boris Johnson and the Russia spat
Stanley Johnson in the jungle
Jo Johnson and university "no platforming" threat
Journalism under attack (T)
Jeff Jones UBER president resigns
Jazz, 100th anniversary of first jazz record

K

Died
Christine Keeler, Profumo affair
Kim Jong-Hyun, K-popper
Gordon Kaye, actor, goodbye goodbye
Bernard Kenny, stabbed trying to protect Jo Cox
Helmut Kohl, former German Chancellor
Adnan Khashoggi, arms dealer
Kim Jong-nam, N. Korean leader's half brother
Robert Knight, singer

Kepler-90i, new planet discovered in solar system
Knee-gate, Julia Hartley-Brewer accuses Michael Fallon of touching
Knee, taking the: US football stars protest police violence (T)
Jared Kushner (T)
Kim Jong-un (T)
Knightscope K5 anti-homeless security robot bullied of San

Francisco streets
Harry Kane, top goal scorer in calender year
KKK (T)
Kensington and Chelsea Council, Grenfell Tower fire
Kaspersky, anti-virus software, Russian exploit warning
Travis Kalanick, UBER CEO resigns
Kiri Te Kanawa, soprano, retires
Robert Kelly, professor interrupted by his children on live TV
Peter Kay cancels tour
Kitchen rolls, "beautiful, soft" Trump throws to Puerto Ricans after hurricane (T)
Colin Kaepernick, NFL, takes a knee during US national anthem (T)
Keystone XL pipeline, Trump v native Americans (T)
Kompromat – information collected for blackmail
Greg Knight, Tory Mp's bizarre campaign video

L

Died
Jerry Lewis, comedian
Martin Landau, actor
Jake LaMota, boxer, "The Raging Bull"
Victor Lownes, Playboy executive
Veronica Lucan, Lord Lucan's widow

Las Vegas country music festival shooting
"The largest audience ever to witness an inauguration, period" (T)
"Little rocket man" Kim Jong-un (T)
London Bridge attack
London Zoo fire
Lettuce shortage
Richard Leonard, new leader Scottish Labour Party
John Lewis gender neutral clothes
Lost documents from National Archives re. Falklands, Northern Ireland etc.
Laptop ban on lanes (T)
La La Land wins best picture Oscar, then didn't in envelope mix up
Las Vegas shooting
Lord's Prayer, Pope's re-translation

Lloyds Bank, last government shares sold
Vera Lynn releases hit new album at 100
"Loot boxes" in video games and child gambling
Leonardo da Vinci's Salvator Mundi, most expensive painting ever sold, $450m
Liverpool car park fire
Lewes Bonfire Night Zulu "black up" abandoned as racist
Louis CK, sexual allegations

M

Died
Roger Moore, actor
Charles Manson, helter skelter
Martin McGuinness, politician
Mary Tyler Moore, actor
Robert Miles, DJ, producer
Erin Moran, Joannie Cunningham, Happy Days
Ronnie Moran, footballer
Bruce McCandless II, astronaut
Michael I of Romania, King
Rhodri Morgan, First Minister of Wales
Sheila Michaels, activist, popularised "Ms"
Brian Matthew, broadcaster
Cormac Murphy-O'Connor, cardinal

Mandalay Bay Hotel, Las Vegas shooting
#MeToo
Robert Mueller's Russia investigation (T)
MSM, Mainstream media (T)
Elon Musk
Meghan Markle
Muslim ban (T)
MAGA – Make America Great Again (T)
Marine Le Pen
Emmanuel Macron, French President
Mar-a-Lago (T)
Maybot – Theresa May
Missteps – euphemism for sex assaults

MOAB, Mother of all Bombs (T)
Gina Miller, Brexit campaigner
Roy Moore, Alabama (T)
Moonlight wins best picture Oscar after envelope mix up
Manchester City FC
Manchester Arena attack
Jose Morinho, not so special
Meerkats killed in London Zoo fire
Momentum, campaigning group
Joe McFadden wins Strictly Come Dancing
Melania wears high heels on Puerto Rico hurricane visit (T)
Melania has a body double? (T)
Melania swats away Trump's hand (T)
Lionel Messi buys world's most expensive car, outbids Ronaldo
Emmanuel Macron wins French election
Million Women March (T)
Angela Merkel wins fourth term as German Chancellor
Monarch Airlines collapse
Theresa May
Micronesia sinking
Myanmar human rights
Robert Mugabe, PM Zimbabwe, forced to retire
"Gucci Grace" Mugabe held by rebels
Chelsea Manning has sentence commuted by Obama
Millennials
Melissa McCarthy spoofs Sean Spicer on SNL (T)
Mental health awareness
Jack Munroe wins Twitter libel case against Katie Hopkins
"Marine A" sentence quashed
Moggmentum, Moggmania, Jacob Rees-Mogg supporters
Microbeads
"Magic money tree", there is none – Theresa May
Muslim travel ban (T)
Microsleep, cause of Croydon tram crash?
Montenegro PM shoved aside by Trump at NATO summit (T)
Multiverse, evidence of parallel universes found
"Mutineers" Telegraph front page headline re. MP Brexit rebels
"Metropolitan elite",
Mosque of al-Nuri destroyed by ISIS

N

Died
John Noakes, Blue Peter
Barry Norman, critic
Geoff Nicholls, rocker, Black Sabbath
Jana Navotna, tennis player
Masaya Nakamura, "father of Pac-Man"
Manuel Noriega, Panamanian politician
Heather North, voice of Daphne in Scooby Doo
Nutmeg, world's oldest cat at 32 (144 in cat years)

National Rifle Assoc. - always too soon after shootings to talk about gun control (T)
No platforming – students refuse controversial speakers
Net neutrality
"Nambia" Trump praises non-existent country (T)
Lee Nelson hands PM P45 at Tory conference
Neymar becomes most expensive player in transfer history
Nokia 3310, classic renewed
Paul Nuttal quits as UKIP leader
Northern Ireland qualify for 2018 World Cup
NHS cyber attack
NHS cancels operations on knees, hips, eyes
NHS parking charges
NHS drunk tanks
Nuneaton bowling alley siege
Nutella changes recipe
Neopalpa donaldtrumpi, new golden headed moth named (T)
Rania Nashar, first female CEO of Saudi bank
Naruto, selfie copyright dispute monkey, PETA Person of the Year
Olive Norris, oldest papergirl retires at 88
National Trust gay pride badge row
Nuclear weapons ban treaty signed at UN, boycotted by countries that have them
Nuclear weapons tested by North Korea
National monuments, Trump cuts protections (T)

O

Oumuamua – asteroid, UFO?
One pound coin, new
George Osborne, new Evening Standard editor
Oscars envelope for best pic mix-up
Obamacare repeal attempts (T)
Jared O'Mara, MP suspended over offensive comments
Orb, glowing, touched by Trump in Saudi Arabia (T)
George Orwell statue at BBC
Ophelia, storm causes red sky
"Oh for God's sake" Brenda from Bristol on hearing about election
One For Arthur wins Grand National
Barack Obama leaves office
Orion, NASA builds craft for deep space missions
One billion pounds to secure DUP support for PM
Bill O'Reilly, Fox News host fired over sex allegations
"Oh, Jeremy Corbyn" chant at Glastonbury
Obstruction of justice claims re. Trump and Michael Flynn firing (T)
Oxford Junior Dictionary removes words related to nature
Online abuse

P

Died
Tara Palmer-Tomkinson, socialite
Tim Pigott-Smith, actor
Tom Petty, rocker
Anita Pallenberg, actor
Robert M. Pirsig, Zen and the Art of Motorcycle Maintenance writer
Bill Paxton, actor
Ruth Pearson, dancer, Pan's People
PC Keith Palmer, Westminster Bridge attack hero
Slobodan Praljac, Bosnian general takes cyanide in war crime court
Stephen Paddock, Las Vegas gunman

Prince Philip retires
Prince Philip's death wrongly announced by Daily Telegraph
Oscar Pistorius' jail sentence extended

Paris Climate Accord (T)
Puerto Rico devastated by hurricane Maria
Marine Le Pen loses French election run-off
Pepsi advert using protest movement images pulled
Poverty affects 1 in 4 children in UK
Plastic pollution
Pope looks glum on meeting Trump (T)
Paddington Bear film a hit
Paradise Papers
Paris Climate Change Accord ditched by Trump (T)
Poland v the EU over judicial independence
Putin believed by Trump on Russian meddling in US election (T)
Putin announces he will run again for President
"Pocahontas", racial slur made by Trump at ceremony honouring
Navajo veterans (T)
P45 handed to Theresa May during conference speech debacle
George Papadopoulos, White House advisor pleads guilty to lying to
FBI (T)
Productivity, poor UK levels fall further
Piegate, footballer Wayne Shaw charged with influencing betting
market
Penis drawn in sky by US navy pilots
Passchendaele 100th anniversary of battle
Pyongyang
Parsons Green tube explosion
Price Waterhouse Coopers blamed for Oscars mix-up
Carles Puigdemont, Catalonia's sacked President
Polymer £10 note
Pollution in UK too dangerous according to UN and WHO
Reince Priebus Whitehouse Chief of Staff fired (T)
Mike Pence, USVP's pre-arranged walkout of NFL game when
players take a knee (T)
Mike Pence says Trump has "fulfilled miracles" (T)
Priti Patel, MP resigns after unofficial Israeli meetings
Psychiatrists warn about Trump's mental state (T)
Post-truth (T)
Pound coin, old one out of circulation
Valdimir Putin announces he is running for President again
Christopher Plummer replaces Kevin Spacey in Ridley Scott film

Q

Queensferry Crossing over Firth of Forth opens
Qatar diplomatic crisis v Saudi Arabia
Queen's broadcast tops Xmas day TV ratings
Queen's grandson's company paid £750,000 to organise Queen's birthday
HMS Queen Elizabeth launched, leaks
Queen invested £10m offshore, Paradise Papers revelation
Quantitative easing, US Federal Reserve calls an end
Quantum computing
Q#, Microsoft quantum programming language
Quinoa

R

Died
George Romero, director
Don Rickles, comedian
James Rosenquist, artist
David Rockefeller, banker, aged 101
Hans Rosling, physician
Derek Robinson, "Red Robbo", trade unionist

Regulations, ending of (T)
Christiano Ronaldo wins Ballon d'Or
Russia investigation (T)
Russian interference
Russian troll farms
Russia banned from Winter Olympics
Russian Revolution 100th anniversary
Ringling Brothers and Barnum & Bailey circus closes after 146 years
Rohingya Muslims attacked in Myanmar
Rallies, Trump's safe space (T)
Rhianna's cousin shot in Barbados
Ryanair pilot strike

Robots to take half of jobs?

"Remoaners"

Reformation, 500th anniversary

S

Died
William G Stewart, Fifteen To One host
Sam Shepard, actor
John Surtees, racer
Peter Skellern, pop star
Peter Sarstedt, pop star
Alan Simpson, writer with Ray Galton
Carol Lee Scott, actor, Grotbags
Bunny Sigler, singer
John Surtees, racing driver
Jill Saward, sex assault campaigner
Keely Smith, singer
Carl Sargeant, ex-Welsh Minister
Tim Piggot-Smith, actor
Joni Sledge, Sister Sledge

Sutherland Springs, Texas church attack
Snap election
OJ Simpson released
Star Wars: The Last Jedi
Sean Spicer (T)
Snowflakes, those easily offended
"Strong and stable", Tory refrain
SAD! Often used in tweets by (T)
Skywalker hoolock gibbon, new species discovered
Submarine, Argentine, lost
Saudi princes detained for corruption
Anthony Scaramucci, Whitehouse Communications Director, fired
after 11 days (T)
Smart speakers
Soft Brexit
Sexual assault allegations (T)

South China Sea Islands territorial disputes
Southern Trains, many strikes
Spanish constitutional crisis
Standing Rock, Sioux Tribe protest Dakota Access pipeline
Soft drinks levy - Sugar tax announced in Budget
Spice, drug affecting communities
Sophia, first robot granted citizenship, Saudi Arabia
Swatting, video gamers prank call police over online disputes, deaths result
Sixtus Dominic Boniface Christopher Rees-Mogg, Jacob names sixth child
Social care cap of £72,500 scrapped
Social Mobility Commission quits
Kevin Spacey sex assault allegations
Selfitis: obsessive need to post selfies
Sanctions on North Korea (T)
Safe spaces for students
Stalking sentence doubled
Nicola Sturgeon
Sharks freeze in US East Coast cold snap
Stirling's Brexit fuelled depreciation "worst in history"
Grant Shapps, MP ringleader of failed coup attempt of PM
Scooter thefts
Sleeping Beauty banned from primary school for inappropriate sexual behaviour
Somalia famine
Anna Soubry, MP receives death threats over Brexit stance
Smacking children to be banned in Scotland

T

Died
Butch Trucks, rocker, Allman Brothers
Jay Thomas, actor
Graham Taylor, footballer

Tiki torches in Charlotesville (T)
Time's Person of the Year sex abuse silence breakers (T)
Tweets (T)

Trump says he refused Time's Person of the Year (T)
T-Charge for diesel vehicles
Traingate – Corbyn v Virgin Trains
Tax cut in USA - "biggest ever" (T)
TTP trade deal withdrawal (T)
Twitter troll farms in Russia
Twitter employee deactivates Trump's account for 11 minutes (T)
Tramadol, Laura Plummer jailed for import of 290 tablets into Egypt
Transexuals
Transgender recruits allowed in US military, Trump drops opposition (T)
Twitter increases message character limit to 280
Trident, Government admits missile test malfunction
T-Charge, London anti-pollution measure
Tesco's green turkeys "ruin Christmas"
Tian Tian, Edinburgh Zoo panda not pregnant
Tesla car company overtakes Ford in market value
Donald Tusk, President of the European Council
Trump v TTIP trade talks (T)
Trump v TPP trade talks (T)
Trump says he turned down Time's Person of the Year, Time denies offering it (T)
Malcolm Turnbull, Trump hangs up on Australian PM (T)

U

Unpopular – least popular President ever (T)
Uber's various problems
UNESCO, US withraws from (T)
UKIP new logo like Premier League's
UKIP vote collapse
Unicorn – food that is dyed rainbow colours
Uniform, gender neutral in school in Lewes
Universal Credit roll out
UFOs existence "beyond reasonable doubt": ex Pentagon official
UN says UK welfare cuts are a "human catastrophe" for disabled
United Airlines settle compensation with passenger Dr Dao dragged off plane
Unisex toilets

United States of Europe
Universal basic income

V

Died
Frank Vincent, Sopranos, Goodfellas actor

Leo Varadkar, politician, a key to Brexit
"Very fine people on both sides" Trump on white supremacist rally, Charlottesville (T)
VX nerve agent killed Kim Jong-nam
Guy Verhhofstadt, European Parliament negotiator: Brexit "waste of time"
Virtue signalling
Venezuela economic crisis
Virgin Care sues NHS
Virgin Care wins £1bn NHS contract
Viagra cleared for over the counter sale from next year
Vaping said to be as dangerous as smoking
Volunteers considered for UK border control
Volcanic activity
Leonardo da Vinci painting, Salvator Mundi, most expensive ever sold

W

Died
John Wetton, rocker, King Crimson
Don Williams, singer
Adam West, actor, Bat Man
Heinz Wolff, scientist
Deborah Watling, actress
Adam West, actor, Batman

Harvey Weinstein
Wall at Mexico border (T)
WannaCry cyber attack
Women's March, much bigger crowd in DC the day after the

inauguration (T)
Lavinia Woodward, medical student stabbed boyfriend, spared jail
Wagamama staff threatened over Xmas sick leave
Water cremation, dissolving the dead
Walnut Whip, Nestle removes walnut
White supremacists
Serena Williams wins Australian Open while pregnant
Claudia Winkleman revealed to be BBC's highest paid female presenter
Wheat, running through fields of: Theresa May confesses to naughtiest childhood act
Jodie Whittaker, new Dr Who
Tiger Woods arrested for driving while intoxicated
Westminster Bridge attack
Wall at Mexican border (T)
Whitehouse, "a real dump" according to Trump (T)
Whitehouse leaks (T)
Whitehouse Xmas decorations look like "house of horrors" (T)
Frederica Wilson, congresswoman's feud with Trump (T)
Winery – Trump boasts he owns one of largest in US, winery denies it (T)
Gavin Williamson, Defence Secretary keeps tarantula in office
Wood-burning stoves face crackdown

X

Xi-cc++ - new particle
Xenophobia on rise world-wide
Xi Jinping, President's ideology enshrined into Chinese constitution, like Mao

Y
Died
Malcolm Young, AC/DC

Yacht lotto, 50 Tory MPs want public to buy Queen new yacht
Youthquake – Oxford Dictionaries' word of the year
Milo Yiannopoulos, controversialist's book deal cancelled
Malala Yousafzai attends Oxford University

Yemen war
Yarl's Wood detention centre abuse
"Yank-shake", Trump's weird dominance handshake
Yellow car "ruins" tourists photos in scenic Bibury, Gloucestershire
Yiwu-London, longest freight train route in the world

Z
Nanzin Zagari -Ratcliffe, detained in Iran
"Zombie drug", spice, synthetic marijuana
Zimbabwe military takeover
Zero-hours contacts, Labour's manifesto pledges to ban them
Mark Zuckerberg admits to Facebook fake news failings
Zulu dancers defend blacking up at Lewes Bonfire Night
Summer Zervos, Apprentice contestant sues Trump for sexual misconduct defamation (T)
Zealandia recognised as seventh largest continent

17087186R00150

Printed in Great Britain
by Amazon